OUT OF SECONDS

SHANNAH BASSETT
MARIAH STREET

Edited by Hilari Cohen

Book cover design by Ever After Cover Design

Formatted by Shannah Bassett

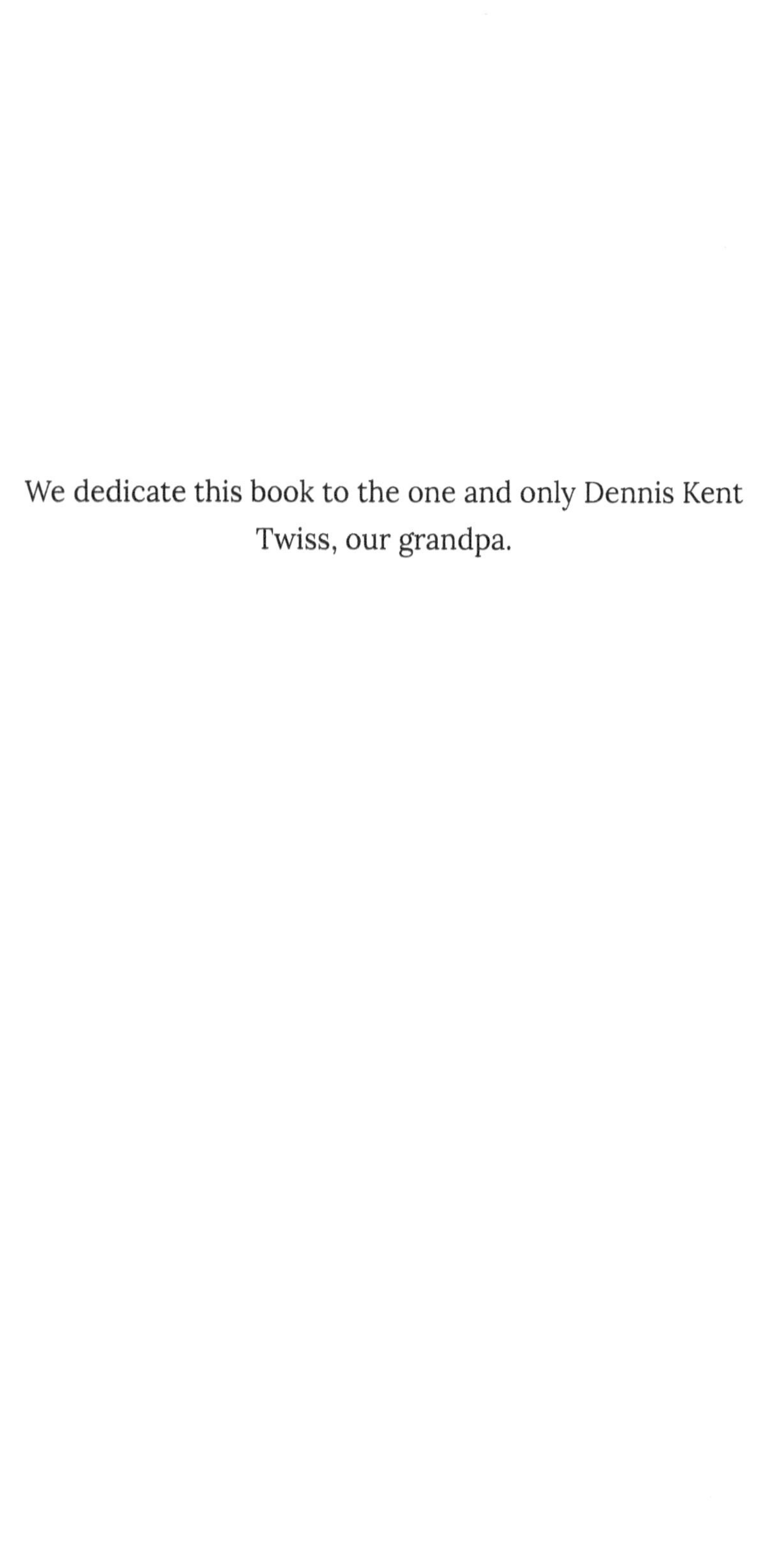

We dedicate this book to the one and only Dennis Kent Twiss, our grandpa.

Prologue

Harper

I don't want to die.

I've never had thoughts about taking my own life. But for a moment I think about staying here forever, in this cool water that feels better and better as it pulls me under. There's something peaceful in the depths of the lake. I need to be here. Ironically, I don't feel like I'm being suffocated. I'm alone. I feel free. And if I don't come back up I won't have to say goodbye. I won't have to see the look in Will's eyes anymore. The look that tells me just how bad he regrets what happened between us. The look that crushes me over and over again.

I don't want to die.

But I don't want to leave.

Chapter One

Harper

S unset is my favorite time of the day. The different hues of pinks and oranges are breathtaking and are the only colors I care to see. I wish the sunset lasted longer but unfortunately, it's brief. Perhaps it wouldn't be as special if I were always looking at it.

It's been a boring day today since Will never came over to play. When I went to ask my mom if she would play a card game with me, she was in her room on the phone. She pressed the phone to her chest when I asked her who she was talking to.

She just said, "Nobody. You're ten years old now sweetie. Go play out back like a big girl."

So now I'm here. Dangling my bare feet while sitting on top of the haystack I'm not allowed to be playing on. Looking up at my favorite sky colors. There is no way my mom was talking to *nobody*. Certainly, it was somebody. She doesn't play pretend the way I do. Unless the person on the phone's name is Nobody. That would make sense. What a strange name. I'm glad my name isn't Nobody.

"Harper!" Will yells up to me, "What are you doing up there? Your dad said we're not allowed to play up there anymore. You're going to get in trouble. I have to show you something at the lake before it gets too dark. We have to hurry!"

It's about time he showed up.

I know I have to get down. My dad will be home from work soon. But I hate walking through the rocks with no shoes and I can't imagine how bad it would hurt jumping down on them. I knew I shouldn't have taken off my sandals.

"Harper! Come on," Will yells.

"I can't! I lost my shoes somewhere up here," I yell back. I frantically look around the hay for them. If my dad finds me up here I'll be in big trouble. And I really want to see what Will has to show me at the lake.

I squeeze my eyes shut tight and think about the sharp rocks at the bottom. When I open them again, Will is climbing up the haystack. He sits next to me and begins taking off his shoes. Great. Now we'll both be stuck if he loses them.

"Here. Take mine. But not because I want you to be my girlfriend or somethin'," he says, handing them to me.

"Duh," I say, putting on the torn-apart sneakers. "They're a little big, but they'll work. Thanks. What are you going to do?" I ask.

"I don't need shoes. I'm tougher than you." He laughs.

I roll my eyes and jump off the haystack. Will follows me and doesn't even look like he's in any pain when his bare feet hit the gravel. I hate that he's right. I hate that he's tougher than me.

As if he can tell I'm mad, Will smiles at me and says, "Don't worry. You're still tough. My feet are just used to being barefoot. It takes practice. Let's hurry, the sun is going down. Grab your bike. I'll meet you on the road," he says, running straight through the sharp rocks. I guess I need to practice walking on the pointy gravel so I can be as tough as Will someday.

Running like a duck in the sneakers that are too big, I grab my bike out of the shed. I pedal as fast as I can to the front of the house where I see Will sitting on his bike anxiously waiting for me by the road. I pull up next to him. "Okay, show me the way, Turbo."

Will has been my best friend since he moved here when I was in third grade and he was in fourth grade. I saw him sitting alone on the grass at recess on the first day of school and sat down next to him to ask if he wanted to play with me.

As I flash back to the memory two years ago, I can hear the sounds of the other children in the school yard as I pick at the grass.

He says, "Sure. I'm Will. Well, my first name is Frank but that's my dad's name, so I go by Will. My middle name is William."

"I'm Harper. Do you want a dum dum sucker?" I ask, pulling the contraband out of my pocket. We aren't allowed to have candy at school so I bet he'll think I'm pretty cool.

"Sure, thanks," Will says, taking the sucker.

He doesn't smile back at me.

"Are you sad?" I ask. "Because you seem sad."

"No, I'm not sad. Just nervous," Will mumbles. "Being in a new school, making new friends. It's hard." He's picking at the grass now too.

"I'm your new friend." I stand up and offer him my hand. "Come on, let's go play on the swings. They go so high, it feels like you're actually flying."

And we've pretty much been inseparable since.

We bike to the peaceful lake that sits in between both of our houses in the center of the valley. Nobody lives around the lake and it's big enough to have plenty of space for all of its visitors in the summer. It's surrounded by lots of trees so most of the time it's so hard to find each other when we want to meet here and play.

Will leads me down a little trail and I feel thick, long grass tickle my legs as I pedal through it. He stops when we get to this big rock sitting underneath a tree.

"Isn't it perfect?" he asks.

I'm confused about what he thinks is perfect.

"Um, the rock?"

"No. Well yeah, the rock. There is this huge rock right here. It can be our meeting spot at the lake. Now we can just say, "*Meet you at the rock.* It's the biggest one I've seen at the lake. It's the perfect meeting spot," he explains.

I think about all the times we've gotten lost trying to find each other here. I love this idea. I love this spot. *Our spot.*

"Oh yeah! I like it! The rock. Can we call it something else? Make it sound cooler?"

"Yeah, what's a cooler word for a big rock? A boulder?" he asks.

"I like it!" I shout, full of excitement. "Boulder sounds way cooler. This is going to be our spot. And the grass doesn't look too thick down by the lake."

I set my bike down and make my way toward the clear water.

"There's even some sand right here, like an actual beach! I know what we'll call it. Boulder Beach. We'll have to clean up some of the little rocks but you're right Will, it is perfect!"

Chapter Two

Harper

Seven years later...

I would never describe myself as a popular girl in high school. My circle consists of my cousin Claire, a few friends in some classes, distant friends who I went to junior high with who would now be considered popular, and then my best friend Will. He's the only friend who really stuck with me since grade school.

Will is definitely popular, no matter how often he tries to convince me that he's not. He is most certainly not the same shy kid I saw sitting in the grass all alone in fourth grade. He plays varsity football and is close with his teammates, but he's really friends with everybody. He takes time to talk to the smart kids, the kids with special needs, the trouble-makers, the religious kids, and basically every single kid that goes to this school. Since he's a grade above me, we've never had any classes together. But we sometimes see each other in the halls and obviously during lunch and before and after school.

I see how all the girls look at Will. They basically take off his clothes with their eyes. They're always staring as he walks by and he's either used to it or never even notices.

Although Will has never been able to afford the best clothes or shoes, he is still the most attractive guy in Wood Lake High. He has thick blond hair, a strong cleft chin, deep brown eyes, and a tall athletic build. To me, his good looks are just a bonus. The real attraction is his genuine personality and his kind heart.

Will

I'm sitting in History class, trying hard not to fall asleep. My dad brought some friends over last night. I assume they were drinking because they always are. Although they were extremely loud, I'm glad my dad didn't pull me and Jameson out of bed like he does most nights when there's a party.

"Please take out your World War II assignment," Mr. Thompson says, "you're allowed to work on it until the end of class. Whatever you do not finish is homework and will be due tomorrow."

"There's no way we'll finish this long ass assignment in class," a deep voice groans.

Shit. I left it in my locker.

I ask Mr. Thompson if I can go get it and he surprisingly says yes.

I'm about to walk up the stairs to my locker on the top floor when I see Harper in the gym with her P.E class. I stop and watch as the loud students play kickball. Has Harper always looked that good in shorts? Her long, golden brown hair is pulled back into a ponytail and she's talking to her cousin Claire. Harper is so naturally pretty. It's a different kind of pretty from all the girls I've been with. She wears a little makeup but I know for a fact she doesn't need it. I've seen her plenty of times without it. I don't think she even realizes just how pretty she actually is. She has shiny, hazel eyes and dimples that appear on the corners of her mouth only when she smiles, a dark beauty mark that falls just beneath her left eye. *What the hell is wrong with me?* We're best friends. That's all we can ever be. We're too close to ever be anything else. I'm not about to ruin that.

I notice someone else in her gym class looking at her. Robby McKinney. He's on the other side of the gym. Is he checking her out? My blood boils as I see his eyes roaming all over her body. He's definitely checking her out and I feel the sudden urge to gouge his eyeballs out. When he finally peels his eyes off of Harper, he looks at the window and sees me looking at him. He waves, and I walk off.

I have to walk off.

Harper

I'm dragging my feet to Math class on the senior floor, as a friend of Will's from the football team, Robby, asks me if

I have a prom date yet. Completely caught off guard, I look up to see Will staring at me from his locker.

I say, "No. No, I haven't been asked. To be honest I'm not sure if I'm going to go."

"Go with me," Robby says with a charming smile. He puts his arm up on the wall blocking me in so that I don't walk away. He is wearing so much cologne that it's giving me a headache. He always has a buzz cut and he's the type of guy who thinks he's way hotter than he actually is.

"I'll think about it."

"Oh come on, Harper. You know you want to go to prom with me. We'll have a good time," he says.

My books feel heavy in my arms. I wanted to talk to Will, not Robby.

"I promise I'll think about it, Robby, okay? I'm going to be late for class. We'll talk later." I say, feeling a little annoyed that I have to duck under his arm and walk around him.

"Okay but I won't take no for an answer!" he yells.

I look back up at Will's locker and Will is no longer there.

After school, I walk out the main entrance doors and Will is leaning his back on the brick wall, waiting for me. He's waving to someone when I walk up beside him.

"Hey dummy, how was school?" I ask.

He looks at me with a wide grin. "It was alright. I think I passed my English test. You?"

"I hate school. I can't believe you graduate in five weeks, Will. We're going to have the best summer yet."

"Of course we are."

His sweet smile warms my heart.

"Hey Will!" I hear a girl yell. He waves back at her and she glares at me.

"Being your best friend sure gets me some dirty looks," I tell him and he rolls his eyes with a smile.

"What was Robby talking to you about earlier today in the hall?" Will asks.

"He asked me to prom and I told him I would think about it. I know he's your friend so I might. Are you going?"

"Robby is not someone who I think of as a friend," Will snaps. "You shouldn't go with him."

"Why?" I ask, feeling confused. Why does he seem so pissed off?

"He's not someone I want you alone with. If you're going, I'm going," he demands.

"Don't be ridiculous. That would be weird." As much as I want Will to come, I can't imagine how awkward the three of us going to the dance together would be.

He groans and runs his hand over his face. Like he's trying to wipe his expression off. It's not working. "How about if you decide to go, I'll offer up a group date and take somebody and we will all go together?" he asks.

"I don't think so. I'm sorry Will, but I've gotta be honest. I don't think you'll get a single girl in this school to go with you," I tease, trying to lighten the mood. He's so tense.

We both laugh and he tells me to think about it. But I think I see a glimmer of jealousy in his eyes and I kinda want to see more. So right then and there, I decide I want to go to prom with Robby.

Will

After school today, when Harper told me Robby had asked her to prom I tried to hide how I felt. I shouldn't be jealous. I'm being absolutely ridiculous. Harper isn't mine. She can never be mine. I think I have jealousy confused with just being protective. I know some jerks have wanted to get with Harper in the past. The ones who only want one thing from girls. But she's smart enough to recognize those jerks. I wish she would recognize Robby for who he is. I don't want her to go with him. But I can't control what Harper does. I don't have a say on who she dates. I have to go with them if she decides to go, whether she likes it or not. Robby comes off a little sketchy to me. The way he talks about girls sometimes makes me cringe. I haven't really decided who I'm going to ask to the dance yet.

When I first started seeing Harper as attractive, I told myself *it's just all the girls*. All the girls are attractive and you just happen to be best friends with one. When I found myself fantasizing about kissing her at age fifteen, I decided to kiss other girls to get my focus off Harper. I didn't want to think of her like that. We're only friends and I promised myself I wouldn't ever ruin that by trying to kiss her. That would just make our friendship complicated and Harper is the only thing in my life right now that isn't complicated.

My first kiss was with Emma. The girl who glared at Harper today after school. Milton invited all the freshmen to his house one night for a bonfire. Emma kept flirting with me and I tried to flirt back. I probably sounded like an idiot but I really wanted to get Harper out of my mind. After eating a dum dum sucker, I made out with Emma Bradley at my friend's house that night. The next day I told Harper I had my first kiss. She started laughing uncontrollably when I told her I ate a cherry dum dum sucker first.

"Of course you did," she said.

Then I wanted to kiss her. I wanted to kiss her way more than I ever wanted to kiss Emma. I was so frustrated. But I kept trying. I tried with Callie the next week. I made out with her at the football stadium underneath the bleachers after our first home game. I tried with Tammy Henders at another freshman party. Each time, eating a sucker first.

Harper bought me a big bag of dum dum suckers once as a joke.

"You really like kissing girls, Will. In fact, I bought you a whole bag of dum dum suckers. And since you eat so many dum dum suckers I'm going to have to start calling you 'dummy.'"

We laughed so hard and I wanted to kiss her again. By my junior year of high school, I had kissed so many girls at Wood Lake High. Then I started kissing the girls I'd meet at our away football games. My friend Milton got a car and we would drive to the next town over just to kiss those girls. None of them got me to stop wanting to kiss Harper. No matter how far I went with them. But I eventually got used to it. Now, as a senior in high school I hardly ever kiss any more girls. I just want to kiss the one girl that I know I never can.

When I get home, my dad is sleeping in his chair with the TV on. Being careful not to wake him up, I quietly make my way into the kitchen to find something to eat. I settle on a bag of ramen noodles and quietly shut the microwave door and hit the button. My dad flinches but thankfully, he stays asleep.

I'm doing homework on my bed with my noodles when Jameson quietly walks into our shared bedroom. Just like me, he also wants my dad to stay asleep.

"Hey," he says, "Oh good, you found some dinner. How was school?"

"It was okay."

"I talked to my boss and he said he can try and get you a job at the car wash as soon as you turn eighteen. But I think you should get the hell out of here instead. Maybe we could both move to Columbus, or back to Cincinnati. We could get a place to rent together," he suggests.

I don't turn eighteen until October. I skipped a grade as soon as we moved here when I was a boy and now I regret it. I don't know what the hell to do since nobody will hire me until I'm eighteen. It's really fucking stressful.

"Yeah, that sounds great. But don't stay here for me James. If you want to move somewhere just go now. I'll be fine."

I hate that I'm the one holding him back. I know he wouldn't be living here if it weren't for me.

He just shakes his head and pulls off his work clothes.

"Everything is going to work out brother. Just focus on getting your diploma for now."

Harper

"Hey Taffy. How are you doing, girl?"

I open the gate and walk out onto the field to pet my horse. When my Grandpa Pearson died six years ago, he left me his brown and white pinto horse he knew I adored, Taffy. He had only had her for a few years when he got sick. I had no idea he was planning on giving her to me until my parents and grandma surprised me after he passed away. Taffy and I have a bond I can't really explain. It's like we mirror each other. When I'm happy she's happy. When I'm sad, she seems sad. Somehow this helps me deal with my feelings. I love my horse.

"What do you think? Should we go for a ride?"

I gently put the saddle on her and hop up on the back of the most compassionate companion I'll probably ever have.

I'm trying to do my homework but my mind keeps wandering. Did Will actually look jealous today when I told him about Robby? Or did I make it up in my head because I wanted him to be jealous? I'm trying not to think about it. And it's making it hard to focus on my homework. I do the best I can and finally I'm finished. It's already almost ten o'clock. I'm still thinking about him as I shower and get ready for bed. I crawl into my bed and finally doze off..

Will is staring at my mouth again. Why can't I talk?

My heart is racing as Will looks at me and asks, "What is your favorite dum dum flavor?" He smiles.

I still can't talk but he pulls a strawberry sucker out of his pocket and sticks it in his mouth.

"This one is for you Harper."

I feel my mouth water. I want to taste it. On Will. But I can't tell him because I can't talk. He takes the strawberry sucker out of his mouth, tucks my hair behind my ear and as he leans in to kiss me, I wake up. It was just a dream. Thank goodness.

"Ugh! What is wrong with me?" I bury my face into my pillow.

Lately, all I ever do is think of Will. I catch myself taking the long way to class, just so I can see him in the hallway. I get a little jealous when I see him talking to girls. I get more excited than usual to hang out with him. I dream about kissing him. What have I turned into? I don't want to be one of the hundred girls that want Will. He's my best friend. When I finally feel convinced enough that my feelings for Will aren't actually real, I get out of bed and get ready for school.

Chapter Three

Harper

Butterflies swarm inside my stomach as I get ready for prom. I've never felt so nervous. Thank goodness Will and his date, Flora Pederson will be there too.

Flora is someone I've known since junior high. We've never hung out outside of school, but I remember laughing with her about how a lot of the girls in eighth grade would sneak makeup to school and spend so much time putting it on in the girl's bathroom only to wipe it off before they got home to their strict mothers. And how when our math teacher, Mr. Jones was writing on the chalkboard, he always tapped the chalk on his head when he would pause to think, leaving white chalk dust marks all over his face. Although I wouldn't necessarily call us friends now, she's not so bad. She's a really nice and popular cheerleader. I just hope Will isn't planning on eating any dum dum suckers tonight.

I look in the mirror at my new navy blue prom dress. It's a little longer in the back and shorter in the front with a slit up the hem. Since we live in such a small town, there isn't anywhere to dress shop, so my mom and I went to downtown Columbus last week, and she insisted I get this one since I loved it so much.

After we bought the dress, I asked my mom if she liked growing up in the city. She said that she did but that she likes living in a small town better.

Then I said, "I think I want to come to school here. It's close to home and Copper Hill University has a great social work program."

My mom looked around. "Really? Here? I don't know if this place is the right fit for you. What if you spread your wings a little higher and went to a different state? I just know it would be good for you. I would still obviously love having you close to home though, if that's what you think you'd prefer."

She has always wanted me to go somewhere far away. I think she believes that the further you get away from home, the more successful you are. But I don't believe that's true at all. Happiness and success aren't measured upon the distance you go.

I felt a little unnerved but I just said, "I'll think about it."

Even though I'd already made up my mind.

I'm in my bedroom finishing up with lipstick when my mom comes in.

"Harper, you look stunning! Will is here with his date," she says.

Anxiety rushes through me again.

"Thanks Mom, I'll be right there."

"I really wish your father didn't have to work tonight so he could see how beautiful you look."

There's a pit in my stomach as I can't help but wonder if my dad had to pick up an overnight shift just to pay for this dress. If so, they would never tell me that.

"I wish dad was here too."

"We'll get some pictures of you to show him. I better go back outside! Will sure looks handsome," she says as I hurry and pin my hair back with my special silver hair clip that Will gave me.

When I step outside, Will is wearing a nice black suit and I've never seen him look so handsome. He looks like a man. He's talking to my mom and when we exchange looks, he does a double take. An encouraging smile spreads across his lips and I'm not even nervous anymore. I have Will. My best friend.

Will

Harper looks amazing. The blue dress that kind of hangs off of her bare shoulders looks beautiful with her olive skin. Her hair is pulled back but some curls are hanging down in the front of her face. I find myself wanting to touch her plump pink lips to see if they feel as perfect as they look. Who am I kidding? I want to *kiss* them. She is making it hard for me to focus on my own date, Flora.

I'm on a date with Flora.

After Robby finally showed up in his Camaro, and Harper's mom got enough pictures of us, we all got in to drive to the dance.

Last week, I spotted Kyra Brown walking out of the lunchroom when I decided I was going to ask her to prom. She's also a senior and didn't get asked last year. I thought she deserved to go to the school dance her last year of high school. Kyra keeps to herself and doesn't have many friends, but is the smartest girl in our senior class.

"Hey Kyra, wait up!" I yelled and ran up to her.

"Oh. Hey Will," Kyra said shyly.

"How's it going?" I asked. "Are you getting excited for graduation? I'm sure you have big plans coming up."

She smiled. "I'm looking forward to going to Stanford in the fall."

"Wow! That's amazing Kyra. Hey, I was going to ask you if maybe you'd want to go to prom with me next week?"

"Sorry Will, I'm already going with Liam."

I smiled as I pictured Liam getting to go to prom as well. He's also a senior who wouldn't be considered popular. I knew it took a lot of courage for him to ask Kyra to prom.

"Oh that's great! I hope you guys have a good time. I'll see you around Kyra."

When I turned around, I heard a girl call out, "Hey Will! Ask me to prom."

I saw Flora Pederson with a grin on her face.

She must have heard my conversation with Kyra. I smiled back at her. "Alright Flora, will you go to prom with me?"

And now here we are. In Robby Mckinney's car, with the music blaring.

"Hey man, maybe turn down the music a bit?" I ask.

He rolls his eyes and turns it down.

"Did you guys hear about the school break-in?" Flora asks, sitting next to me in the back seat.

"Someone broke into the school?" Harper asks.

I say, "Yeah, they might've. There was a shattered window so they assume someone was trying to get in. My brother told me he talked to a police officer in town. Nothing was taken, no computers were tampered with, and nothing inside was damaged."

"That's so strange," Harper says.

"Super creepy," says Flora.

"I'm sure it was nothing," Robby says. "So Harper... my buddy Stan is having a party after the dance. Do you want to go?" he asks, sliding his hand into Harper's.

My teeth clench together. Just the thought of him touching her is pissing me off.

"Sure. My curfew is at midnight so as long as I'm home by then."

"Hell yeah! I'll show you a good time babe." He leans down and kisses her on the hand.

I've never wanted to rip someone's head off before. Robby looks at me in the rearview mirror and gives me a condescending smile.

Once we get to the school, I can see the shattered window out front that they have blocked off. What's the point of breaking into a high school?

In the gym, everyone is admiring the decorations and having a blast. I hear laughter and excited conversation over the music. Streamers, colorful lights and balloons are everywhere.

Harper pulls me onto the dance floor. We're laughing and pretending like we know what we're doing.

"Are you having a good time?" I ask her loud enough for her to hear me.

"Yeah, are you?" she asks with a smile.

I try and show her I'm having a good time by doing a hideous dance move and she hunches over, laughing hard.

It looks like Kyra and Liam are having a good time too. I smile at them and wave.

A slow song comes on and Harper looks at me but Robby comes up behind her and grabs her in a blink of an eye. She smiles at me, letting me know that she's okay.

When I spot Flora, I ask her to dance. I pull her in close and I notice Robby has got Harper pushed all the way up against him. I try to keep a straight face as every muscle inside my body tenses. Harper takes a step back for some space as they continue to sway to the music. *Good girl.* I realize I'm still staring at Harper so I immediately look back down at skeptical looking Flora.

"Are you and Harper just friends?" she asks.

"Oh yeah definitely."

I leave out the fact that I think about kissing her 24/7.

"Sometimes it seems like you're into each other," Flora says.

"No, that's weird. She's like my sister."

Flora lets out a small laugh. "Thanks for bringing me to prom, Will. I've had a lot of fun."

"I'm having fun too. Thanks for coming with me. You look great by the way."

She smiles. "Thanks."

Robby and I have never really been friends. Sure, we played football together in the fall and share a lot of the same friends. We both played quarterback. Maybe that's why he's never really liked me. I've always been the starter and played most of the game. But I'm a senior and he's a junior so it just made sense. Robby was the one who was always initiating the vulgar locker room talk all season too. That's why I didn't want Harper coming alone with him. And I'm definitely not letting her go to the house party alone with him either.

After the slow dance with Flora, she tells me she's going to go talk with some of her friends.

I spot Milton, Paul, and Michael at the snack bar and make my way over to them. "There's the man!" yells Paul and I can already tell that he's been drinking.

"Hey guys, how's it going?" I ask.

"We're having a good time," Michael answers as I feel someone grab my shoulders and I look behind me. It's Robby.

He's laughing. "Are you guys already wasted? Are you all coming to the party?" Robby asks.

"Milton and I will be there for sure. Paul's getting some with his girl tonight, so I doubt he'll make it," Michael jokes.

Paul gives him a playful shove and says, "You're just jealous."

We're all laughing when Robby looks at me and says, "Hey speaking of getting some, do you think Harper will put out for me tonight?"

I clench my jaw. It takes everything I have not to beat this piece of shit up. The only reason I haven't smashed his face in already is because of Harper. I don't want to embarrass her.

"Shut up," is all I manage to say.

"What? Oh, so you *are* hooking up with her! I was under the impression you guys were just friends. I've got to know, is she that good in bed?" Robby asks.

Milton grabs me by the arm just as I'm about to hit Robby.

"He's not worth it man," he says, "let's go cool off." And he pulls me outside before I get Robby's blood on my hands.

Harper

After that extremely awkward slow dance with Robby, my cousin Claire runs up to me and gives me a big hug. She's in the same grade as I am. She's just a lot more boy crazy and has more friends. But she lives just down the road from me so we grew up playing together.

"You look so pretty Harper. How's Taffy doing?"

Claire loves horses too. Her family has a few of them.

While I'm talking to her, I notice Will being dragged out of the dance by Milton.

"I'm going to go check on Will. It looks like Milton just took him outside."

"See ya, Harper!"

As I'm walking out of the dance to go see what's going on with Will, Robby grabs me by the arm. "Hey babe, you ready to get out of here? This dance is kind of boring."

"Um, sure. Let me find Will and Flora and see if they're ready to go," I say, walking away.

"Wait Harper, I already did. They're not coming with us anymore. Will said he and Flora are going to go hook up somewhere else. Let's go."

I'm really disappointed that Will left but I understand that he's on a date too.

"I'll make sure you're home by midnight Harper I promise. Come to Stan's party, have a drink. Maybe Will and Flora will show up after all."

I nod. "Okay."

⁂

So many people are already at the house party when we get here. I'm sitting on the couch with Robby as he chugs his fourth beer. A couple is making out next to us and some guys are right behind us on the staircase, having a contest to see who can stand up while riding down the railing.

"Are you ready for a drink yet?" Robby asks through the wild laughter and loud party music.

"No, I already told you I don't want a drink," I say, feeling irritated.

"Would you drink if Will were here to offer it to you?" Robby slurs.

"No, it doesn't have anything to do with Will. I just don't like to drink. I think I'm going to take off. My house isn't too far from here. I can walk," I say.

I was hoping Robby would stay sober enough to take me home but he's clearly had too much to drink. I really wish Will had a cell phone right now so I could call him to come get me.

"We just got here! Let's go outside," Robby says, standing up.

"Okay but after that, I just want to go home."

"Fine. I'll take you home after I show you what's out back," he says.

"That's okay. I'll be fine walking."

We sit down next to the house in the dark. The lights from inside shine through the windows and I can see a huge open lawn. I think I see Flora's bright orange dress as she stands with some other cheerleaders in the distance. Will must be here somewhere. I look around, wondering what the heck Robby wanted to show me out here.

"You're such a pretty girl," Robby says with his eyes glued everywhere but my face. "And that dress is straight up sexy."

He licks his lips before leaning in for a kiss. Feeling uncomfortable, I get up and step into the light from the window of the house.

"Thanks Robby. It's been a fun date. But I'm ready to go home now."

He stands up next to me and pulls me against his body. We slip back into the shadows of the house. His hands grip my wrist so hard it hurts.

"Come on Harper. I don't want you to go home before I have a chance to kiss you."

Just as Robby leans in again, I shock myself. I slap him across the face and run.

"Bitch!" he yells out.

I run through the house and out the front door when I see a car pull up. Will jumps out and comes running over to me. I see the muscles in his neck twitch. He's angry. "What did he do to you?"

I ignore his question. "I'm walking home. Flora is in there, probably waiting for you," I say coldly.

"I already told Flora I wasn't coming to this party. I was looking for you everywhere at the dance and decided Robby must have brought you here. Are you okay?"

I nod just as Will lifts my wrist and sees the red mark from Robby's tight grip. I've never seen Will look so mad. He storms toward the house and I run after him and grab his arm.

"Please don't," I beg.

He ignores me and walks faster. I jump in front of him to stop him. "Will stop. This is exactly what he wants. Please don't humiliate me."

"He hurt you." His nostrils flare. "He doesn't deserve to live."

My heart races. "Please. Don't do anything stupid."

Milt comes up to us and thankfully grabs a hold of Will. "She's right man. Let me give you guys a ride home. We can deal with Robby later."

My eyes shoot up at Milt. *Deal with him later. What does that mean?*

Luckily, Milt helps me drag Will to the car before he does something he'll regret.

Will

I'm still fuming but I'm relieved Harper is okay. I was really nervous when I couldn't find her or Robby at the dance and even more nervous when I noticed his car was gone. Robby is lucky Harper convinced me not to pummel him tonight. I knew he would try something with her. Stupid prick. If Harper thinks I'm just going to let it go that he touched her, *hurt her*, then she's wrong. I won't actually kill him but after I'm done with him, he'll leave Harper alone. If he doesn't, he might wish he was dead. But I'll worry about him later. Harper deserves a proper date.

"Hey thanks for the ride Milt, do you mind taking us to the convenience store?" I ask him. It's not too far from Harper's house.

"Sure," he says.

"Then we can just walk to your house from there?" I ask Harper.

"Yeah, but that's a lot of walking for you considering your house is on the other side of town."

"No worries." I smile.

"Thanks again, man," I say to Milton when we get to the store.

"Yeah, thanks Milton," Harper says, climbing out of the car.

I had to clean Jameson's side of our bedroom for him to give me a little money to rent this suit for the dance. With that little change I had left, I bought a Twinkie and a 7up, Harper's favorite comfort food. There is a little picnic table set up outside the store under some street lights.

"Let's sit," she says, "it's not that cold out and we have another hour before my curfew." We sit down on the bench on the same side of the table and she splits the Twinkie in half. Handing me part of it, she asks, "How was your night?"

"It was alright. I feel bad you didn't have much fun."

"I had fun at the dance. Afterward, not so much," she says.

"I need you to tell me what happened." The rage inside of me somehow stays hidden. I'm worried it will unleash when she tells me but I need to know. I'll go to the goddamn police myself if he assaulted her.

Harper sighs. "Robby wouldn't let me go home. Then he tried to kiss me, so I slapped him."

I can't help but smile. "Wait, you slapped him?"

She nods.

"Thatta girl." We both laugh.

Harper says, "Let's talk about something else. The first word that comes to your head. And... go."

I laugh and say, "Okay. Fireworks."

"Fireworks?" Harper laughs. "That's the only thing you could think of?" She pauses while she thinks. "Okay I have an idea! How about this year, on the Fourth of July, we watch the fireworks from Boulder Beach? We can make a fire, roast marshmallows, and watch the firework show from there. Doesn't that sound fun?" She smiles, revealing her cute dimples. I could never tell her no.

"Let's do it."

Talking about the Fourth of July reminds me of being a kid.

"Do you remember when you, Claire, Jameson and I used to run around and play night games when we were little?" I ask randomly.

Harper's eyes widen as she smiles. "Those days were the best. Remember when we stole my grandma's hen eggs to try and "rescue the chicks?" For some reason we thought we could take better care of them than the hen."

We both laugh hysterically.

"Your sweet grandma had never been so angry in her life."

"I think that's the only time I ever saw her get mad," Harper says.

"She always used to tell me that I would want to marry you someday. It used to gross me out so bad," she says, looking slightly embarrassed.

I laugh. "Well, do you? Want to marry me?" I tease.

I don't think I've ever seen Harper blush before, but I love it.

"Not yet," she says, laughing.

I don't know if I'm on high alert because of Robby or because my instincts are actually telling me something, but I feel like we're being watched. I don't want to tell Harper because I don't want her to worry. I look around and Harper touches my hand.

Her eyes tell me all I need to know.

Harper

I can tell Will is still paranoid about Robby. He's a jerk but I don't think he would've followed us here. Will keeps looking around, like he's waiting for him. I touch his hand and change the subject.

"Did you eat a dum dum sucker tonight?" It's my way of asking Will if he kissed Flora.

"I didn't," he says.

"You haven't eaten any dum dums lately. At least none that you've told me about. Did you finally make it through every girl in Ohio?"

He laughs. "I haven't kissed anyone since last year. It just got old I guess. Kissing girls who I don't have feelings for, that is. Girls who I hardly even know."

I wonder if you ever want to kiss me. I press my lips together.

"I had a dream a couple weeks ago. You tried to kiss me," I confess.

Will looks completely shocked that I said this. His laugh sounds slightly nervous. It makes me wonder if he's thought about kissing me too.

"That would be crazy," he says quietly. He touches the side of my face and looks down at my lips. "Us kissing," he whispers.

I forget how to breathe in this moment.

You want to kiss me. I want you to kiss me. So kiss me. I'm trying to tell him with my eyes. He's definitely thinking about it. His expression is telling me he wants to but that he can't. He looks conflicted. Will's mouth gets so close to mine, his breath hits my lips. I can feel my heart as it rapidly tries to thump right out of my chest.

Then Will stands up. I feel both relieved and devastated at once.

"It's probably getting close to your curfew," Will says, "we should start walking to your house."

I stand up too. "Yeah, good idea."

Will

Harper has never looked at me like that before, like she wanted me to kiss her. How I somehow managed not to is beyond me. But we can't risk our friendship. We grew up together. When we were kids she really did basically feel like a sister. I can't risk losing her no matter how deeply I feel the need to kiss her. She means way too much to me.

She deserves the world. She deserves someone who knows what the hell they're going to do in life after graduating high school. She deserves way more than I'll ever be able to achieve in life. I have to be careful.

We're walking down Harper's street when she says, "I'm glad this is how the night ended. With you."

She smiles. If she keeps saying stuff like this I won't be able to stop myself from kissing her next time.

"Me too," I tell her.

We walk in silence for a minute.

"Harper. Some guy is going to be so lucky to be with you one day. But that guy could never be me. You know that right?"

She stops walking and I turn around to look at her. I can't read her expression.

"Why would you say something like that?" she asks.

I wish I would've just kept my mouth shut.

"I don't know. I just felt like there was some tension at the store. Sorry."

"It's fine," she says and storms past me, visibly upset.

I don't know what to do to make this right. I run up to her and stand in front of her. "Harper, I'm sorry."

I glance over her shoulder. That's when I notice a random truck parked down the road from Harper's house. I don't tell her that because even though I feel like something is off, I still wonder if it's just my nerves from my fight with Robby. There are two other houses on this street that the truck could belong to, even though it's parked closest to Harper's.

"I shouldn't have said that. You're my best friend. I never want to risk losing you," I say and she shakes her head.

"You just caught me off guard. You've never said anything like that before. I get it, Will. You never want to be that guy and that's completely fine with me," Harper says as we make our way up to her front door. She's still clearly upset with me.

I don't even know what to say to her. So I just look at her. *I wish there was some way I could be that guy Harper. But I can't. You deserve better than me.*

"Goodnight Will," she says before stepping inside and shutting the door.

The moment I saw Robby's handprint on Harper's wrist, I really felt like I could kill him. Now that I've cooled off, I start walking back to the party. I'm dealing with him tonight.

Chapter Four

Will

"Don't forget the stuff to make a fire. Oh! And I'll bring the marshmallows and chocolate bars to make s'mores. I hope we can see the fireworks from Boulder Beach. If so, we're watching them from there every year. Are you sure you don't want to stay for dinner? My dad's grilling burgers," Harper says in a rush of words after the Fourth of July parade.

We're walking back to her house since the parade route was only a couple of blocks away. But it's so damn hot outside I can barely breathe. Or maybe it's the cutoff shorts Harper is wearing and the way she left all of her long, wavy hair down. That's definitely making it hard to breathe too. We're making our way up the steps to her front door.

"I've been with you guys all day. I'll let you have your family time. Plus, I told Milton I'd come to his cookout he's having for the guys," I tell her.

"Okay, meet you at Boulder Beach at nine?" Harper asks.

"I'll be there."

When I get to our spot right at nine o'clock, Harper is already there looking out at the water. I don't think I've ever seen anyone more beautiful. I sneak up behind her, grab her by the waist and pick her up. She screams and starts laughing.

"Will! You scared me." She turns around and looks at me with a playful glare. I start spinning her around just to hear her laugh again.

"Okay! Okay. I'm dizzy!" she squeals.

I put her down. Then I realize it's still hot outside. Taking off my shirt as fast as I can, I lift her over my shoulder and start running towards the lake. She's laughing even harder now.

"Will!" she screams. I throw us both into the lake and the cold water feels so good on my overheated body. I help Harper up and she pulls me back in, still laughing. We start a splashing fight and then eventually both surrender and drag ourselves out of the lake.

"Not going to lie," Harper says, "the water felt great. It's been such a hot day today. I needed to cool off."

As I'm handing her the blanket I brought so she can dry herself off, I ask, "Should we run to your house so you can get changed quick? We definitely have time. The fireworks don't usually start until like 11 o'clock."

I feel bad I didn't think about her being in wet clothes the rest of the night.

"No worries. I'll just have to be wet the rest of the night. It's a bummer we don't have any supplies to build a fire to help dry me off," she says sarcastically. I guess that's my cue to start the fire.

Then I remember my shirt. "At least put on my dry shirt."

I throw it over to her and she catches it.

"Fine, if you say so. Thanks." She walks into the trees to change.

I'm already finished building us a fire when she comes out wearing my shirt. Only my shirt.

Holy. Fucking. Shit.

The shirt is too big on her so it's covering her butt, but just barely.

Harper says, "I'm just going to set my clothes down by the fire so they'll be somewhat dry when I go home.

I clear my throat with a small cough and muster out, "Yeah, good idea," thinking of how I don't ever want to wash my shirt again.

I can't pinpoint the exact day I started looking at Harper differently. There was a time when we were little kids and just the thought of kissing her would make me want to puke. Then when I was fifteen and sixteen, I figured it was just physical attraction when I wanted to kiss her sometimes. Now that's all I ever think about when I'm with Harper. How badly I want to kiss her. I have to stop thinking of her like this. I can't love her like that. I can't be with her. I can't. Ever. I'll just have to keep telling myself that over and over again.

"Will. Will! Your marshmallow is burning!" she yells, interrupting my thoughts. "Are you okay?"

"Yeah, gosh I'm sorry," I say, blowing out the flame on the now black marshmallow. "I've got a lot on my mind."

"Are you stressed about finding work? About trying to pay for school?"

"Yeah," I say, telling a lie, but also the truth. I am stressed about that stuff. I push it out of my mind. "It will all work itself out though. No worries." I look up at Harper and she's laying the blanket down.

She says, "It's dark. Let's sit down and wait for the fireworks."

The light from the fire is shining on her as my shirt comes up even higher on her long, tan legs as she carefully sits down. Her hair still looks wet, making the natural waves more defined.

Damn it, Harper what are you trying to do to me?

I sit down next to her in silence.

Harper looks over at me and brushes her hand over my shoulder. The feel of her fingertips melt right into the surface of my skin and I never want to forget the feeling.

"What are these scars from?" Harper frowns with her eyebrows pulled down with worry.

I glance over to my shoulder and realize she's touching the round, bumpy burn marks. "My dad's cigarettes," I say bluntly.

"Will, I'm so sorry."

She looks so sad, I regret telling her. "Don't be. It was a long time ago."

"That doesn't make it any better."

I nod my head in agreement and we sit in silence. She lets go of me, the feel of her touch still lingering on my shoulder as I ache to have it back. But goddammit, I have to ignore that.

Harper looks up at the sky. "Do you ever just stop and think about how freaking tiny we are in the universe? All of these enormous, countless stars and planets revolving around us, just doing their jobs. It makes me feel so tiny and little, thinking about it."

I look up too. "I've never thought of it that way. I think that stargazing makes us view things from different perspectives. It is crazy to think about how huge everything is up there. But you, Harper. You may be tiny but you are going to do big things in this universe. I know it."

Her pleased smile exposes her dimples and she says, "You, Will, are also going to do big things in this universe. Enormous things in fact. You'll do so many enormous things, the planets will finally start having some competition. And then, when you show even the planets up with the enormous things you do, they'll finally give up and then you'll have to run the whole universe. Think you can handle that Will?"

I'm laughing too hard to answer straight away. "I'm going to need some help. Maybe tiny, little you can help me one day. Run the whole universe. Think you can handle that Harper?"

"Hell yeah I can." She laughs.

Suddenly, we're interrupted by fireworks. We can see them perfectly. And the reflection of them coming off the water makes it even better.

Harper

There was something so attractive about the way Will's skin glowed when we were sitting by the fire. I'm so glad I took his shirt just so I can look at him without it. I'm going to keep that image burned into my brain forever. I hope he's okay. He seems so quiet tonight. Something is off about him but I don't know what it is. Now sitting on the blanket, I catch Will watching me instead of the fireworks. He looks so hesitant as he looks at me with a tortured expression.

"What?" I ask him.

Then he leans over, brushes my cheek with his thumb and whispers, "I shouldn't do this."

I want him to kiss me so bad it hurts. "Do what?" I swallow.

Without answering me, he kisses me so softly on the lips, I can barely feel it.

But I *can* feel it.

Everywhere.

The feel of Will's lips on mine is better than I ever imagined. Does he feel it too? My heart is beating so fast I think it might burst through my chest.

When Will lets go of my lips, he keeps his forehead pressed on mine. Running his fingers through my hair he whispers, "Sorry."

I can't believe that just happened. Will just kissed me.

I'm trying to catch my breath again, but I don't want to stop. I grab the back of his neck and pull him in, kissing him harder. By the way he's kissing me back I can tell he doesn't want to stop either. My head is spinning as my fingertips make their way down his bare back. When Will parts my mouth with his tongue, an intensity of emotions rip through me. Wanting to be closer to him, I wrap my legs around him to straddle him. I feel the hardness of him through his jeans, causing me to whimper. Will kisses me even deeper as his hands move from my waist and slowly make their way down to my butt, then my legs, then make their way back up again. Will's hands running up my body make me feel something I've never felt before. The way he's kissing me is making my stomach flip over and over again.

Our breathing is getting harder. I never want this kiss to end. I want to stay here forever. I never imagined kissing Will would feel this good. It's like we're trying to tell each other how we feel *without actually saying it*. We're kissing each other so hard before reality kicks in and we have to stop.

Suddenly we hear a splash out into the water, startling us both. We look at the lake and realize it must have been a fish. I keep my eyes out on the water. I don't dare look at Will right now. I'm scared to see the look on his face.

When I finally get the courage to glance over at him, I feel *pain I've never felt before. He regrets it.*

Will looks back at me and says, "We should go. The fireworks have stopped. I don't want your parents to worry."

I stand up. Obviously, he thinks our kiss was a mistake. I'm absolutely mortified.

While I quickly change in the trees again into my damp shorts and t-shirt, Will pours water onto what's left of the fire.

We make our way to our bicycles when he says, "Meet you here tomorrow?"

"Sure." I don't even want to look at him. I turn my back to him just as he grabs my arm.

"Harper. We'll talk about it tomorrow okay? Same time?"

I still don't look at him. I don't want him to see the tears streaming down my face right now.

"Okay," I say, climbing onto my bike with my head down. When I pedal up the trail I can tell Will isn't following behind. Instead, he's watching me go.

On my way home I catch something out of the corner of my eye. I turn my head toward the movement and spot a human figure out in the field. I can tell it's a man as he walks toward me. I swerve my bike the opposite direction and crash into the ditch. I lay there for a moment when I hear what sounds like footsteps coming toward me.

"Shit," I mumble to myself. I quickly stand up off the ground and when I go to grab my bike I realize it's stuck.

"Shit, shit, shit," I whisper. The footsteps are getting closer and my bike is wedged in between a rock and a fence post.

I pull on my bike with all my strength and finally get it out.

I'm absolutely terrified as I jump back on my bike and pedal as fast as I can toward my house without looking back. Being alone in the dark has always made me paranoid, but I know I saw someone. I heard someone. I pedal toward my house faster. I'm pedaling faster than I ever have before.

When I get home, I throw my bike on the lawn and sprint toward the door. I slam it shut when I make it inside, and lock it behind me. I peek out the window to make sure nobody's out there. I'm relieved when I don't see anyone. When I take a step back, I feel pain in my left knee. It's bleeding. I was so scared when I crashed my bike, I didn't even notice I was hurt.

My hands are shaking and I feel completely exhausted as I make my way upstairs to clean and bandage my knee.

Chapter Five

Harper

I've been waiting at Boulder Beach for Will for an hour now. We need to talk about our kiss last night. I'm still a little on edge about seeing that man watching me. I don't want to ride my bike home alone again in the dark, so I hope Will gets here soon.

If he shows up.

I look up at the rope swing my dad tied to the tree when we were kids. Will and I have had so much fun on that rope swing. Sometimes we'd just meet here and do hardly anything at all. We'd eat snacks and just laugh and talk for hours. But sometimes Will doesn't show up. There was a time I didn't understand why he didn't show up or why he was covered in bruises and wouldn't look at me the next day.

Finally, when he was fourteen, he told me everything after begging him one day to finally spill his guts.

"Sometimes my dad invites friends over," Will tells me. "He makes me and my older brother Jameson fight. He and his friends bet money on who's going to win."

"Wh-what? What kind of fights?" I ask.

"The kind that hurt like hell. The kind that leave headaches for days and bumps and bruises for weeks. The kind where I have to pound on my own brother and he has to pound on me until one of us is left unconscious. If we say we don't want to do it, my dad threatens us. My dad's threats scare me so bad, that I hit my own brother." Will looks down feeling ashamed as I'm left speechless for what feels like ten minutes. I feel scared for him.

"You've got to tell somebody. Somebody has to help. What about the school counselor, Mr. Miller? Surely he would know what to do or how to stop this."

"Harper!" he interrupts, "I can't tell anyone. You cannot tell anyone. Do you have any idea what my dad would do if I told anyone? He would probably beat me dead. Do you understand Harper? Please. Please just don't tell anyone."

I grabbed his hands and made a promise I knew I had to keep.

Jameson is only two years older than Will. They lost their mom to breast cancer when they were three and five. Will says he hardly remembers her at all. After her death, Will's dad started drinking a lot. Now, he's a raging alcoholic. He forgot how to be a father, if he ever was one. Before they moved here from Cincinnati, Will and Jameson used to stay with their mom's brother, Uncle Mike. One day Jameson tried to get away and go work with his uncle Mike at an Iron Industry plant after he turned eighteen. When their dad found out, he beat Jameson so bad he nearly killed him.

Then he told Jameson if he left, he'd find someone bigger and stronger to come fight Will. So Jameson stayed.

I'm so angry. So angry at Will's dad for doing this to him and his brother for years. After waiting at Boulder Beach for over an hour, I ride my bike toward Will's house so fast my legs burn. Will always stays true to his word. If he told me he'd be here tonight, then he would've been here. How am I going to get Will out of this nightmare? How am I going to confront his dad? All I know is I have to help my friend.

When I get to the trailer park, I notice a bunch of vehicles parked outside of Will's house. What is wrong with these people? I feel sick to my stomach.

I've only been here a couple of times to pick Will up with my parents. I've never been inside. Will has never *let* me inside. I know that what I am about to do is stupid but I have to do something.

I knock once and barge in as if I've always been welcome. I instantly smell alcohol and there's so much cigarette smoke I can hardly see. Music is blaring loudly I know for a fact that nobody saw me come inside. When I get to the circle of drunk and wildly cheering men, I push my way through the crowd to find Will and his brother fighting in the middle of the room.

"Will!" I call out, but nobody can hear me. "Will! I yell again at the top of my lungs as Jameson hits him so hard in the nose I hear it crack.

Not knowing what to do, I see the boom box on a shelf on the other side of the circle of rowdy men. I run around them to get to it and as I unplug it, everybody looks at me. But I'll never forget the way *this one man* looks at me. I can tell his teeth are clenched so hard they might crack; his face is red with veins so big they might burst. He's wearing a tank top drenched in sweat and booze, jeans, no shoes, and a snake tattoo wrapped around his neck.

He blinks slowly and yells, "STOP!" I look over at Will and Jameson as they're staring at me in disbelief.

"Who is this little lady?" One of the drunken men asks.

"This would be Will's girl. She's a looker ain't she?" says the man in the tank top, now smiling.

When the hell has he ever even seen me? I've never seen him.

"You think I haven't seen you whoring around with my son, always down by that shitty lake?" he yells.

I stumble backward. "I-I'm just here to get Will. We were supposed to meet and he never showed up so I figured I'd come get him," I say, looking over at Will as he's telling me something with his eyes.

He's looking at the door. Telling me to go.

I'm not leaving you, my eyes say back.

I slowly look back at Will's dad and he's glaring at me. I've never in my life seen a man look so mad. I wonder how often he looks at his sons like this. It's absolutely terrifying.

"Will! Get your whore out of this house before I do something I'll regret," he says with a cruel smile, showing his yellow teeth.

"Ahh come on man, let her stay. Like you said, she's a looker," another drunk man says as he smacks me on the ass. Before I can turn around to tell this guy off, Will runs up and punches him in the face. Then he grabs me by the arm and drags me out the door.

"You come back here, you'll regret it! You hear me, whore?!" Will's dad screams at me as we continue running out to our bikes.

As we start riding off, in the distance I can hear Will's dad screaming at him to come back. But he doesn't. Without saying a word the whole way, Will gets me home safely.

❧

I'm feeling so worried about Will. What was I thinking? Barging in, pretending to be a hero last night? I feel so terribly mad at myself that I scream in my pillow. I don't even want to get out of bed yet but my mom has been yelling at me to get up for the past thirty minutes.

I hope Will forgives me. I begged him to stay at my house last night. But he never said anything. When he left, I felt more worried for him at that moment than when I thought I was rescuing him. I imagine he had to wait for his dad to be asleep before he went inside his own home. What if his dad wasn't asleep? A terrible guilt rushes over me again.

"Harper! Are you okay?" My mom shouts out again in her concerned tone. I guess that's my cue to get out of bed.

"Yeah Mom, I'm fine. I'm just about to get in the shower, then I'll be down."

"Okay well, your breakfast is cold, but I'll heat it up for you when you're ready."

I've never felt as grateful for my mom and dad as I do right now, especially after meeting Will's father. They keep me safe. They look after me. I used to beg them to bring me home a baby sister or a baby brother. When my mom would go to her regular doctor's appointments, I always waited for her to come back holding a new baby. I don't know why I thought she was going there to have a baby. They just told me a doctor helped bring me into this world so I just assumed that's why she was going to the see him. But my mom finally had to explain that it wasn't going to happen. They tried for years but they never were able to have any more kids after me. I didn't understand it at the time but I eventually stopped asking questions about it.

Then they would always tell me, "You make our hearts so full Harper, all we need is you. Our miracle baby."

Will

She's going to think this is her fault, but what Harper doesn't understand is I've been thinking about enlisting in the military for quite some time now. Graduating high school at age seventeen kept my options limited. Nobody will hire me until I'm eighteen and I can't afford college, but I have got to get out of here. I'm lucky the Navy will give me the opportunity to enlist at my age. After making sure Harper got to her house last night, I ran into her dad. Usually he just gives me a wave or a smiling nod but last night he pulled his truck over and got out to talk to me. He told me he can get me out of this mess for good. Gord and Dorthea have always been so good to me. Since Harper and I have been best friends and they've known the type of home life I come from, they basically took me in and treated me like family. Gord works for the railroad and told me some guys were headed to Cleveland to enlist with the Navy tomorrow and if I wanted him to, he could get me a ticket. This was my chance. I thought of Harper and her bravery that night. I thought of Jameson. I thought of my dad. I knew I had to get out of here. So I didn't even have to deliberate about it. Getting on that train will be the easiest and hardest thing I've ever done.

I pull up to her house and start walking up the steps. We haven't talked since yesterday. I know she thinks I'm mad at her for coming to my house and confronting my dad. But in all honesty, her courage helped set me free. It inspired me in some way to do what I was meant to do. I don't think I'd be ready to leave yet if she hadn't shown up.

Her mom answers the door and asks with concern, "Will, how are you? Come in, Harper is in the back."

I walk out and see her on the tire swing. A wave of grief washes over me as I think about how much I'll miss seeing her every day. I had never planned on kissing Harper. I didn't want to risk everything. I was planning on apologizing when we were supposed to meet at Boulder Beach the next day, but obviously never got the chance.

Now there is definitely some awkward tension between us. "Hey dummy," she says.

"Hey."

"Will, are you okay? I'm so terribly sorry. I don't know what came over me or why I th-"

"Harper, just let me do the talking okay? I'm not mad at you. At the time, I was mad at you for putting yourself in that kind of danger but I realized you were only trying to help me. You're so incredibly brave Harper. I couldn't ask for a better friend than you. I've got something to tell you."

"Okay." She's looking up at me from the swing with those hazel, worrisome eyes.

"I'm leaving. Tonight."

She's standing up now with a look on her face I think might shatter me. If I stare at her too long, this look she's giving me right now is going to force me to stay.

"What do you mean you're leaving? Where are you going?"

I grab her hands and tell her about the train ticket from her father, about joining the Navy and getting out of this town.

"But what about trying to find work? What about possibly going to college?" she asks with a shaky voice.

"You know I have to leave Harper. I'm going to try to make something of myself. And it's not forever. Maybe the Navy will even help me pay for college someday."

I brush my thumb across her beauty mark as the corner of her eyes moisten and her lip quivers.

"I don't want you to go," she says as she hugs me. Holding her is making it hard to want to leave again.

"I know. Stay strong, okay? I'll be back to visit before you know it," I say looking down at her incredibly pretty face, still holding her. I'm about to tell her I'm sorry for kissing her the other night but then I look down at her lips and remember how good she tastes. We are both staring at each other like we want it to happen again.

It could never work.

As if she can tell I'm unsure of what to do, Harper stands on her toes and kisses me with her soft, full lips. The gentleness of the kiss quickly turns into a deep, passionate one. We can't stop but if we don't, I worry I won't get on the train. So I gently pull away and realize this is a mistake. A mistake I never want to forget.

I can't love her. I can't.

I walk away without looking back.

Chapter Six

Will

One year later...

Dear Will,

I'm so happy to finally be done with high school! A couple months ago, I received my acceptance letter to Copper Hill University. I got in! I can't believe I'm going to college. In the city. I'm so excited! And nervous. How are you doing? I haven't heard from you in a while. I ran into Jameson a couple days ago at the carwash. Oh, I bought myself a car after graduation! I saved up my allowance and babysitting money just to get it. I think my parents are having a hard time with me being away so having a car will make it easier for me to drive home whenever I want. Anyway, Jameson told me about working at the carwash part-time now while he goes to the Police Academy. I think it's so great that he wants to become a police officer. He told me you're doing more training in North Dakota. That's how I got this mailing address. I miss you. I hope to hear from you soon.

Love, Harper

I feel bad for not writing to Harper as much as I should. The truth is, it hurts me. It's a punch in the gut that I can't see her every day. And I think she deserves better. She doesn't deserve to be kissed like that, only to be left behind. But I honestly don't know how to explain it. I know I can't be with her because she's way too damn good for me. So why did I do it?

It's been a year since we said goodbye, but I still think about her every day. I don't think I'll ever stop thinking about Harper. I push my thoughts aside.

She's your best friend, don't mess that up.

"I hereby volunteer for duty in Afghanistan," I raise my right hand and state that simple phrase to the recruiter.

Harper

I've written Will so many letters since he's been gone. He hardly ever writes back. I used to look outside my bedroom window every morning, waiting for the mailman. As soon as he delivered the mail and drove off I ran down the stairs and through the front door, only to be let down. The days he did write back and I finally got a letter I would get so excited. But after opening the letter, I saw that he hardly wrote anything at all. I've also written some letters that I never sent Will. That I never planned to send him. Telling him off for kissing me like he did, and then leaving without any explanation. Writing those fake letters to him makes me feel better.

Dear Will,

I miss you. Do you miss me? Because it sure doesn't seem like it. You hardly ever write to me. Why? Is it because you kissed me? Gosh, the way you kissed me Will, it had me convinced you feel the same way as I do. You shouldn't have kissed me. You can't kiss a girl like that and leave her. If you wouldn't have stopped us that night Will, I would have gone even further. Sometimes I go to Boulder Beach just to imagine our fire and the way you looked with your shirt off. The way you kept looking at my legs when I was wearing just your t-shirt. I loved watching your reaction. And I was completely shocked when you kissed me the way you did. It's like you've been wanting to do it for years. Have you Will? Have you been wanting to kiss me for years? Do I mean anything to you? Or am I another dum dum sucker girl to you? Please explain. Please write to me and tell me how you feel. Please.

Love, Harper

Dear Will,

I think I'm in love with you. I can't stop thinking about you. I can't stop thinking about the way you kissed me. And the way you look at me sometimes. I wish you would tell me how you feel. I wish I had the courage to actually send this letter. I miss you so much it hurts. Like sometimes it physically hurts me that you're not here. I feel like I'm not home. I feel homesick. Is that a thing? To be homesick for someone? Because that's exactly how I feel. Will, why did you do this to me? I hate you for kissing me. But I don't really hate you. Not at all. I could never hate you. You mean the world to me. Do you ever even think of me? Or am I freaking dirt to you? I sound like a crazy person. Goodbye Will.

Love, Harper

Dear Will,

I'm trying so hard to get over you. I kissed a boy last week and it was fun. I even used my tongue. Like you did with me. But it wasn't the same. It's never the same. And the boy was cute, too. Maybe even cuter than you. But he's not. Nobody is as cute as you. Nobody even compares to Will Karter. The cutest boy that ever was and ever will be. Why did you have to make me fall in love with you?

Love, Harper

My senior year of high school was definitely not the same without Will. I never really got over him being gone, but I'm adjusting. Some days I half expect him to come home and to tell me he's changed his mind. There are days I really wish he would come back. I started doing everything I could to keep my mind off of him. My senior year, I hung out mostly with Claire and Flora. I'd go to parties with them and kiss random boys.

Today I'm packing up the rest of my things for college. I leave in two days. I hear my dad knock on my bedroom door. I know it's him because his knock always sounds the same. Four fast knocks, then two slow ones.

"Come in Dad."

He opens the door and asks, "How's the packing going? Can I help?"

"I'm just about finished. But if you want to help carry these boxes out to the car that'd be great," I say.

"Of course. I'll do that now. Oh and before I forget, a letter came for you in the mail." He hands over the envelope and I see it's from Will.

He takes some boxes and heads downstairs. Trying not to feel too excited as I open it, I begin reading it.

Dear Harper,

Copper Hill University! I knew you could do it. I received your letter just a couple weeks before leaving for San Diego. I hope graduation went well. I wish I could have been there. How's Taffy? I'm sorry it's taken me so long to write back. I've been trying to find the right words to tell you. The reason I was training in North Dakota was because I was going through the Fleet Marine Force school as a Field Corpsman. I've volunteered to be deployed to Afghanistan with a Marine Corps unit. I leave in two weeks but by the time you get this letter it will probably be a week. I know it's going to be hard for you but I just wanted you to know. I miss you a lot.

Run the universe.

Love, Will

As soon as my dad comes back to my room and asks if I'm okay, I break. I don't want Will to go to Afghanistan. Soldiers are dying over there every day. My dad puts his arm around my shoulder, "Are you okay Harper?"

"Will is going to Afghanistan," I say and bury my face into his shoulder and cry.

"Oh, I'm so sorry. That must be scary for you," he says, comforting me.

"What if he doesn't make it home?" I ask fearfully.

"I know you are worried about Will and that's okay. It's scary to know that he's risking his life. But what he needs now more than anything is support. The more support he has, the better attitude and head space he will have. Does that make sense?"

I nod and say, "I'm going to go to the lake and write Will a letter. Thanks, Dad."

I kiss him on the cheek before leaving.

I'm sitting at Boulder Beach trying to come up with the right words to say to Will. I'm staring out into the water when I hear something behind me.

When I turn around and look my heart feels like it's about to burst.

"Will?"

Will is standing there looking at me with a big grin on his face. All my feelings come rushing back to me as I jump off the rock and run up and wrap my arms around him as he hugs me back. We stay like this for a moment then I ask, "What are you doing here?"

He looks older. Even better looking than before.

"Did you get my letter?" he asks.

"Yes. I got it today. I was just writing you back."

"Your house was the first place I went when I got home. Your mom told me I'd find you here. They gave me some days off before leaving for Afghanistan. I found out right after mailing your letter or I would've told you." He looks a little sad when he adds, "I've missed you Harper."

"I've missed you too. Will, I'm so proud of you."

He grins, "I'm proud of *you*. For getting into such a great school. That's incredible!"

"Thanks. I have to leave in two days. I wish we had more time –"

"Two days is plenty of time," he interrupts, "I'm happy for you."

I can't believe I'm having an actual conversation with Will. In our spot. It feels like a dream. I've come here a few times since he left, mostly on days that I just really missed him. Sometimes I'd imagine having conversations with him. Sometimes remembering our kiss. I thought about coming back here to watch the fireworks on the Fourth of July last month but it would've been too hard without him.

"You okay?" he asks.

"Yeah. I just can't believe you're here."

Chapter Seven

Will

On my way back home from California, I didn't know if Harper had left for college yet. Part of me was praying she was home so I could see her. Another part of me was hoping she'd left. Only because saying goodbye again is going to be excruciating. And if it's possible, she's even prettier than before.

"You've changed," I tell her as we walk back to her house. I can't stop looking at her.

"Oh really? How so?" she asks.

"You just seem different. More mature, maybe. Older." I say, trying not to offend her.

She laughs as she says, "I'll take that as a compliment, I guess. You've changed too."

We get to her house and her parents aren't home.

"My mom and dad will be back later. They're going to a wedding reception."

"Yeah, your mom told me," I say. "She offered to let me stay in the guest room. But if it's too weird for you I can stay with Jameson."

"Of course not. I want you to stay. So what do you want to do?" she asks. "We can take my car and go see Jameson."

"I'll meet up with him later. I'll have plenty of time to spend with him when you leave for school in two days. For now, I just want to spend time with my best friend."

She smiles widely and I get to see her dimples. Without even realizing it, I'm looking down at her, touching the corner of her mouth. She blushes and looks away.

I hate how much I just loved making her blush.

Harper looks at me enthusiastically and says, "I have an idea. I'll be right back."

After a few minutes she comes back downstairs wearing a tank top and some shorts. *Holy hell.* Harper really has grown up. Her body is not as petite as it used to be. She has developed curves and it takes serious strength to keep myself from looking at them. I have to remind myself I shouldn't be looking at her like that because she's my friend. *Nothing more.* She's holding roller skates in her hand.

"We're going roller skating. I know the perfect place. Don't worry they have skates you can rent there."

I nod. *I'll do anything you want Harper Pearson.*

Harper

Will and I have been skating for an hour now and he's finally getting the hang of it. Sort of. He stumbles and falls on the empty floor. I've come to this roller skating rink a lot with Claire and Flora, so I knew a Tuesday afternoon wouldn't be crowded. I want Will all to myself. I make my way over to him and we're both laughing so hard we can barely breathe. I've missed his laugh so much.

"I am not good at this," he says, still laughing.

"No but you're getting better. And I haven't laughed this hard in such a long time. It's nice."

I don't think I ever laugh this hard with anyone else.

I help him up and he says, "Well, this is fun and all, but I can't feel my ass."

"Let's call it and go get a shake."

We find a bench to sit on. Will slips off his roller skates and takes them back to the counter where he rented them. I'm struggling to get out of my skates that obviously don't fit anymore. I'm grunting as I try pulling one of them off when I hear Will's laugh. I look up at him.

"My roller skates are getting way too small for my feet," I tell him before standing up. I try getting it off with my other foot when Will takes over.

"Let me help you before you hurt yourself," he says, helping me back down on the bench. He sits next to me and picks up my foot with the roller skate that I'm sure is now permanently attached. It takes him a minute as he gently pulls it off and puts it on the floor.

"Gah, thank you. I'll have to remember to buy some bigger skates," I say as I'm about to stand up.

But I can't stand up because Will still has my foot in his hand. I feel his thumb stroking the top of my toes and the sensation causes me to take a gulp of air. His hand tenderly slides up my ankle as he looks at me with a pained expression. Like he's aching for something. Then he gently sets my foot down on the floor. My legs feel weak as I stand up. Not because I was just roller skating, but because of what Will just did to my foot.

When we get to the diner, we sit down in a booth by the window and order a chocolate shake and some French fries to share.

When Will gets up to use the restroom, I notice a man in a ball cap stop him to talk to him. When Will gets back I ask him who it was. "No idea. He thought he recognized me from somewhere."

"So how do you like being a Navy Corpsman?" I ask him, biting down on a hot French fry.

"I like it. The training was hard, working in the hospital was really difficult, but I learned a lot. I like helping people. I just hope I can give those marines the proper medical care they need while we're over there."

I grab his hand. "You're going to do amazing things, Will. They'll be so lucky to have you," I say encouragingly.

"Thanks," he says. Then he moves his hand away from mine.

"Have you decided what you're majoring in yet?"

"Social work."

"Harper, that's brilliant. I can't imagine a better job for you than that," he says smiling proudly.

I think to myself how I don't want to bring up old wounds *literally* but Will definitely impacted my decision on choosing this line of work. I want to help children living in situations like he did. Like, really help them. I don't want him to have to think about his hard childhood so I just say, "Thanks, Will."

My parents are still gone when we get back to the house.

We go outside in the yard and Will is pushing me on the tire swing when he asks, "So, what have I missed since I've been gone? How was your senior year?"

"It was okay. It wasn't the same without you but I had fun with Claire and Flora."

"That's awesome. Did you date anyone? Or are you dating anyone?" he asks.

"Yeah, I have about ten boyfriends now. In fact, one of them will be here any minute," I say and we both laugh.

"Have you kissed anyone?"

I stop the tire swing and stand up. "Yes. As a matter of fact I have." I step closer to him, looking him in the eye as I continue to say, "I've kissed other boys. But no matter who I'm kissing or how many boys I kiss, none of them ever even compare to kissing you. Is that what you want to hear, Will?"

I turn around and start walking inside when Will says, "Harper, wait. I'm sorry. That wasn't fair of me to ask."

I turn around and he looks like he feels bad.

"Why did you kiss me if you regret it so much?" I ask.

Before he can explain, I run into the house.

Will

I'm such an asshole.

What was I thinking? Asking her if she's dating anyone and if she's kissed someone? I'm so fucking stupid. I wasn't expecting her to say that none of them compare to kissing me. I can tell that I've hurt her. It's going to tear me apart. I'm pacing back and forth outside when I notice a light come on, illuminating the back patio.

Harper's parents walk outside and Dorthea says, "Will! We're so happy to have you here." She gives me a hug.

Gord hugs me too. "How are you doing, son?" he asks.

"I'm okay. Thanks for letting me stay."

Then Dorthea says, "Where's Harper? Have you both eaten dinner?"

"Harper went inside. Said she needed to clear her head. It might have been a mistake, me coming here."

Gord grabs my shoulder and says, "Of course it wasn't a mistake. You have to say goodbye before you leave for Afghanistan. That's important."

I smile and Dorthea says, "We are so proud of you. Now come in and let me fix you a sandwich before you starve to death."

We go in the kitchen and I spend time with the two people who have always treated me like their own son.

Harper

I can hear my parents and Will laughing downstairs. I know I overreacted earlier. It's only ten o'clock. I don't want to sit up here and sulk all night while he's here. I've got to make the most of the time I have left. I swallow my pride and walk downstairs.

Nobody is in the living room but the light is on out back. I walk outside to the lit up back patio and my dad is messing with the stereo while my mom and Will are sitting on the patio chairs. My mom is laughing and Will is holding a beer in his hand. A string of bright yellow lights hang from two trees. It's so beautiful out here on summer nights. My dad smacks the stereo and says something about fixing it tomorrow. Will notices me and gives me a look that says *I'm sorry.*

I smile and my mom stands up and says, "We're going to bed. You kids have fun."

She motions for my dad to come with her inside as she opens the back door. After telling them goodnight, I lean up against the railing as one arm comes across my chest to hold the other arm. Slowly, I look up at Will as he stares at me.

"Do you remember when you and your dad would dance together out here?" Will asks.

I nod my head and laugh at the memories.

"I remember him blasting that stereo to some music from the 80's and teaching you all sorts of dance moves," Will says. "The way he used to flip you back over his arm and about gave your mom a heart attack every time was hilarious."

"Oh my gosh." I say as I can't help but laugh. "I don't think I ever landed on my feet when my dad would flip me over his arm like that. But it was so much fun dancing with him. No matter how ridiculous it probably looked as I stumbled through every dance move he taught me."

Will laughs and awkward silence takes over. I press my lips together and inhale as I'm about to tell him goodnight. Even though I really don't want to.

"Harper," Will says quietly.

Music comes on from the stereo, startling me.

It's definitely on a station my dad would listen to. Some old, slow love song with so much static on the radio you can barely make out the words.

"We better let your dad know he doesn't need to fix it after all," Will says with a grin as he stands up out of his chair.

"Dance with me?" he asks.

I take his hand and Will backs up so our arms are straightened out before twirling me back to him.

"Your dad isn't the only one with the moves," he says, making me laugh. He pulls me in his arms and holds me close from behind.

"I'm so sorry about earlier," he whispers, "you didn't deserve that. It isn't any of my business who you kiss."

I turn around to face him as I say, "I'm sorry too. I overreacted."

"No you didn't. And I don't regret kissing you, Harper."

I hold on tight to his hopeful words as he bandages my heart. *He doesn't regret it.*

Then Will rips off the bandage when he says, "But I know that it can't happen again."

I've just got to accept the fact that Will only wants to be friends with me. Nothing more. "Friends?" I ask as we continue to sway to the low quality music.

"Friends," he says.

Will

I know I'm probably holding Harper too close as we dance. She wraps her arms around the back of my neck as I pull her face against my chest. I could stay like this forever. I smell a hint of citrus shampoo in her long, wavy hair. It goes halfway down her back now. She's still pressed up against me when she looks up. I can feel her breath on my chin. It sends chills down my spine. *I want to kiss her again.*

"Are you nervous? To go to Afghanistan?" she asks softly.

I think about it for a moment and say, "Not yet, but I'm sure I will be. Are you nervous about school?"

She laughs. "That is not even remotely the same and I feel silly telling you that I am a little nervous. How am I the nervous one? It's pathetic."

"No, it's not. I'd be nervous for college too. It's way scarier than war," I make her laugh. Laughing with her all day was something I didn't even realize I desperately needed.

"God, I've missed you," I accidentally say out loud.

She looks hard at my face with her pretty golden eyes. I know she wants to know how I feel. I can't give that to her right now. Not before leaving. I don't even know if I know how I feel. Or if I want to admit what I'm feeling. It's too much.

"Sometimes you're so hard to read," Harper says quietly.

I feel bad she has to try so hard to understand me. I wish more than anything I could let her in. But I can't.

I playfully twirl Harper around and dip her back down. When she comes back up, her smile almost destroys me when I realize I *can't kiss her.* We're no longer moving with the music as we hold each other's gaze. Harper's expression is serious now and I want to kiss her so bad it hurts. The painful urge causes me to let go of her. She steps back and clears her throat. I can't help but notice the disappointment in her eyes but I have to ignore that.

The radio is almost completely transmitting static now as some jazz song tries to play in the background. Harper walks over to shut it off.

I know if we stay out here any longer, I'll end up breaking my word and kiss her, so I say, "I guess I better go to bed. I had fun today."

"So did I," she says as we make our way inside.

It's probably a good thing that the guest room is downstairs. The more distance between us, the better.

I'm standing at the bottom of the stairs watching Harper as she's slowly walking up to her bedroom. She stops and looks back at me over her shoulder. We just stare at each other. Her eyes are inviting me to follow her. Her eyes are longing for me in an almost painful way. I want to take her pain away. But *I can't*. I'm doing it for her, I've got to remember that.

I can't come to your room. I'll kiss you. I'll do more to you than kiss you. I want to do more to you. I want to feel you. I want to explore every part of you. I want to taste every part of you. I want to hear the sounds you make when I'm inside of you. I want to tell you how beautiful you are. But I can't. I leave her longing eyes on the staircase and I walk away.

How many times can I walk away before I fucking break?

Chapter Eight

Harper

It doesn't sound like anyone else is awake yet. I jump out of bed, brush my teeth and go downstairs. As I'm making coffee I hear the front door open quietly. It's Will. All sweaty and breathing heavy. He's not wearing a shirt and I see muscles on him that I've never seen before. Why does he have to look so good?

"Good morning dummy," I say.

He jumps when he hears me.

"Geez, Harper you scared me. I was trying to sneak in so I wouldn't wake anybody up. I went for a run early this morning," he says, making his way over to me.

Will is ripped... and is that a tattoo?

A line of thick pine trees are wrapped around his upper arm and cover his shoulder. It reminds me of Boulder Beach and I can't help but smile. "Nice ink."

"Thanks."

I'm imagining what it would feel like to run my hands across the black trees and over his muscles when he asks, "How was your night?"

Terrible. I couldn't sleep knowing you were right downstairs.

"Good. Want to help me make breakfast?" I ask.

"Yeah let me go take a quick shower then I'll be down to help."

Now I'm imagining Will in the shower, *naked.*

"Harper? Are you okay?" Will asks, smiling at me like he just heard my thoughts.

I can't help but continue to look at him and his beautiful body.

I stumble over my words then cover with a question. "Do they make you work out every day in the military?"

"Pretty much. It's more of a habit for me now. It helps me clear my head," Will says as he walks into the guest bedroom to gather his clean clothes.

"I'll be back!" he says, making his way up the stairs to the bathroom.

As I'm mixing up the pancake mix, I hear the water running. Running over Will's body. *His naked body.* I think about how badly I wish I was in my shower right now to witness the water running down his... muscles.

Will

Harper was checking me out so hard downstairs that I can't help but smile. I quickly shower and change.

She's sitting on the counter drinking her coffee when I get back to the kitchen. She's still wearing her black pajama short set. I'm imagining what it would feel like to wrap her bare legs around me and kiss her warm vanilla-flavored mouth when she says, "You just missed my dad. He left for work. My mom went back to bed when I told her we were making breakfast."

I smile. "What are we making?"

Harper hops off the counter as I'm taking a step toward her and we bump into each other. I think my eyes just gave away how sexy I think she is right now because she's blushing.

"Sorry," she giggles. *She's so unbelievably gorgeous in the morning.*

She tucks her hair behind her ear. "We're making pancakes, eggs and bacon. I already mixed up the pancake batter. I'll have you make the eggs since you're the scrambled egg pro," she winks.

I'm whisking the eggs while Harper is flipping pancakes. I hear the bacon grease pop and turn off the stove because the bacon looks nice and crispy. I turn back around and Harper is looking at me playfully with a spatula covered in pancake batter.

"Don't you dare," I say, walking around the kitchen counter to take cover.

"Fine, but your eggs are burning and I'm not touching them. My mom loves your scrambled eggs. She'll be so disappointed when they're burnt." She smiles slyly.

I quickly make my way back to the eggs and I'm flipping them as fast as I possibly can when I feel a wet spatula slide across my cheek. I turn around, wrap my arms around Harper as I push her backward and pretend like I'm about to dip her hair into the bowl of pancake batter. Both of us are laughing.

"Will!!" she squeals.

I release her then scoop some batter with my finger and tap her on the nose.

"Now we're even." I turn around to stir my eggs again.

"What's the plan for to-" I start to say as I feel something hit the back of my legs. "What the?" I say and look down at my pants. They are covered in white powder. Flour. She threw a handful of flour at me. I spot the bag of flour and dart toward it as she runs away. After grabbing a handful, I chase her with it. She goes running up the stairs and I'm right behind her as she slips into her room. She buries herself under the covers on her bed. I quietly walk over to her so she doesn't hear me. I'm beside her bed as she lifts up the covers to peek and I dust her in the face with the flour. She screams and we are both laughing uncontrollably.

Harper's face is covered in flour so I kneel down next to the bed. She's not laughing anymore when I wipe some of the white dust off underneath her eye with my thumb. This causes her chest to rise as she takes deep, nervous breaths.

That, and the way her lips are slightly parted are pulling me in closer. *I can't want her like this.*

I stand up when I smell something burning.

"Shit," I say and run down the stairs leaving Harper in her bedroom.

I'm throwing the burnt eggs in the trash when Harper comes walking down with a clean face.

"How are the eggs?" she teases and I glare at her playfully.

"I'm making your mom new ones."

After we finally finish making breakfast it's already ten AM. Harper's mom walks into the kitchen and joins us to eat.

"Grandma Pearson called and invited us over for lunch later if you guys want to go," Dorthea says as we are cleaning up our breakfast mess. "And how did you guys manage to produce such a mess making breakfast? I knew when I heard you two laughing there must be a food fight going on down here. My sister and I used to have those all the time," she says.

"Sorry about that, Dorthea," I say, getting the broom out of the pantry.

Then Harper says, "We'll come to lunch with you Mom. Will and I are going to town. We'll meet you there afterward."

Chapter Nine

Harper

"We are going to stuff this bag so full of candy," I say to Will as we walk around the new candy shop in town. "These are my favorite. Rock candy suckers. You need at least three," I say, dropping one of each color into the bag.

"That was like five." He laughs.

"I know you like your sweets. And like I said, they're my favorite," I say as I scoop all kinds of chocolate covered nuts into our bag. "What else?" I ask him.

"Gummy bears?" he asks.

"Oh yeah they have some covered in chocolate right here," I say, opening the container.

Then I spot some dum dum suckers in a huge jar.

"Are you going to need any of these while you're in town, dummy?" I tease him.

He laughs. "I definitely do not need any of those."

"I can't believe you sucked on a dum dum sucker every time you kissed a girl just to help your breath."

I wonder why Will never sucked on a dum dum sucker before kissing me. Then I realize it's obviously because it was an unexpected kiss. The rest of the girls were intentionally kissed.

"Wait. I didn't suck on a dum dum sucker because of my breath," Will says.

I turn around and look at him.

"Why else would you eat a sucker before putting your tongue in someone else's mouth if not to taste good?" I ask.

"No. That's actually not why at all. You gave me a dum dum sucker when we were kids the first day we met. I was so nervous being at a new school. That sucker seemed to help calm me down. I didn't only eat a dum dum sucker before I kissed girls. I eat them before anything that makes me nervous. Hell, I ate one before enlisting with the Navy," Will says.

Looking into his eyes, I can't help but fall even more in love with him. Why does he have to say things that make me want to devour him right here in the candy shop?

"You're definitely going to need some of these before going to Afganistan, then."

After dropping some dum dum suckers in the bag, we find even more candy, and by the time we're done, our bag is overflowing.

"We're going to be sick," he says.

We pay for our candy and make our way downtown.

I spot these beautiful turquoise beaded bracelets in the gift shop but when I look at the price my jaw drops. Definitely can't get one of those.

I look up to see Will staring at me from the corner of the store. I smile at him. He smiles back when I see a man with gray hair walk up to him.

I hear the stranger say, "Is your old man still locked up?"

Will nods.

I recognize him as I get closer. He's the creep who slapped my butt at Will's trailer home the night I stopped the fight. The guy Will punched in the face before we left.

Will glances over at me. His eyes are telling me to stay away. I try to eavesdrop from across the store.

"Why don't you come with me to the bar tonight? I told your pop I'd watch out for you. He sure was mad when you left without saying a word," says the gray-haired man.

"No thanks. I have plans," Will says.

The man looks offended. "Are we not good enough for you? Why do you think you're better than us? Come on. We'll call up your brother. He's still around. He shows up to fight nights from time to time to earn some extra money. We have a place set up in my pal's basement. It's like an actual ring you see on TV. Maybe the two of you could fight again. Each fight was always so unpredictable with the two of you. I'd bet on you now. Look how big you've gotten."

My blood is boiling and I've got to help Will get out of this situation. When I begin walking toward them, Will looks up at me and shakes his head.

The man looks over his shoulder to see what Will is looking at when he spots me. That's when I notice the man has a huge black eye. He immediately recognizes me and laughs. He looks back at Will.

"I see. I see why you don't want to come near us anymore. This tramp has you brainwashed. Is that it?"

Will clenches his jaw. He looks pissed but he holds back.

The man continues, "Is she telling you we're bad people and that you're different? Well I'll tell you what. You're nothing."

Then the man leans in and whispers something to Will and I can't make out what he's saying. Then he spits on Will's feet and says, "That's from your Pop."

I've never seen Will look so mad. He grabs the man by the collar and says something aggressively into his ear. The man tries to push Will back, but Will is too strong. He's gripping the man's shirt so hard I can see the veins in Will's forearms. Will shoves the man backward when the cashier grabs the phone, probably to call the cops.

The gray haired man is red in the face when he says, "I ain't scared of you boy. Hit me. I want you to hit me."

Will fake laughs and says, "I'm not going to hit you Bert. Why are you even here? Did my dad send you to spy on me? Is that it? Well, you can tell him that I'm going to war. I leave for Afghanistan in a few days. So he can quit sending his friends my way. And stay away from Jameson. He's training at the police academy and soon will be able to arrest your ass if you go near him or Harper."

The man mumbles something to himself and walks out of the gift shop.

I walk over to where Will is still standing.

"Sorry about that," he says, turning away.

I touch his warm face and make him look at me.

"Are you okay?"

"I'm fine. Let's get out of here."

Will

I can't believe Bert came into the gift shop to threaten me. To threaten Harper. He's such a piece of shit. I'm so pissed off. I wish I could have beat his ass. He deserves it. He also deserved the threat I gave him about touching Harper ever again. I thought I was going to kill him. Especially after what he whispered to me, that he'd do a lot more to Harper then slap her ass if I hit him again. Then the perverted piece of shit wanted me to hit him. He was trying to anger me and I know my dad had something to do with it. How I held myself back is beyond me. James and I have always promised each other we'd stay away from my dad's crowd. I've got to make sure he stays away from them when I'm gone. What was he thinking? Fighting illegally to make some extra money? That could ruin his career as a police officer. I can't spend the rest of today feeling like this. I have to get over it. We walk back to Harper's car.

"Are you sure you're okay Will?" Harper asks again.

I smile at her, "Of course I'm okay. I have a bag full of candy and I get to see Grandma Pearson today."

The smell of baked bread fills the little house as we walk into Grandma Pearson's for lunch and I instantly feel nostalgic. I used to come here with Harper a lot when we were kids.

"Hello, Will!" Grandma says excitedly, "I was so excited to hear that you're in town, I just had to have you over for lunch. How are you?" she asks, giving me a welcoming hug.

I say, "Thank you for having me. I'm doing well. How are you doing?"

"You're just the sweetest. So polite. And I'm not going to give credit to the military because I know you always have been. Look how grown up you are. You're a man now. And a man's gotta eat!" she says, "Harper, Dorthea help me in the kitchen will you?"

I think I knock Grandma Pearson's socks off when I join them in the kitchen to help.

After lunch, Dorthea leaves but Harper and I stay to play card games with Grandma Pearson for hours.

"What do you want to do now?" Harper asks as we pull out of her grandma's driveway. "Do you want to go see a movie?" I ask. "Now that you have a car, we can go to the drive-in."

"Yes! That sounds fun," she says.

The movie is playing on a big screen in front of us. We have the sound on the radio and it's taking everything I have to watch the movie instead of Harper. I can't help but look at her. I honestly could watch Harper all day long and never get sick of it. When we were all cooking in the kitchen at her grandma's earlier I just couldn't stop looking at her. As I was staring at her, I saw someone in the corner of my eye and turned to see her grandma smiling at me. I was caught. I felt like an idiot. Then she slipped me a picture of Harper to take with me to Afghanistan. I pull out a chocolate gummy bear and chew it. It's weird but it's good. Harper is enjoying a rock candy sucker. The way her lips move on the bumpy sucker makes me crave the taste of her mouth. *I'm jealous of that sucker.* She looks over at me.

"How's your candy?" I ask, feeling like a creep ass I've been caught watching her again.

"It's good. Want to taste it?" she asks, handing it over to me.

I want to taste it on you.

Taking the sucker, I take a bite out of it and the sugary rocks fall apart in my mouth.

"It tastes like cotton candy," I say as I hand it back.

She smiles. "It's my favorite flavor."

You're my favorite flavor.

I try really hard to keep my eyes on the screen for the rest of the movie.

Harper

After going to the drive-in we decide to go back to my house. My parents told me they were meeting with friends and they'd be home late.

"It's been a fun day," Will says, sitting down next to me on the couch.

"Yeah it has. My grandma sure was happy to see you."

"I love your grandma. She's always been so nice to me. And I didn't know she was so competitive. Playing card games with her was kind of intimidating."

The fact that Will loves my grandma just as much as I do is heartwarming.

"I just realized I'm starving," I tell him. "We never ate dinner. Unless you count all the candy we had. I'm going to go wash up and then I'll make us something."

After washing my hands, I decide I want to get comfortable. I quickly change into my soft pajama set with the button up top. When I'm done brushing through my wavy hair, I head back downstairs to find Will in the kitchen.

"I hope you still like grilled cheese," he says when he sees me.

"I love grilled cheese."

We're sitting at the table eating our grilled cheese sandwiches and tomato soup.

"I remember making you dip your grilled cheese sand-wich in your tomato soup when we were young. You didn't want to try it. But I knew you'd love it so I told you if you tried it I'd try a pickle dipped in mustard. You must have really wanted to see me eat a pickle dipped in mustard because you agreed. When you tried the grilled cheese dipped in tomato soup, you of course loved it. Then I really wished I hadn't made that deal when I realized what I got myself into. I pulled a pickle from the pickle jar and you said I didn't have to eat it."

Will laughs and says, "I tried to stop you but you dipped it in mustard and took a bite anyway."

We are both laughing and I say, "I must have made a funny face because you laughed so hard you could barely breathe. Then I couldn't breathe either because I was laughing so hard. It was one of those laughs that you feel in your gut, one that you can't control."

He nods knowing exactly what I mean because we've had so many of those laughs with each other.

I wish I could go back in time and pause it in our child-hood. We have so many good memories together.

We stop laughing and look at each other, knowing we won't be able to look at each other for much longer. I'm going to miss him. I'm going to miss everything about him.

Please make it back to me Will.

Will

"Have you made any friends in the military?" Harper asks, as she takes a hair band off her wrist and wraps all of her hair into a ponytail.

When I glance down at her bare neck, I feel a sudden urge to run my mouth over it. I want to feel how soft her skin is on my lips. I clear my throat when I realize I've been staring at Harper's neck for way too long.

"Yeah. My closest friend there is Noel. We're not in the same unit but we trained together. He's deploying too. He was the one who got me to come back home to see you."

"Really? You almost didn't come home?" she asks.

"No. I was worried it would be too hard but then Noel told me I'm a pansy if I don't come back and say goodbye."

She smiles. "I like the sound of this guy. Tell me more."

I laugh and tell her the story of him trying to find a gift for his fiancé, Laura before going home to Pennsylvania.

"We walked through so many shops until he finally found some lingerie that he liked. Then he tried it on in the dressing room just to make sure it was actually see-through."

She laughs with me. "He sounds like fun. I'm glad you came home."

"Me too."

Then she stands up. "I want to show you something."

I follow Harper upstairs into her room. She opens up her jewelry box then pulls out an old, little piece of paper and hands it to me. *To Harper. Happy birthday. From Will.* I read my sloppy handwriting from when I was a boy as she hands me a silver hair clip.

I flashback to when I was a kid. I remember worrying about Harper's tenth birthday. She was having a birthday party and I really wanted to get her a gift. I knew my dad wouldn't let me buy one, so one day when my dad left the house, I started going through some of my mom's old things. I knew it couldn't be something my dad would notice was missing, so I was looking for something small, something that Harper would like. After finding the hair clip, I wrapped it up in some newspaper and wrote her the note.

"This was my favorite gift that I got on my tenth birthday. Do you remember giving it to me?" she asks.

I nod and say, "I do remember. It's the hair clip I snuck out of my mom's things. I can't believe you still have it."

She knows this was my mom's hair clip that I took from my dad because I told her. What Harper doesn't know is my dad noticed the hair clip was missing a couple weeks later. He was always selling things for more booze so I'm sure that's how he figured out it was gone. When he asked me if I had taken it, at first I lied out of fear. Then he told me I could tell him the truth, that he wouldn't be mad about it if I would just tell him. I told him I did take it but lost it at school. He punched me hard in the face, giving me a bloody nose.

"Take it with you," Harper says. "It was your mom's."

"No. I want you to have it. It's yours Harper."

"You can give it back to me when you get home. Please Will, let me give you something to take with you."

I know she's not going to take no for an answer, so I take it from her and tell her thank you. And it means more to me than she'll ever know.

I look down at her mouth. I hate what her smile does to me. I can't feel this way.

Don't think.

"So, since you asked me this last night," she says, "I feel the need to ask you. Have you kissed anyone since you've been gone?"

"Just Noel, occasionally," I joke and we laugh. "No, I haven't kissed anyone."

As I'm thinking she's the last girl I kissed, I notice her lips are pressed together. They slowly come apart and she's looking at me like she did last night on the stairs.

She's got to stop.

She groans.

"What's wrong?"

"Nothing Will, I'm just really struggling," she says.

"Oh yeah? Struggling how?" I ask.

She gets closer and if she takes one more step I'm going to have to kiss her. I can't not fucking kiss her. I look deep into her eyes, trying to read her. *What do you want Harper?*

"Will," she whispers, stepping even closer. She's so close I can almost taste her already. "I want you to kiss me."

I'm a goner.

Our bodies come together as I grab her and crash my mouth down onto hers. She's cupping my face, pulling me even closer. I can't get enough of her. The way she moves her lips, the sounds she makes, the way her tongue feels as it slides against mine. Harper is kissing me so hard I can barely keep up as she backs me up onto her bed. I sit down and she straddles me. We are kissing like we've been waiting for this moment since the last time we kissed. Neither one of us stops for air. I'm worried that if we do, we'll realize what we're doing. Then she grabs my shirt and rips it off over my head. She runs her hands over my shoulders and slides her fingertips across my tattoo of trees. "You covered your scars," she says.

It was a statement, not a question so I don't correct her. The tattoo represents the trees at Boulder Beach. This tattoo is for the touch of her fingertips from that night on the Fourth of July. Harper will never know this tattoo is for her.

She looks like she's trying to inspect everything about me. Her eyes focus on my chest and she slowly picks up my dog tags. She's looking at them like they're the most important thing in this world. Then she completely destroys me when she kisses them, her eyes landing on mine when she does it. She wants me to remember this moment. And I will.

After she sets them back down on my chest, she brings her soft lips to my face before she climbs off me. I watch her as she slides her shorts down, leaving her only in her shirt and panties.

I take a good look at how beautiful she is but I don't wait too long before grabbing her by the waist and pulling her into me. I slowly unbutton her pajama top and I'm at a loss for words. She's taking big, slow breaths as I stand up off the bed and drop her shirt on the floor.

My mind is torn between looking at her or kissing her. I'm just going to have to figure out how to do both. I brush my lips against her soft skin on her neck and shoulders. She smells so freaking good. When my lips finally give my eyes a turn with Harper, I watch her as she brings her arms up to her head and her thick hair comes tumbling down her shoulders.

It's *fucking ridiculous how good she looks.*

I can't decide if I like watching Harper pull her hair up or take it down better, because each movement made me want to put my mouth all over her.

"Harper," I whisper as I move her hair out of my way and frantically kiss her neck. I quickly undo her bra and it falls off of her. My eyes and lips can't seem to stop their battle. The more my eyes look the more my lips want her. My lips win again and land on her chest.

I slowly skim my tongue across one of her breasts. When she gasps, I pull her down on top of me and she brings her mouth to mine. Our chests are pressed together and feeling her bare skin on mine makes me want to explode. She feels so good. She feels like *mine.*

I want her to keep making these noises. She's straddling me now as I run my hands down her back, and grab her hips. I draw her toward me and she moans softly into my mouth. It's the sexiest sound I've ever heard in my life. She's grinding on me slowly as she kisses me. I want to take her all in. I want to watch her and hear every single breath and sound she makes. I want to feel her. I want to savor every single thing she does before it has to end.

By the way Harper is moving and tensing her body, I can tell what's about to happen.

I grab her hips and pull her harder against me to help her finish.

Holy fucking shit.

Her whole body shakes as she moans and I never want her to stop.

"Is that the first time that's ever happened to you?" I ask, touching her rosy cheek.

She nods shyly, making my head spin.

"Can I make you do it again?"

The way she bites down on her lip and nods makes me crazy.

I get on my knees and look down at Harper. All that's left on her body is light purple panties with a dark purple butterfly in the center of them. I slowly slide them off her. The timid smile on Harper's face forces me to kiss her. "I want to taste you. Is that okay?"

She opens her legs and as I make my way down her body, I make sure to taste her *everywhere.* I memorize how each part of her feels on my lips and tastes on my tongue.

And just like before, I make her whole body quiver, but with my mouth this time. I have to hold her steady as she arches her back and moans my name. I make my way back up to her lips and kiss her softly. She takes hold of my hair on the back of my head desperately wanting me to keep kissing her. My head is telling me to stop but my heart is telling me we both need this.

I stop kissing Harper and look down at her face. I want to kiss it again but the way she's looking at me and the feeling I get absolutely terrifies me. If I don't stop now I won't be able to. I can't let this go any further. I'm only going to hurt her.

"Harper," I say as gently as I can. "We can't do this. I'm sorry. I can't risk losing you."

The heaviness I feel in my chest is so sharp, making it hard to breathe.

I look away from her so I can't see the look on her face and sit up on the bed. I rest my eyes in the palms of my hands. *What the hell am I doing?*

"You won't lose me Will. Please," she says. I can feel her standing in front of me but I can't move my hands. I can't.

"Will look at me," Harper says as she moves my hands away from my eyes. I do and realize that looking at her was a terrible mistake. She's right here in front of me, *naked*. *Dammit*. I wish she knew I need her even more than she needs me. I can't tell her that.

"You'll never lose me Will. Never."

"I'm sorry," I tell her before doing the hardest thing I've ever had to do. I get off the bed and leave her room without looking back. *She can never be mine.*

Harper

Will leaves me in my room, alone.

I take out a piece of paper and write Will another letter for my DO NOT SEND box.

Chapter Ten

Will

I hardly got any sleep last night. I wanted to sneak up to Harper's room and finish what we started. I wanted to give her what we both desperately need but I knew I couldn't. I feel like such an asshole right now. How could I have done this to Harper? The one person in the world that means the most to me and I almost screwed her before leaving her. I knew I had to walk out. I knew if she kept saying those things I'd give in. I knew if we kissed even one more time, I'd give in. I know I probably hurt her, but I had to get out. I had to get out before we made the worst mistake we could possibly make right now. I can't make love to Harper. I wish I could have stopped myself from everything else that happened. And now I have to face her. She probably hates me.

I get out of bed. Harper isn't downstairs. Nobody is. I walk upstairs and knock on Harper's bedroom door but she doesn't open it. I don't blame her. I slowly open the door and notice Harper isn't in her bed. I'm about to walk out when I notice a piece of paper on Harper's night stand. I get closer and see that it's folded up and says *Will.* So I open the letter.

My feelings came back to me as soon as I saw you yesterday at Boulder Beach. Who am I kidding? They never left. I'm not sure they ever will. Today I decided that I'm a hypocrite. Why am I so mad at you for not telling me how you feel when I haven't even told you how I feel? It goes both ways. I think we are both too afraid. Afraid of losing what we already have. A friendship so strong that we can't risk messing it up. After our fight, we made up and you held me as we danced. The way you held me is a memory I'll never forget. Why do you have to keep making me fall in love with you Will? I wanted you to come to my bedroom and show me just what you were thinking about when you were watching me on the stairs. I saw the desire in your eyes. You wanted me. You want me. I want you. I don't know how you possibly believe we are just friends. You are so much more to me than my best friend. If only we can overcome our fear. Our fear of losing each other. I can't lose you. But maybe loving each other would be worth it. Why not take the risk?

I hate how painful it is to love you Will. Do you realize what you're doing to me? You almost made love to me tonight. I told you that you would never lose me and you still wouldn't give me what I needed. I needed you to show me. Since you won't ever tell me. Show me and I won't make you tell me. The way you looked at me and touched me had me convinced that you feel the same way. But then when I saw the change in your eyes when we stopped, it completely shattered me. How do you just shut it off? You make it look so easy. I don't want to feel it either. But I do. And I know you do too. You're hurting me. You hurt me more and more each time you pull away. I wasn't expecting you to just walk out. I never knew just how bad you could hurt me until you left me naked on my bed.

You completely stole my heart Will. You continue to steal it over and over again. I wish you would stop stealing it just to break it.

I'm so in love with you. If only I could shut it off the way you do.

Love, Harper

I hate myself.

I hate what I've done to her. I hate what I'm doing to myself. Why did I ever let things go so far? I'm losing Harper more and more every time I'm with her. I'm hurting her. What is wrong with me? I knew by the way she looked at me last night that we were in too deep but I never expected this. I don't know what to think. I don't think she wanted me to read this until after I left.

I leave the letter where it was and go find Harper. I see her out in the field resting her head on Taffy, and Taffy is resting her head on Harper.

I make my way to where they're standing and Harper lets her horse go and looks at me.

Her sad eyes this morning might just break me. This is all my fault. I can't tell her I found the letter. Not yet.

"I took Taffy for a ride this morning."

I know Harper likes to be around Taffy when she's sad. I hate that I'm the one doing this to her.

"Harper, I'm so sorry for last night. It never should have gotten that far."

Devastation is written all over her face when she says, "it's okay. It's not all on you. It was a mistake."

That's exactly what it was. The biggest one I've ever made. But it could've been bigger. I'm so glad I stopped it when I did.

I change the subject. "What time do you have to leave?" I ask. Even though I really don't want to think about that right now, I have to be prepared. And I know I'll have to bring up the letter eventually. But I don't want to ruin our last day together. As hard as it is to see Harper now, it would be way harder not to. I have to be with her today. I just hope I haven't lost my best friend.

"Orientation is at five o'clock. I need to leave by three-thirty," Harper says.

Those words make my heart sink.

"Okay. What do you want to do today, before that?" I ask her cheerfully. I have to make the most of the time I have left with her.

"Do you want to go to Boulder Beach one more time?" she asks. "It's supposed to be nice today. Maybe we could swim and have a picnic? We could invite Jameson to go with us."

I'm relieved she wants my brother to be there. It will make it way easier to just be best friends today. Nothing more. Ever again. I can't keep breaking her heart.

"Let's do it," I say and she smiles.

Harper

Will is looking at me like he's trying to read me. He knows he hurt me by walking out last night without saying a word. I sense he's trying to figure out how to fix the damage. I'm trying not to be upset today, I really am.

Jameson says, "Shit, it's hot out. I'm getting in the water."

"Yeah let's swim," Will says and offers his hand to pull me up off the ground. I'm wearing my black swimsuit under my clothing. I slip out of my yellow sundress and I see Will turn away. He can't even look at me.

I glance at Will as he takes off his shirt and my eyes fall down to his dog tags and I remember the way they felt pressed up against me last night. I quickly get that thought out of my mind and turn my head. I can't even look at *him*.

When we get to the water, Jameson splashes us after he jumps off the rope swing and into the lake. Jameson yells out cheerfully. We laugh and I realize I really need to cheer up. It's my last day here. Will runs up to the boulder rock and grabs the rope that's hanging from a tree. My dad helped us hang it when we first discovered this spot on the beach.

"Wahoo!" he yells, swinging himself into the lake. He's now in the water next to his brother.

I guess it's my turn.

I climb up on the rock to reach the rope swing and realize it's been a while since I've even done this. I feel a little nervous. I'm stalling when Will yells, "Come on Harper!"

I smile as I hop on the rope and swing out over the lake, making sure to let go when I see Will and Jameson under me. The cold water hits me and I let it pull me under, deeper and deeper.

I don't want to die.

I've never had thoughts about taking my own life. But for a moment I think about staying here forever, in this cool water that feels better and better as it pulls me under. There's something peaceful in the depths of the lake. I need to be here. Ironically, I don't feel like I'm being suffocated. I'm alone. I feel free. And if I don't come back up I won't have to say goodbye. I won't have to see the look in Will's eyes anymore. The look that tells me just how bad he regrets what happened between us. The look that crushes me over and over again.

I don't want to die.

But I don't want to leave.

I'm letting the water take me further under when my instincts kick in and I'm forced to swim to the surface for air. I feel a hand grab my arm and help pull me out and I gasp when my head comes up out of the water.

I cough.

"Harper, are you okay?" Will asks with his hand still gripping my arm.

"Yeah, I'm fine."

Will's eyebrows are pulled together. He looks worried and I see fear in his expression.

"I'm fine Will. I promise," I assure him. "The water just felt really good."

"It does feel good, doesn't it? Let's swing off the rope again. But this time don't forget to come back up," he teases as we climb out of the lake.

Jameson is already swinging himself out over the water again.

And we do too. Over and over. Until we feel like kids again. Before life splits us up in different directions. Until we are only left with our goodbyes.

Will

The day at the lake was almost perfect. But I'm worried about Harper. She really scared me today when it took her so long to come up out of the water. I was about to dive down and get her when she finally came up. I just hope she's okay.

After what I did to her last night, I had to try and keep my eyes off of her. If I look at her long, I forget why I can't have her. I'm starting to think distance will be good for us. She'll be so much better off without me here.

We were dreading this moment all day. I hate it. I hate that it's here already. Harper rests her head on my shoulder and cries. We're standing out in the driveway next to her car when she says, "This is so hard."

Saying goodbye to Harper might just break me. This *day* might just break me. I hate that she's hurting and there isn't anything I can do to stop it. I hate that I'm the reason she's hurting. I touch her hair.

"I know," I say.

I'm going to miss you so damn much.

I press my lips against her head and close my eyes.

"When I get back, can I come visit you? At college?" I ask.

"Of course you can Will. I can't wait for that day."

I've never seen her look so sad.

"Harper," I whisper. "It's going to be okay. I'll see you again soon."

Her hazel eyes are red and glazed over with tears. "Will. Please be safe. Please make it back home."

"I will. I'll be back," I know I can't promise that to her but I'm doing my best to reassure her.

She slowly nods her head.

I glance down at her full glossy lips. I know I shouldn't kiss her so instead I just sigh and desperately take her in my arms. We hold on to each other. I'm wishing that time was endless and we never have to pull apart. But we do.

We look at each other. I swallow when I think about last night. My stomach is in knots as I think about the letter. I hate that I broke her heart. I've always tried to protect her from assholes. I never imagined I'd be the one to hurt her. I'm the one asshole I should've been protecting her from and I realize that I have to confess.

"Harper. I found the letter."

Her eyes widen. "What letter?" she asks.

"The letter you're probably about to give me. For me to read after you leave. I already read it. I found it in your room when I was looking for you this morning."

Harper looks completely shocked.

"Will, you were never supposed to see that. It's more like a journal than a letter. I do that sometimes."

I feel terrible. I read her journal? I'm the biggest jerk on the planet.

"Harper, I'm so sorry. I just saw my name on it and assumed you wanted me to read it."

She shakes her head. "You know what. No. I'm glad you read it. Now you know exactly how I feel. Now it's your turn."

I have to look away. I can't look at her. I can't believe this. What the fuck have I done? I can't love her. I just can't. I feel so frustrated. I lock my fingers behind my neck and turn back around.

"Harper, I'm so sorry. Last night never should have happened. You have to understand that I was caught up in the moment. I'm so sorry I let it get carried away. I never wanted to hurt you. That's what I was trying so hard not to do. But I messed everything up. It was not your fault. It's mine. I let my attraction toward you take over. I never should've let that happen."

Tears are streaming down her face. I can barely look her in the eyes. *I hate myself.*

"That's what you're going to call it? Attraction?" she scoffs and looks up toward the sky. She doesn't even want to look at me right now and I don't blame her. She hates me too.

"I see it in your eyes," Harper says. "I see it all the time. Why can't you just say it? You didn't have any problem with almost showing me last night. That was more than attraction and you know it."

She steps toward me and I have to step back. I can't hurt her anymore.

"I love you Will."

"Stop," I whisper. She's got to stop.

"Say it," she says and the agony in her voice is ripping me apart.

"Harper, stop."

"Say it back." She's crying harder now. "I need to hear you say it back."

"I can't do this to you," I tell her.

"Say it," she says louder as she starts to cry harder. I hate seeing her like this. It's going to kill me.

"Please just tell me that you love me," she whispers.

"I do love you Harper. Too damn much to ever be with you in the way that you want me to. I can't love you like that. I love you. But I can never be in love with you."

She's staring back at me, like she doesn't even recognize me. *I don't even recognize me.* I hate what I've done to her. My hands slide into my pockets as I stare at the ground. I can't even look at her anymore. Especially when I tell her this.

"I love you too much to love you," I say, feeling so much shame crashing down on me.

She doesn't say anything back. This is it. Exactly what I didn't want to happen. This is why I never should've let anything happen between us.

I say, "I'm sorry." I look up at her just as she turns her back to me.

My eyes close because I can't stand to watch her walk away after what I've done to her. After what I just said. I hear her car door shut. I hate that I've ruined this goodbye. I hate that she's leaving.

I bite down on my knuckle to stop myself from screaming. I've never been so mad at myself in my life.

As Harper drives off I think about how I wish more than anything I could go back in time and stop her from falling in love with me.

Chapter Eleven

Harper

I 've had to pull over a few times on the way to Copper Hill University because I couldn't see through my tears. I haven't felt pain like this before. This much heartache. The way Will and I said goodbye is not how I wanted us to leave things. I've waited for this day for a long time. To leave home and go to college and have my own freedom. I'm ready for this new chapter. I just wish I could turn off my sadness and be as happy about this day as I should be. But that's not how life works.

I get out of my car and wipe my tears away because it's time to pull myself together.

After orientation, I pull out my cell phone to double check the address to Student Den Apartments. It's going to take some time getting used to driving in the city. I like my privacy so I chose to stay in a student apartment on campus instead of a dorm since there are two bedrooms instead of sharing one.

I take a deep breath as I turn the key and open the door to Apartment 5A. There's a girl with short black hair sitting on the sofa, putting on some tennis shoes. She's wearing black shorts and a light pink tank top. She looks up with her bright green eyes and smiles at me with a mouth full of straight, white teeth. Immediately, I notice how gorgeous she is.

"Hi! You must be my new roommate. I'm Scout. What's your name?" she asks.

I'm instantly flooded with relief that she seems so nice.

"Hi Scout, I'm Harper. It's nice to meet you."

"What a pretty name," she says as she finishes tying her shoe. She hops up off the couch.

"Here, let me help you with your bags," she says, lifting one of my suitcases off the floor. "I'll show you around. I moved all my stuff in yesterday."

After setting my bags down in my room, Scout continues to play tour guide around our new home. The apartment is really nice. What is that amazing smell? It smells like vanilla and flowers. There are two bedrooms, one bathroom, and a little kitchen with a bar and two stools. The apartment is furnished with one twin-size bed and a dresser in each room. There's a couch in the living room, along with a rocking chair, a coffee table and a TV mounted on the wall. A purple candle is burning on the little side table next to the couch.

"You have amazing taste in candles," I tell her, "it smells so good in here."

Scout smiles proudly and shows me her room. A pink bedspread covers her mattress with fluffy white throw pillows. A full length mirror covers one wall. It's adorned with flower stickers and what looks like red lipstick kisses. *Did she actually kiss her own mirror?*

"I love this place," I say, following Scout back into the front room.

"I love it too. So, what brings you to CHU?" she asks as we both take a seat on the couch.

"Oh, I'm majoring in social work. I only live about an hour away from Columbus, so I'm close to home. What about you?"

"I'm far away from home and the boys there."

We both laugh and her positive energy is helping lift my depressed mood.

"I picked this school because of they offered me an athletic scholarship. Only way I was able to afford it. And lucky for me, track doesn't even start until March, so I have plenty of time to focus on the boys here." She stands up. "But the team does meet up at the gym twice a week for workouts. That's where I'm headed. Wish me luck."

She grabs a duffel bag and a water bottle off the kitchen counter and heads out the door.

"Good luck Scout." I shout after her.

***

I'm carrying the last box from my car. I'm struggling to open the entrance door when someone pushes it open for me. The stranger's bright blue eyes are staring back at me. I have to remind myself to breathe, his gaze is so strong and intense. The silence between us is so loud, that I don't even hear myself tell him thank you.

He clears his throat and walks out without a word.

When I get back to my apartment, I unpack my things. I'm doing my best trying not to think of Will. I try not to think of his words, but they're drowning me. I just have to remember how to come back up for air.

***

Scout gets back from the gym while I continue putting away all of my stuff. It sounds like she's in the shower. Hanging up my mirror, I realize it's very boring compared to Scout's. I walk over to my suitcase and pull out some lipstick. Stepping back over again to my mirror, I look at my reflection. My eyes are swollen and red. I rub them as if that will take the puffiness away. Then after applying my pink lipstick, I kiss the side of my mirror. When I pull away I see my lip print.

Scout knocks on my bedroom door and says, "Hey Harper. I made a friend while I was at the gym. He just lives upstairs and he's having a party tonight. Do you want to come?"

I open the door and smile politely.

"No thanks. I want to unpack the rest of my clothing tonight. Thanks for the invite though."

She watches me with a sincere look in her eye. Like she can tell that I'm off. I feel a little embarrassed. She probably thinks I'm such a downer.

"Are you okay?" she asks.

"Yeah. Sorry, I'm not usually like this. I just had to tell my best friend goodbye today. He's leaving for Afghanistan. It's just been hard."

I'm worried that I just overshared because I hardly even know her. But I see pain in her eyes too. Immediately I can sense that she knows how it feels to hurt. Maybe even more than I do.

"He's going to war?" she asks.

I nod.

"I'm so sorry."

She pauses. "You know what. The parties can wait. I'm going to help you unpack," Scout says as she stands next to me in my bedroom. "What can I do?"

I don't even know what to say. "Um. Are you sure? I don't mind doing this on my own. I don't want to ruin your night."

"I hate being alone when I'm hurting. If you want to be alone, I'll leave but I want to be here with you. I honestly don't feel like getting ready anyway."

I smile at my new friend. "Okay. Thanks."

"I'm hanging out with a cute guy from work tomorrow. His name is Luke. If you want, I can ask him to bring a friend and we can double," she suggests.

I take a deep breath and feel that crack in my chest.

Scout says, "Oh, I know that look. You're still trying to get over someone. Don't worry, I get it. When you're ready, there will be plenty of men who will line up to date you."

Am I really so broken that people can actually see it?

"You're right on point," I tell her. "I can't wait to hear all about your date. Where do you work?"

"I work at the gym. I feel like I'm always there between work and the track team, but I like it."

"I need to go job hunting. I want to stay as busy as possible. And I need the money," I admit.

"Something will come up. I'll keep an eye out for you."

***

We're done unpacking all of my things two hours later.

"Wow," I exclaim as we both stand back and examine my new bedroom.

"I can't believe how fast we got that done," Scout says.

"Yeah, thanks to you." I give her an appreciative smile.

"I bought a whole tub of ice cream yesterday. Let's go eat it," she says, walking out of the room.

I follow behind her.

"You could use some sugar therapy," she continues, opening up the freezer.

"I definitely could."

We both plop down on the couch and Scout puts the tub of mint chip ice cream in between us and hands me a spoon.

I ask Scout what she's majoring in.

"Education. I want to be a teacher," she says.

"That's great. What made you choose that career?" I ask.

"I had a teacher really help me through some tough times when I was a kid. Miss Caddel in the fifth grade. One day after school, I waited for my mom to pick me up for hours. This happened before. I didn't understand it at the time when I was a kid but when I got older I eventually figured it out. My mom would be too high in the middle of the day to remember to come and pick me up. Miss Caddel sat down next to me and told me that she didn't mind waiting with me. She didn't even complain about having to take care of me. That day just stuck with me. I want to be the same type of teacher someday. A safe place for my students. When my mom finally sent my brother to pick me up, I didn't want to leave Miss Caddel's side. She made me feel safe. At least school was decent."

"You're going to be the best teacher someday."

Something in Scout had changed from when we first started talking. She's quieter now.

"Are you okay?" I ask.

She looks up at me with a forced smile.

"Yes. It's getting late. I better get to bed before I talk your ears off," she says, standing up.

Then, after saying goodnight, she leaves the couch. She shuts her bedroom door behind her.

At two in the morning, I go to bed feeling happy, knowing that I've already made a friend.

Chapter Twelve

Will

After getting vaccinated myself and then as a Medical Corpsman injecting marines for two weeks in Ukraine, I was finally flown with a few other medics into an expeditionary airfield in Afghanistan to join my unit. The division surgeon told me they were set up in a forward operating base about eighty miles away.

Several attempts were made to contact their HQ to arrange the transfer, but they were unable to get radio contact with them. The Chief said he would get me there the next day with a group that would be headed that way. Since it was getting late and there was no room in the main bunker of the battalion aid station, I was given a cot to sleep on in an ambulance.

Now, here I am trying to get comfortable enough to rest. I'm wearing my sweat-soaked t-shirt, pants, and boots I've had on since yesterday. It's so damn hot and dry here I can hardly breathe. I can't stop tossing and turning. I'm worried my nervous energy will keep me awake all night. I hold on to my dog tags tightly and try to keep still so I can get some sleep.

"We couldn't find you anywhere Will! You scared us," says twelve-year-old Harper as she's walking away from me in her backyard. She's kind of mad and I feel bad.

"I can't believe you hid in the shed that long. Aren't you scared? I'm scared for you." She turns and looks at me but now she's older and she's crying.

"How could you hurt me like this? Wake up, dummy."

I wake up to the sound of an explosion. Reality kicks in as the dream fades away quickly and I remember where I am. There is a searing pain behind my left ear, I reach up to touch it and immediately feel the wet blood. "Holy shit!"

I jump out of the ambulance and begin running to the main bunker. I hear another mortar go off. Everything fades to black.

I wake up lying in the dirt. It takes me a minute before my memory comes back to me. I've been hit twice. My lower back is on fucking fire. I can't move. I think I must be paralyzed.

Eventually, I pull myself together and somehow begin crawling over to the aid station bunker.

"The kid's been hit!" I hear someone yell.

"Let's get him some meds."

I hear footsteps running up to me so I lay back down in the dirt. They push a needle in my arm and then everything goes black again.

Everything is a haze when I wake up, but as it becomes clear the first thing I notice in the hospital is that my dog tags are missing.

"Where are my dog tags?" I ask a doctor behind me, as he's sticking something in my wounded back.

It's his finger.

The doctor doesn't answer me. And he's digging his finger into the wound in my back.

"What are you doing? Answer me, please. Where are my dog tags?"

"I'm Dr. Abner," he finally speaks up. "I'm going to put you under anesthesia and get these pieces of shrapnel out of your back. You were hit by a mortar last night. Don't worry, you're going to be okay. And the nurse took your dog tags for paperwork. She'll bring them back."

"Was anyone else hurt?"

The nurse comes in with my dog tags and I feel bad for acting like a dick. Those dog tags just mean something to me. Ever since Harper put her lips on them.

"Nope. You were the only one," says the doctor.

I'm relieved when he tells me this.

The next morning when I open my eyes, I see something pinned to my pillow. A purple heart.

After recovering for three weeks in the medical facility in Bagram, I was finally able to join my unit at the assigned forward operating base. A senior corpsman at Lima company is taking the stitches out of my back and behind my ear.

"Thanks man. What did you say your name was?" I ask the corpsman when he's done stitching me up.

"Shaun. How old are you? You look like a kid."

I laugh and remember the battalion back at the last base saying the same thing. "That's what they call me. The Kid." And the nickname stuck.

Chapter Thirteen

Harper

S tudents are scrambling around campus as I make my way out of my psychology class. When I first got here, I felt overwhelmed not knowing where each of my classes were. I've been here for over a month now and I'm finally getting the lay of the land.

I hear the sounds of cars whizzing by and breathe in the brisk fall air as I walk down the sidewalk. There are bright red and orange trees lined up down the busy street. The fallen leaves crunch beneath my shoes with each step. I told Scout I'd meet her for coffee after class.

I make my way into the little bakery that's about a block away from my apartment. A cozy feeling warms my soul as the roasted coffee bean aroma surrounds me when I open the door. The smell takes me back home.

There are a few tables set up but I'm sure most people probably just take their coffee to go. I find Scout sitting at one of the tables chatting with a very well dressed blond man with facial hair.

"Hey Scout," I say.

Then I look over at the man and notice his almond shaped eyes. "Hi. You must be Luke. I'm Harper."

They both laugh.

"No, no, no. This isn't Luke. This is Rafe. We're just friends. And I'm done with Luke," Scout says.

Then Rafe says, "I'm your neighbor from upstairs. And trust me, I'm not Scout's type and she's definitely not mine." He stops talking and looks around. Then he cups his hands so nobody can see his mouth as he whispers, "No woman is in fact my type." He moves his hands and leans back in his chair with a crooked smile.

Apparently this is a secret. I think anyone should be able to be open about who they love. But I get it. People are jerks and I hope someday Rafe can feel like he can be who he is without being judged for it.

"Well Rafe, feel free to be who you are around me. It's nice to meet you." I wink.

I get up and walk to the two baristas at the counter.

"Welcome to Steamin' Mugs. What can I get for you?" says a cute blonde lady with glasses.

My parents told me not to get a job while I go to school. They told me they would take care of everything financially so that I could focus on my classes. But I don't want them to have to pay for everything. I know that they've basically been saving every penny that they could just to afford my tuition. I don't want my parents to struggle and I don't want to have to rely on them anymore. I'm here to learn how to be independent and I just realized how much I love this coffee shop.

"Hi I'll take a coffee with vanilla creamer please. And a job application? Are you guys hiring?"

She smiles wide and says, "We are hiring! For the morning shift. It's early. It starts at five-thirty a.m. but you're off by ten a.m. We need someone on Mondays, Wednesdays, and Fridays. Maybe some Saturdays. Are you interested?"

"Yeah, that's actually perfect. My classes don't start until eleven."

"You're hired!" she says. "Can you start tomorrow?"

"Yeah of course! Thank you so much."

"I'm the manager. You'll hardly ever see the owner come in. My name is Tracy," she says with a warm smile.

"I'm Harper. I can't wait to start," I say smiling back.

"Let me get you some paperwork to fill out and an apron to wear tomorrow for your first shift. I'll be here to train you bright and early."

I turn around and Scout and Rafe are giving me a thumbs-up.

Chapter Fourteen

Harper

Today is October twenty-second. I wonder if Will even realizes today is his birthday. I wish I could talk to him. I've gone months without hearing a word from him.

As I'm getting home after my night class, I smell something delicious coming from the kitchen and realize I'm starving.

"Hey, how was your day?" Scout asks.

"Wednesdays might just break me. Waking up before the sun is even up for work and getting home so late is exhausting." I plop myself down on the bar stool and lay my head down on the counter.

"Are you liking your job at the coffee shop?" she asks.

"Yeah. I'll like it more when I get my first paycheck on Friday."

"I made chicken noodle soup," Scout says.

"It smells amazing. You like to cook?"

"I taught myself how when I was little. The cooler weather today made me crave soup," she says, handing me a warm bowl.

"Wow, this looks great. Thanks Scout."

Scout and I have become such good friends, I can't imagine being here without her.

I take a bite of the soup.

"Hot," I whisper and take a drink of water from my water bottle.

Scout is leaning over the bar, smiling at me like she's waiting for my reaction.

"Hot and delicious," I tell her, blowing on another spoonful to take a bite.

"Speaking of hot and delicious, have you seen Rafe's new roommate yet?" she asks.

I almost spit out my soup as I burst out with laughter and say, "No. He already has a new roommate? What happened to his other one?"

"Rafe said his roommate just up and left without a word two days ago. College must not have been for him I guess. I saw Rafe and his new roommate at the gym yesterday. And ho-leee. He's gorgeous. Rafe introduced us."

"If he's that good looking he probably already has a girlfriend."

She shakes her head. "Definitely not by the way he looked at me. He looks like a player though. I could tell because I caught him staring at another girl's ass just before he looked me up and down."

Scout is so observant, especially when it comes to men. She has at least one new boyfriend every week.

"I don't know how you notice these things." I laugh. "I'm going to go get ready for bed," I say standing up. Oh and you know you're a player too right? Just a female version," I joke.

Scout chuckles. "Damn straight. But since you said that, I get to finish your soup."

I slide my bowl over to her and give her a wink before stepping away.

I'm scrolling through my phone looking at pictures of Will and me while I lay in bed. I laugh out loud when I find the selfie I took of us when we were roller skating. I feel a pit in my stomach thinking of the night before he left. And everything we did. I think about that night a lot. And the way he made me feel. But then I remember his exact words the next day: "*I can never be in love with you*" and I feel like my heart shatters all over again. I put my phone away and try to go to sleep. How was I so tired before I came to bed and now I feel restless? I'm so sick of feeling this way. They say time heals all wounds but I still feel broken. I wish someone could tell me how long it takes but I guess you can't put a timeline on the healing process. I'd do just about anything right now to get my mind off of Will. I'm not going to sleep so I get out of bed and throw on some jeans and a sweater.

"I'm going for a drive," I tell Scout who is watching reality TV on the couch. Before she can even answer me, I'm out the door.

I don't know why, but I'm drawn to a bar. It's not like I can order a drink being underage. But it was the only place open and I didn't know where else to go. This particular bar and grill isn't too far from the apartment. Feeling a little ridiculous sitting here like a child, the bartender brings me over a drink. After setting the pretty red drink down on the table in front of me, he walks off.

"Wait, I didn't order anything."

The bartender doesn't hear me. Someone else must have sent the drink my way. They must be able to tell how much I could use one right now. I look around when I notice an attractive man across the bar looking at me. I've seen him before. My face gets hot so I look away. I take a gulp of my drink and feel flustered when I can still feel him staring at me. *Mmm. Cranberry. I love cranberry.*

When I look up at him again he smiles slightly. I smile back. This cranberry drink has him written all over it. As much as I like this eye flirting game we're playing, I want a closer look.

It seems as though I do irrational things when I'm hurting. At least that's what I'm about to do. This guy can't seem to keep his eyes off of me and it's intriguing.

When I get the nerve to walk over to him, I almost turn around when I see the hesitant look on his face. He definitely wasn't expecting me to confront him. He was attractive, even from afar. He's tall and has broad shoulders, his shirt is tight around his arms and I'm a little intimidated when I realize just how blue his eyes are.

"How do I know you?" I ask him as I take a seat next to him at the bar.

His demeanor changed. His focus is now on his drink instead of me. After he swallows he says, "You don't."

"Oh. Well thanks for the drink." I hold it up and take another sip.

He practically tackles the drink as he rips the glass off my lips and slams it on the table. "Don't drink it. I didn't send it to you!"

What the hell is this guy's problem? I realize now that he's the person who opened the door for me when I was moving into my apartment. He was a gentleman then. Definitely not now.

"Sorry," he says, "you just never know. Somebody could've put something in it."

"You think someone drugged my vodka cranberry?" I ask.

I'm about to take another drink but realize it's now spilled all over the table. Ugh, I needed that. I don't say anything else before he gives me a look that takes me by surprise. *Definitely not a gentleman.* He doesn't even have to say he wants me. I see it on his face. *I kind of want him too.*

I just nod towards the women's bathroom. He follows behind me.

My heart is pounding but as soon as we enter the bathroom I take a hold of his shirt and pull him into me as we kiss. He grabs my ass and sets me on the countertop behind me. I'm taken back at how much I'm enjoying his lips and tongue. They're soft, and he tastes like mint gum. *Why do I love that he put gum in his mouth?*

He stops and says, "My name is –."

"Shut up," I say feeling annoyed that he stopped kissing me to introduce himself. I don't care what his name is. Did I really just tell him to shut up? Whatever. I need this.

This will never go anywhere and that's exactly what I want. A distraction for one night. I grab his hair just as he grasps my ass even tighter. His hands are warm, and I can feel my body throb against his. He pulls away for a split second, looks down at my lips then back up at my eyes. Without even thinking I whisper something in his ear I might regret.

"Fuck me."

He steps away and it takes me by surprise. He looks at me like I'm the broken and ridiculous child I am. It's like he knows.

"I'm sorry, did you just tell me to fuck you? We're in a public bathroom and something tells me this isn't you."

I take that as a no and jump off the counter with an annoyed sigh. By the way he was looking at me, I thought he'd be up for it. But I guess not.

He says, "Wait," as I hurry out of there.

But I don't. I'm done waiting on other people. I'm such a mess. I can't believe I just about gave myself to a complete stranger. Was I actually going to go through with it? I just don't care about anything anymore. I wanted to feel something even if it meant giving up the thing that's supposed to be special. I guess that's what happens when you get your heart broken for the first time. That's my excuse for my behavior tonight anyway. *Who the hell even am I anymore?*

Chapter Fifteen

Harper

When I get to Steamin' mugs for my shift, Tracy is starting up the espresso machine.

She sees me and says, "Morning, Harper. Are you ready for our morning rush?"

"Bring on the craziness," I say.

I flip the sign to open at the glass window up front. Someone walks in as I'm putting on my apron behind the counter.

Then I see his bright blue eyes. *Shit. Shit. Shit.* The guy from the bar. For a moment I contemplate ducking behind the counter but he's already looking at me. He looks at me so intensely that I feel nervous.

"Can I get a black coffee to go please?" he asks when he gets up to the counter.

It's only been like a week. Does he not remember me?

"You bet. Can I get a name?" I ask as I grab the marker to write it on the coffee cup.

"Oh now you want my name?" he asks with slight smirk on his face.

Dammit. He does remember me.

Before I say anything he says, "Ardyn."

I feel flustered as I pour his coffee. I wish this man would stop looking at me the way he does.

My hands are so shaky when I'm handing him his cup that I spill a little on the counter.

"Oops. Sorry."

I hand him a napkin.

"Don't mention it," he says.

I watch Ardyn go sit at a table far in the back. He pulls out a laptop and a textbook. Great. If he comes in here every time he needs to study we're going to need a lot more napkins. I'm trying not to make it too obvious when I glance at him. Every now and then when I do, he's already looking at me. There's something so mysterious about him. A girl comes in with bleached blonde hair and rushes over to him. I can tell they are flirting from here. She must be his girlfriend. I bet she has no idea her boyfriend had his tongue in my mouth just last week. *Jerk.*

I'm so thankful more customers walk in so I can focus on them instead.

When I get home after class I find Scout rummaging through the kitchen.

"Hey. Want to go to the library with me?" I ask. "I have so much homework to do."

"Yeah, I should study," Scout says. "Have you been to the Bar and Grill?"

"What do you mean?" I ask. *What does she know?*

"I mean that I'm starving and we have no food. Well nothing that sounds good anyway. Let's go eat there after the library."

She doesn't know. Not that she would ever judge me but I'm embarrassed of how I acted that night. I'd be okay if I could just delete that experience all together. Wouldn't that be nice?

"Sounds good to me."

After studying at the library for a couple hours, we drive my car to the Bar and Grill. We're sitting at a booth eating burgers when a group of college students walk in and wave at Scout.

"Some people from the track team, " she explains.

They sit down at a booth on the opposite side of the restaurant when one of the women with a high ponytail in her hair comes walking past us.

"Oh, hey Scout," she says. "We totally wanted to invite you to join us tonight, but nobody had your number."

"Don't worry about it," Scout says.

The woman turns and walks into the restroom.

"A friend from track?" I ask.

"She's a teammate. I would have introduced you, but she actually doesn't even like me."

Scout is probably the sweetest person I've ever met. So it surprises me that someone could not like her. Some women are funny like that.

"She's probably just jealous. Does it bother you?"

"Not really. What bothers me is that I used to act just like her. Well pretend to anyway. In the past, I'd probably be friends with someone like her. The bitches who are only nice to my face. That type doesn't like me now that I'm myself. You should hear the names they call me when they think I can't hear them. But do I give two shits? Nope," she says before sipping down her water with a straw.

Scout has a mysterious side some people don't understand. I noticed she doesn't like to open herself up a lot. I don't think many people understand that about her.

Their loss.

"You are one of a kind Scout. As closed off as you seem sometimes, you're still yourself around everybody. I love that about you."

She smiles. "I've never had a friend like you, Harper. You see me for who I really am. Thank you for that."

"Well I've never had a friend like you either." I smile back.

One of the men from the track team walks over to our table.

"Hey Scout," he says sitting down next to her, "who's your friend?"

"This is my roommate Harper. Harper, this is Matt."

"Hey," I say to him.

"Are you single?" he asks me. "My friend sitting with us wearing the red shirt wants to know." Matt points to the man in question.

He's kind of cute. I smile and wave at him.

"I'm single. But I'm not interested in dating right now. I'd be happy to get to know him as friends though," I say.

"Cool. Are you guys doing anything tomorrow night?" he asks.

"No plans yet," Scout tells him.

"There's a bonfire going on up Green Canyon if you're interested."

"We'll be there," Scout says eagerly.

I say, "Sounds fun."

Matt pulls out a pen and writes something on a napkin and hands it to Scout.

"Here are the directions. See you guys there," Matt says as he gets up and walks back to his booth.

Scout says, "See ya, Matt."

Chapter Sixteen

Harper

The next day, I do my usual Saturday morning routine. I straighten up my bedroom and help Scout tidy the rest of the apartment. Today is my turn to clean the kitchen and vacuum while she tackles the bathroom.

Afterward, I call my mom. She tells me she hopes I can come home soon for a visit and that she's proud of me for getting a job. When she tells me that I haven't gotten any mail from Will yet, I'm really not that surprised, because of how we left things. He probably doesn't know what to say to me after what happened between us. And I honestly don't know what to say to him.

When I get off the phone, Scout asks me to go to Target with her to get a new outfit for the bonfire tonight.

"Please come with me. I'll drive," she says.

"I love Target. Let's go," I say.

Scout drags me straight to the clothing section when we get to Target. I'm poking around the shirts but not loving anything that I find. Scout looks like she's on an important mission. I've never seen someone so serious about shopping.

"What are you hunting for?" I ask.

"I want to wear something hot tonight," she says, keeping all of her focus on a rack of skirts. "I've never shopped here before, but Target actually has some pretty cute stuff."

"You've never shopped here before? Where do you usually shop for clothes?"

"Gucci. Ralph Lauren. Dior," she names the expensive stores and my mouth drops.

"How? Wasn't your track scholarship the only way you could afford school? I thought you said your family doesn't have a lot of money?"

"I never said that. I don't have a lot of money. But my family does."

"They wouldn't help you pay for college?" I ask.

"It's not that. I just don't want their money anymore."

"I never would have guessed you were a rich girl. I mean that in the nicest way. Do you miss it?"

"I used to have a cool car and way more expensive clothes and shoes. I sold them all to move here. To start life on my own. It's exactly how I wanted it. And I'm loving it, honestly. So no, I don't miss it."

I truly admire Scout for being so brave.

She holds up a light blue denim skirt and a pink one. "Which one?"

"Don't you think it will be a little cold for a skirt?" I ask. "It's October."

"That's what the fire is for. To keep me warm. And I'm wearing my leather jacket. Which one?" she asks again.

"Denim."

She looks pleased when I say this. After throwing it in her basket, she walks over to the rack of shirts. She flips through the hangers faster than I can keep up. After handing me a couple of them she says, "You should try these on! I think the black one would be so cute on you. And it's got long sleeves."

"I do kind of like the black one. I'll go try it on."

Once on, I realize that it reveals more cleavage than I'm used to. I walk out of the fitting room to see what Scout thinks of the top.

"Harper, you're a babe!" Scout exclaims. "If you don't buy that shirt, I'm buying it for you. I wouldn't have the boobs for it. That's the only thing I hate about being a runner."

"It's cute. Are you sure it's not too low cut, though?" I ask her as I look in the mirror again on the fitting room door.

"No, you look hot!" she says standing next to me. "And you should wear your hair down. I'm so jealous of your natural waves."

"I'm jealous of your straight hair. My hair can be a pain in the butt sometimes," I say.

"Do you consider your hair dark blonde or brown?" she asks.

"Probably light brown. I do have some natural highlights. Especially in the summer, it looks more blonde."

After buying our not so essentials, we go back home to get ready for the bonfire.

It looks like the whole school is at the bonfire. As we walk around, I spot a tall skinny guy with a buzz cut. As soon as I see him from a distance, I recognize him. Robby McKinney. I heard he was coming to college here but hadn't run into him yet. He looks at me and whispers something to his friend. Trying to ignore him, I keep up with Scout to meet with her friend Matt and some other people on the track team.

"You girls ready for some shots?" Matt asks us.

"Absolutely," Scout says.

I already decided to let Scout drink and I'd drive. "None for me. I'm the designated driver."

Matt's friend, the one from the Bar and Grill, who wanted to know if I was single, looks at me and says, "Hey." He smiles shyly. "I'm Jake. You're Harper, right?"

"Hi. You actually decided to come talk to me yourself this time?" I wink and he laughs.

"Sorry about that. Pretty girls make me nervous."

"It's nice to meet you Jake," I say as I feel someone else's eyes on me.

I look behind where I'm standing and see Ardyn. He's with a different woman than the one I saw him with at the coffee shop. *Seriously?* I roll my eyes. *What a player.*

"Hey, neighbor," Rafe says.

"Hey Rafe."

"Come here, I need to introduce you to my new roommate," he says.

I follow him over to the fire where Ardyn is sitting with the girl. Rafe says to his roommate, "Ardyn, this is my friend Harper. She lives below us. With Scout. Harper, this is Ardyn."

Ardyn is Rafe's roomate?

"Hi," I say and he nods at me. *Not even a hello. I guess we're just going to pretend we've never met.*

"And this is Julie," Rafe says, pointing to the girl.

"Hi. I like your top," Julie says as she wraps her hands around Ardyn's arm and rests her head on his shoulder. At least she's friendly.

"Thanks I love your shoes," I respond, looking down at her black boots.

"Thanks, girl," Julie says.

I look back at Rafe. "Come meet Scout's track friends."

I introduce Rafe to Matt and Jake. "Professor Granite's English class right?" Matt asks Rafe, handing him a shot glass.

"Oh yeah. I know you," Rafe tells him before tossing the shot of alcohol down his throat.

I hear music start to play and I scan the crowd. Some people are dancing, some people are all over each other by the fire, some are drinking, and some are getting high. It's a typical college party.

I sit down on the ground near the bonfire alone while Scout mingles. When I look up, Ardyn is staring at me with a stoic expression across the fire. Julie is all over him, kissing his neck. I didn't realize I sat directly across from them. I look down at my feet, feeling a little uncomfortable.

When I glance back up, Ardyn is now staring at me like he was the night at the bar. And he has a girl sitting right next to him! A minute later, I see him and Julie get up and walk out of the light from the bonfire and into the trees.

Jake sits down next to me and I talk to him for a while. He really is a great guy. I like getting to know him, even if it is just as friends. Then I see Robby talking to Scout in the distance. I jump up and quickly walk over to her because I know she's been drinking and I don't want Robby to try to take advantage of her.

"Scout, there you are." Then I force myself to turn and say, "Hi Robby."

"Harper! I haven't seen you since graduation!" he exclaims.

He looks over to his friends who are standing nearby and says, "See. I told you she's a tease. Look at the top she's wearing."

I grab Scout by the arm. "Let's go."

"It's too bad Will isn't here to threaten me again huh?"

I jerk my head back to him. *Will threatened him?* His smile convinces me that he wants me to react. I don't give him that satisfaction. I ignore him and turn back.

We're walking away when Scout turns around and yells out to Robby, "Dick face!"

She's obviously really drunk at this point. Robby says something back but we can't hear him.

"Are you ready to go?" I ask Scout.

"Not yet. I was hoping to run into Billy. Maybe he's not here yet," Scout says, looking around.

"Is Billy the new flavor of the week?" I tease.

Scout throws her head back, laughing hysterically, "Sorry. I just think it's funny you think it will last a whole week."

I hear someone yell out in the distance.

"What was that?" I ask.

"I don't know. Let's check it out," Scout says as we walk over to where the noise and crowd of people are.

Rafe is lying on the ground. Did someone just push him?

"I just don't understand why you're always hanging out with girls," says some jerk I've never seen before, looking down at Rafe. "It's a little weird man. Do you like dudes or something?"

Then he kicks Rafe hard in the stomach. Rafe groans.

I see Ardyn run up and grab the jerk by the back of the neck and throw him back hard on the ground. "What the hell's the matter with you?" Ardyn yells at the guy bullying Rafe. "Back off!"

Ardyn helps Rafe up as the jerk is now backing away because he's not about to fight Ardyn who is way bigger than he is. Matt and some other track guys ask Rafe if he's okay and Matt looks at the bully and says, "Fuck off."

Without saying anything else, the guy walks off with his friends and they leave. I'm not at all surprised when I see that Robby was a part of that mob.

I feel so bad for Rafe. He must be humiliated.

"Are you okay?" I ask him.

"Yeah. Ardyn and I are headed out. Thanks for inviting us," he tells me and Scout. "Don't worry about me. I'll see you guys later."

"Bye Rafe!" Scout shouts, as Rafe and Ardyn make their way down to the parked cars.

Scout finds Billy after that and I let her make out with him in the trees for fifteen minutes. *What is so special about the trees?*

Ardyn

I'm so pissed off at myself for bringing a date to the bonfire tonight. I didn't know that *she'd* be here. I don't want her to see me with other women. She has no idea what she means to me. Julie is all over me and all I can do is admire how good Harper looks across the fire from us. I can't describe how badly I regret that night at the Bar and Grill right now. That I didn't just do what she said right then and there. By the way she's looking at me now, I don't know if I'll ever get that chance again. But it's probably for the best. That's exactly how I need it to stay. She deserves way better than a one night stand in a bathroom anyway. I can't pursue her. I've got to remember to keep my distance.

I just have to accept that I can't have Harper.

"Let's go somewhere private," I tell Julie who can't keep her mouth off of me. I can't do things like this in front of Harper. She's different.

After having some fun with Julie out in the trees, I find myself looking for *her*. That's when I see Rafe being shoved by some asshole. As I'm running over to him, I see the guy kick him in the gut.

I grab the worthless piece of shit and tell him to back off. I hate pussies like him who are up to fight anyone smaller than them but as soon as someone bigger comes in, they back off like a little bitch. I'm feeling way too pissed off to be here right now and I think Rafe just wants to go home. Julie tells me she's going to stay longer and catch a ride with someone else.

I'm not as pissed off when I spot Harper. She and her roommate Scout tell Rafe goodbye and I'm pleased to see that Harper gave me an appreciative smile.

I see you Harper.

On the drive home, Rafe is quiet as he looks out the window.

"Don't worry about assholes like him," I tell him.

He turns to look at me. "Thanks for having my back. I really need to start coming to the gym with you. You scared the piss out of them. I'm glad Briar moved out. You're a way better roomie. Even if you do keep me up at night with your assortment of women."

I laugh. "Sorry about that. You're a good dude Rafe. And for what it's worth, you had a lot of people backing you up back there. Let's start lifting weights together."

It got too hard driving back and forth to school from my parents' place. Student Den Apartments were completely full when I enrolled for school here at the last minute. Rafe doesn't know that I paid off Briar to leave so that I could move in. There were other student housing options available, but it had to be the Student Den Apartments.

Chapter Seventeen

Harper

It's already November and I haven't been back home yet. I'm just really not looking forward to going to the place I last saw Will, where we said goodbye. But Thanksgiving is coming up and I miss my mom and dad. I look up at Scout as we sit at a table in the library to study.

"Thanksgiving break is next week. Are you going home?" I ask her.

She says, "No, I'm not. I'll probably just order Chinese food and enjoy some alone time." She looks at me seductively. "Maybe I'll invite Billy over for a sleepover."

I laugh quietly. "Or you can come to my house. My parents really want to meet you."

"Really? Are you sure? I'd love that!" Scout blurts out.

We arrived at my parents' house late the night before Thanksgiving. They had waited up so they could meet Scout. As I expected, they met us with open arms.

It feels good to be home, even though it feels different.

Scout and I are laying in my bed at midnight, still jabbering. Even though we live together, it feels like this is our first slumber party. I have my back against my headboard and she is lying on her stomach on the other end of the bed, looking up at me.

"Your mom and dad love you so much. They're the type of people who were made to be parents. And I can't believe how much you look like your mom," she says with a smile.

She's right. They really are great.

"Thanks. I'm lucky to have them. But they aren't perfect. My mom and I definitely have our moments," I admit.

"You and your mom don't always get along? I never would have guessed," Scout says.

"Well, we do. We just butt heads sometimes. She can be a little controlling. What is it about when parents try to force us not to do something, it only makes us want to do it more?" I ask.

"I wouldn't really know. My mom didn't even care what the hell I was doing most of the time," Scout says.

"I'm sorry Scout."

She shakes her head and stands up. "Don't be. It made high school fun."

There she goes again, covering up her emotions.

"Scout. You deserve better."

She pauses as she looks at me over her shoulder.

"I know," she says.

When she turns back around she changes the subject. "We definitely need one of these for the apartment," she says as she admires my pink and purple lava lamp on a shelf.

I laugh.

"Oh my," Scout says as she picks up a framed picture of Will and me when we were kids. "Look at all your curly hair. This is adorable. Who is the little blond boy?"

"That's Will," I tell her.

She turns and looks at me. "Wow. I didn't know you grew up together. You must miss him so much."

More than I want to admit.

Scout tells me she's going to go brush her teeth and heads for the bathroom. She shuts my door and I think of the last time I slept in my bed. I think of what happened. I close my eyes and try to stop my brain from thinking.

Thanksgiving Day was really fun with Scout at home with me. We helped my mom make dinner and she got to meet my grandma. Later in the evening, I show Scout the back yard and introduce her to Taffy. Scout absolutely loves her.

"Want to take her for a ride?" I ask.

I've never seen Scout look so excited. And I've seen an excited Scout, a lot.

"Yes! Can I? I've never ridden a horse before though."

"That's okay. I'll teach you."

Scout is riding Taffy in no time. I can hear her laughter as she rides the horse around the field.

After their ride, we go back inside and I slice up some pumpkin pie and put huge heaps of my mom's homemade whipped cream on each piece. Then we go out on the back patio and eat our desert.

Scout says, "This has been the best Thanksgiving ever. I adore your family Harper."

I smile. "I'm glad you came home with me."

I almost ask her what her family usually does on Thanksgiving, but I decide not to.

Scout interrupts my thoughts. "You're so lucky you're an only child," she says.

"Really? I always wanted siblings. Lots of siblings. But my parents were only able to have me."

"They tried to have more?" Scout asks.

"They wanted to have more. But my mom wasn't able to get pregnant again."

"Wow. That must have been difficult," Scout says.

"Didn't you like having a brother?" I ask.

"No. He's ten years older than me," she says, looking down at her feet. "Like I said, you're lucky to be an only child."

"So, tell me more about Will. Were you ever more than friends?" she asks.

I feel my face go hot as I bury it in my hands.

"I knew it!" Scout yells.

Then she must see it all over my face. She's a lot more serious now when she says, "You love him don't you?"

"Yeah but he made things clear before he left. He just wants to stay friends."

"Is he the reason you don't go out with anyone?" she asks.

"I guess. But speaking of which. I made out with a guy in the women's bathroom at the Bar and Grill a few weeks ago."

Scout jumps up out of her chair. "What? And you didn't tell me? Give me all the detes right now," she demands.

I pull her back down to sit with me. "It was Ardyn."

Scout jumps back up again. "What?! The hottie from upstairs? Okay, now I really need all the details." She says, sitting back down.

"I actually hate the thought of that night. The kiss was great. He's a really good kisser. But I wasn't in my right mind. It was Will's birthday and I wanted a distraction. I got one for a few minutes but he shot me down when I practically begged him to do it right there in the women's bathroom. So that's how my love life is going. How's yours?"

Scout's mouth drops open before she smiles. "I'm so proud."

"You should not be proud. I made a fool of myself and now it's mortifying every time I have to see him."

"His loss. Screw men. We found each other," Scout says.

Chapter Eighteen

Harper

When we get home the next day after Thanksgiving, we are walking down the hall to our apartment when Rafe runs up behind us.

"Hey guys, how was Thanksgiving?"

"Great! I got to go home with Harper," Scout says, holding on to the pink lava lamp we brought back with us.

"How was yours?" I ask him.

"It was good. I'm having a game night tomorrow at my place. You guys should come."

"We'll be there!" Scout responds immediately, not giving me a chance to say no.

***

Rafe, Matt and Jake have become good friends since the night of the bonfire. They're all in Rafe's apartment waiting for us when we walk in for game night.

"Hey guys," Rafe says, greeting us at the door.

We say hi back and Scout adds, "I invited Billy over if that's okay. He'll be here when he gets off work at ten."

"Oh yeah. The more the merrier," Rafe says.

Matt brought a cute girl tonight. She has long red hair and her name is Lucy. They're cuddled up on the living room couch and Jake is sitting on a bar stool in the kitchen.

After a wild round of poker in the living room, Billy shows up.

"Let's play truth or dare!" Rafe shouts, as he's getting more beer from the fridge. I'm sitting on a bean bag chair next to Jake, who's sitting on the floor.

"Good idea. I'm sick of playing poker," says Scout as she sits on Billy's lap next to Matt and Lucy on the couch.

"Me too. It's too confusing," Lucy says.

Matt says, "Okay, Scout, you first. Truth or dare?"

"Dare." She smiles playfully.

Matt says, "I dare you to go out in the hall and yell out your best friend's name as loud as you can."

Without hesitation, Scout walks out into the hall and yells, "Harper is my best friend!"

We're all laughing when she sits back down. She looks at me and I give her a wink.

Scout says, "Rafe, truth or dare?"

"Dare," he answers competitively.

Scout leaves the room and walks back out with a hairbrush. "From now on, every time you speak tonight, you have to put the brush up to your mouth and talk into it like a microphone."

Rafe dramatically grabs the brush, stands up and puts it up to his mouth, "I'd just like to thank ya'll for comin' tonight."

Laughter fills the room again.

"Harper," Rafe says with his brush microphone, "Truth or dare?"

"Truth."

Rafe looks at me and shakes his head, "No. I dare you…"

I can't help but laugh, "I said truth! But fine, I'll do a dare."

"I dare you to get up on the bar and dance without music for two minutes."

I hate this game. I get up on the bar in the middle of the living room area and dance like an idiot for two minutes while they all holler at me.

"Jake, truth or dare?" I ask him.

"Dare," he says.

I look at Rafe. "Do you have ice?"

"A whole tray of it," he answers again with his microphone brush.

I smile mischievously and look back at Jake. "I dare you to dump the whole tray of ice down your pants."

Jake walks over to the freezer and pulls out the ice tray and looks at me. "Not cool Harper," he jokes. He begins dumping the ice down the front of his pants and he's squealing because it's so cold.

I'm laughing hysterically when Jake grabs some ice that fell on the floor and begins chasing me with it. I try to run from him but he grabs my arms and puts a handful of ice down the back of my shirt and hugs me so it won't fall out.

I'm screaming for help and everyone is laughing at us.

Except for Ardyn, who must have just walked in.

I don't know how long he's been standing there looking at us, but he looks mad. He leaves the living room to go to his bedroom and slams his door shut.

Rafe picks up his microphone brush, "What's his deal?" he says into it.

What the hell? What was that about? Ardyn is such a grump.

⚘

When we get back into our apartment Scout says, "I'm bored with Billy. What is wrong with me?"

"Nothing is wrong with you," I reassure her.

She stares at me. "I think Ardyn is into you."

"What? He is not. I'm pretty sure he hates me. Did you see the way he was looking at me?"

"Exactly," she says, "he seemed jealous because Jake was all over you. It was intense."

I shake my head. "I don't think so. You see how he is with the women he likes. He definitely doesn't act like that with them."

"I guess," she says with a shrug.

"Are you going to break up with Billy?" I ask.

She sighs, "Probably."

Chapter Nineteen

Harper slips off her summer dress and she's wearing her black bikini.

"You okay?" She smiles at me as we walk out into the water.

"Yeah, why do you ask?"

"You just look uncomfortable is all," she says.

I'm going to tell her the truth. "Honestly, Harper, you look way too hot in that swimsuit."

She looks shocked that I even said that.

I shrug my shoulders. "You asked," I remind her.

She laughs and says, "Thanks Will. You look good too."

The sun is setting behind her as we step closer to each other in the water. She's making my head spin. I want to kiss her so badly, but I don't want to hurt her.

"I wish I could kiss you," I say before I rest my lips on her cold cheek. My God, she smells amazing.

"Come home and kiss me then," Harper whispers.

I wake up from my power nap on the rocky, uneven ground and rub my eyes. "Shit, I thought that was real," I mumble. We were on a late patrol last night and I didn't get any sleep. But I've hardly felt like I've gotten any real sleep here at all.

Private Batra shoots a look at me as he chows down on an MRE. "You thought what was real?" he asks.

"The dream I was having."

He smiles from ear to ear. "Was it about a woman?"

I sit up and brush the dirt off the back of my head. "How did you know that?"

"I didn't until now. Who is she?" he says with curiosity.

"My friend back home. We were swimming."

"Your friend?" he asks.

"My best friend. Her name is Harper," I say, and he smiles again.

"Oh shit man. You have a crush on your best friend? I have someone back home too. Her name is Danielle," he says, showing me a picture.

"She's pretty. Think you'll marry her?" I ask him.

"Already did. She's my wife. Do you have any pictures?"

I remember the picture of Harper that Grandma Pearson snuck in my hand when she caught me staring at her grand-daughter. "I do," I say, handing it to him. "My best friend, Harper."

"Whoa. She's very pretty. You better snatch her up quick before someone else does."

I laugh. "She's definitely pretty but it's more about her personality. She's so much fun to be around. I can't wait to see her again."

All of a sudden, I hear someone yell, "I get to go first!"

Private Batra and I make our way over to the noise. Private Wallace is getting undressed by a barrel of water. He's about to get in to take a bath. Wondering where the hell they found the barrel, I look over at Private Pillar laying in the dirt with his head propped up with his jacket.

"Have you taken your meds?" I ask him. He still looks sweaty and uncomfortable. A week ago he had a fever after being bit by something. He's been vomiting and sweating for days. I've been giving him a drug for malaria.

"Yeah Doc. I feel better today," he says.

I lean down and check his temperature. He still feels a little warm but his fever has definitely gone down.

"You going to get in Doc?" he asks me.

"In the barrel bath?" I ask. "After Private Wallace's filthy ass is done soaking in it? Probably not."

He laughs and suddenly we hear machine guns. We're being shot at.

"Goddammit! They always gotta ruin the fun," I hear someone yell as I go running toward a convoy to take cover.

After a while, the shooting stops and I look up. Luckily this time, nobody was hit. Everyone laughs when Private Wallace pops his head up out of the barrel of water he was hiding inside of.

Chapter Twenty

Harper

S cout begs me to go to this cardio gym class with her that she teaches. She's been the instructor there for a week. I've never been that interested in working out. I'm not a lazy person and I like to stay active, but I'd much rather go hiking, horseback riding or for a jog and enjoy the outdoors than go to the gym.

"Please come with me. I need to know what I can do to make the class better. You're the perfect observer." Then in a sing-song voice she says, "the class is really fun."

I sigh. "Why do you have to be so persuasive?"

Ardyn

I'm on my way to the supply store to get some material for the new project for work. I've always known I'd take over my dad's construction business one day. He told me going to school would be a waste of time. And even though I didn't have to, I think it will be beneficial to have my finance and business degree.

I'm passing the gym when I notice Harper walking in with Scout.

I take the next U-turn and head back to my apartment. When I get home Rafe is planted on the couch like a potato.

"Get up," I tell him. "We're going to the gym."

Harper

After the exercise class Scout teaches, I'm left feeling more energetic than I had before we started, even though I'm also incredibly tired at the same time. I'm surprised it felt so good. Therapeutic almost. I can see why Scout likes it so much. I take a drink from the water bottle I brought with me.

"That was actually really fun. You made it so simple and easy to follow the steps. I'm glad I went," I say to Scout as we walk out of the studio and into the gym loaded with intimidating equipment and ripped people.

"I'm glad you liked it! I have to teach it again in five minutes if you want to join in," Scout says.

I open my eyes wide. "No wonder you're in such good shape. One time is definitely enough for me. I'll wait for you though."

While Scout teaches her next class, I wander around the gym feeling like an imposter for even being in here. I've never lifted weights but I kind of want to try.

I observe a girl as she pulls down on something while sitting down. That seems like my kind of workout. When she gets off I take a seat and try it out.

After attempting that machine I notice Ardyn helping Rafe with a bar with weights on each end. Ardyn looks up at me and I feel slightly self-conscious about how I must look. But why should I care?

Then Ardyn's eyes scan up and down my body. *Don't check me out.* We've already established I'm *not your type.* He looks me in the eye and quickly looks away, like he just read my mind.

After trying out a couple more machines, I walk into the studio to watch Scout finish up her cardio class.

***

We get back to the apartment and Scout tells me I can shower first while she makes us a protein smoothie. When I get out of the shower and get dressed I go join her in the kitchen.

"I've been really stressed about my statistics class. Math is the only subject I really struggle with," I tell Scout as she hands me the smoothie she made for me. "Why is it green?" I ask as I lift the glass to my lips.

"It's the spinach. You won't even taste it," she assures me.

I make a funny face because it tastes awful and I think I hate spinach.

Scout notices my grimace because she says, "It's good for you."

"As soon as I finish this delicious smoothie," I say sarcastically, "I have to go study for my math test on Monday."

"I hear you. I have to study today too," she says while walking into the bathroom.

When I hear her in the shower, I take one more sip from my glass and dump the rest of the contents into the sink.

Chapter Twenty-One

Harper

I think my parents expected me to come home every weekend, but that definitely hasn't happened.

Will has been gone for almost five months now, and I still haven't gotten a single letter from him. When I'm in Columbus, it hardly seems like it's been that long. But now, being home it feels like he's been gone forever. I imagine he'll have the worst Christmas of his life this year. I wish he could come home.

I pull up to my house on the night of Christmas Eve and it's decorated with the same Christmas lights as always. Snowflakes are falling down lightly in the dark night and the yard is covered in a thick white blanket of snow.

I usually love the holiday season, but this year I'm struggling.

I invited Scout to come home with me for Christmas but she decided to fly back home to Tennessee. She never wants to go home so that took me by surprise. Hopefully she has a good Christmas.

"There's our girl!" my dad says as I open the front door.

Christmas music is playing and I smell cinnamon candles and ham baking in the oven. He gives me his awkward one-arm embrace he gives me every time we hug. I missed him.

My mom walks into the room from the kitchen. "Oh, we've missed you so much, Harper. How's school?" she asks.

"It's pretty good," I say, "I'm sorry I haven't been home for a while. I've been so busy."

"We understand honey," my mom says.

My mom has made a big dinner just like every year on Christmas Eve.

After dinner is cleaned up, I help my mom frost the sugar cookies. I can't imagine what it'd be like to have a mom like Scout has. Feeling lucky, I look up at her and smile. "I love you mom."

When we were kids, every Christmas day, Will would come over and we would play with all of my new toys. He usually didn't get much and if he did, it was from his aunt and uncle who sent him some gifts. And my parents would usually get him something. We would always go outside and play in the snow until we couldn't feel our fingers and toes. One year I remember we made a huge snowman. We named him Giant. We were so proud.

It's Christmas night and I'm lying on the couch, cuddled up with a warm blanket, reading a book when my dad sits down on the couch next to me.

"I have something for you. From Will."

I sit straight up and he hands me a sealed envelope that says *Christmas*.

"He wrote me a letter?" I ask.

My dad stands up to give me some privacy. "Yeah. He came over to say goodbye the day he flew out. Then he handed it to me before he left. Asked if I would give it to you on Christmas. I'm glad I remembered."

I open the envelope and begin reading:

Dear Harper,

Merry Christmas! I hope you are having a wonderful time with your family. I know Christmas will be different this year, with me being away at war. I'll be thinking of you. I'll be thinking about our Christmas memories. I'll be thinking about all of it. I'll close my eyes and it will feel like I'm home. Please don't feel sad today. It's Christmas. I'll be home next year. We'll build another snowman. I hope school is going well and that you are loving every minute of it. More than anything I hope you're happy. I'll see you soon.

Love, Will

A tear runs down my cheek. This letter was just what I needed.

Will

An Army helicopter got shot down by the Taliban on Christmas Eve. We were ordered to go see if there were any survivors. I thought winters were bad in Ohio. Winters in Afghanistan are brutal but I guess that could be because we're outside most of the time. I don't know if I'll ever like snow again. I wonder what Jameson is doing. Maybe he went to see Uncle Mike and Aunt Charlie in Cincinnati. I hope he's not alone. I wonder what Harper is doing. The homesickness I feel when thinking of Harper and Christmas back home is absolutely gut-wrenching. I'm sure she went home to be with her family. My stomach grumbles at the thought of fudge. We haven't hardly eaten anything in two days. Our rations didn't show up last week so we've been trying to save what we have left. This morning we all licked a spoonful of peanut butter. Not each. We each licked and shared the same spoon of peanut butter. They say we should be getting a shipment in right after Christmas. I know I've probably lost some weight by now.

I hear a marine mumbling next to me while we're on our march to find the Army helicopter.

"Stick it up your ass," I hear him say. *What?*

Then he starts to chant. "Jingle Bells, Mortar Shells, hiding in the grass, Take your Merry Christmas, and stick it up your ass!" he shouts louder. I hear a few laughs.

"Jingle Bells, Mortar Shells," he begins again and some marines repeat after him. After the third time, I join in with the rest of the marines and we repeat the words over and over again until we see the smoke.

We run to the helicopter where it looks like another unit is already helping the few survivors from the crash.

We set up a perimeter and take cover behind a rock hill for protection because we suspect the Taliban is close by.

As I'm helping a soldier whose in bad shape but knowing he'll make it out alive I ask him, "Do you have family back home?"

He mumbles, "Yeah. A wife and four kids if you can believe it."

"Wow. Well they're going to have the best Christmas ever this year," I say loudly as I apply pressure to what's left of his ear. "Their dad gets to come home."

That causes him to smile and I know this conversation will help him fight to get home to them. At least by the new year.

"What's your name?" I ask.

"Chris," he musters out before he starts to cough hard.

When he takes his hand off his mouth, it's covered in blood.

Shit. "I need you to lay down flat on your back Chris."

After helping him lay down he begins coughing again as I raise his legs up and set them up against the rocks.

"I need water," Chris mumbles.

"Sorry, you can't drink anything yet. Are you experiencing any chest pain?"

"I can hardly breathe," Chris answers painfully.

Chris's breathing eventually comes to a stop so I begin CPR.

"Come on Chris," I say during compressions.

Someone jumps down next to me. I look up to see Noel checking Chris's pulse.

"Noel?"

He ignores me and says, "It's weak. Do you need me to take over?"

After giving Chris two breaths and continuing compressions I say, "I've got it."

I'm relieved when Chris begins coughing.

"He's stable but he needs a doctor to control the internal bleeding," I tell Noel. "We've got to get him to a hospital."

"They've already radioed an ambulance in from the nearest FOB. Should be getting here any minute now," Noel says.

"Am I going to be okay?" Chris asks.

"Sure you are, you've made it this far," I say just as the ambulance arrives.

Noel and I help get Chris to the Army's tan humvee ambulance. Before the doors shut, Chris grabs me by the arm and says, "Thank you."

I smile down at him. "Merry Christmas."

When the ambulance drives off, Noel holds his hand out with a grin.

"Didn't expect to see you here," I say, taking his hand as he pulls me into an aggressive hug.

"I missed you so much, they finally let me join your unit," he jokes. "But really, they merged our units together. At least for the time being, we're teamed up, buddy."

I can't put into words how good it is to see such a good friend of mine here. We got to be really close at basic. I haven't seen him since he talked me into going home to see Harper. Noel is the kind of friend I know will always have my back. Christmas turned out to be better than I thought it would.

Chapter Twenty-Two

Harper

I went back to the apartment on New Year's Eve because I told Scout I would. She's really excited about the party at Matt's family cabin. Scout is lying on the couch when I open the door. Her head is down and there is a bottle of vodka next to her. She won't look at me. Right away, I can tell something is wrong.

"Scout? Are you okay?" I ask.

She looks at me with her swollen eyes and flushed face.

"Have you been crying?"

Scout says, "I came back to the apartment on Christmas. I was only in Tennessee for one night. My mom promised me he wouldn't be there. But she lied."

She takes a drink straight from the bottle of vodka. She's wearing a tank top underneath her jacket that's hanging off her shoulder. Tears are rolling down her cheeks and this is the first time I've ever seen Scout cry. She lays her head back down on the couch.

"Do you want to talk about it?" I ask. She shakes her head no.

"Scout, I'm so sorry. I just wish I would've known you've been here since Christmas. I would've come back for you."

I bend over and wipe the hair out of her face and sit down on the couch by her head. She scoots herself back and lays her head in my lap.

What have you been through, Scout?

"I should've come with you and spent Christmas with Taffy," she says as she laughs through her tears.

Then she sits up and looks at me. "How was your Christmas? You seem a little upset too," she says.

Scout's problems seem way bigger than me just missing a boy.

"Harper, you can talk to me. It makes me feel less alone. It's better for me when I'm not the only one with the issues," she says.

"It's just Will. I miss him. Maybe we should just stay here tonight," I suggest.

"No way. We need this party now more than ever. You're drinking with me tonight," she says as she stands up. "I'm going to go shower and pull myself together."

We arrive at Matt's cabin and it's huge. He gives us a tour and there are at least twelve bedrooms, five bathrooms, and a huge balcony that wraps around the whole place.

"I hope you guys remembered your swimsuits," he says when he shows us the giant hot tub.

Matt already told us when he invited us we could pick a bedroom to stay in tonight. We picked the room in the loft upstairs decorated with pine tree wallpaper.

We change into our swimsuits and go out to the hot tub with Matt, Lucy and a bunch of others.

Lucy says, "Oh my gosh I love your white bikini, Harper! How are you so tan in the winter?"

I thank her and Scout says, "I know I'm so jealous of her skin tone! Lucky genetics."

After about fifteen minutes of soaking in the hot tub, I realize that we'll eventually have to get out and dry off.

"Shoot, Scout, we forgot our towels."

"Oh, I can go grab them," Scout says.

"No it's okay. I need to cool down anyway. I'll go get them," I tell her as I climb out of the hot water.

When I get inside the cabin through the balcony door that leads into the kitchen, I get a glass and drink some water when I hear the front door open. I feel embarrassed standing here soaking wet while being basically half naked. I grab a hand towel and begin wiping up the water I had dripped on the kitchen floor. I'm finishing up behind the kitchen counter when Rafe and Ardyn come into the kitchen.

"Damn girl!" Rafe says then whistles.

This is so awkward.

"Hi. I was in the hot tub but I forgot my towel. I'm going to go get it," I mumble to them.

I have to walk past them to get to the guest room. As I'm about to go up the stairs, I realize Ardyn is standing right in my way.

I'm inches away from him and I don't even dare look him in the eyes when I say, "Excuse me."

He moves to his right and I still manage to bump into him somehow.

"Sorry," I say feeling embarrassed as I begin walking up the stairs.

Please don't be staring at my ass.

I turn around and they are both still looking at me.

Whipping the loft door open, I say, "The show is over boys."

I may have even seen Ardyn smile at me for once.

⸙

When I get back into the hot tub, Rafe and Ardyn are already in there. Everyone is talking and Rafe hands me a beer.

"Thanks."

Scout is now sitting next to some guy I don't know.

Lucy asks me what I'm majoring in.

"Social work," I tell her.

"That's amazing. I could never do something like that. That would be a depressing job. Is there a reason you chose that career path?" Lucy asks.

I think about it for a minute in silence. *There are children all around the world who don't feel safe in their own homes.*

Who don't feel safe with their own parents. Children like Will. There are some children who go to bed hungry and wake up hungry. There are children who are abused. Some are struggling with depression and anxiety so badly that they're willing to take their own lives. There are children everywhere suffering from trauma. I want to help them. I want all children to remember that they matter. That there are people willing to help them. That's why.

But instead of explaining all of that I just say, "I'm just really passionate about helping kids. What are you going into?" I ask her.

"I'm still trying to figure that out," Lucy says.

I turn to look over at Ardyn when I feel him staring at me. *What is it with him and staring?* He's flirting with a girl. Always a new girl. She is practically sitting on his lap. I look away.

We start laughing when we see Matt, Jake, and Rafe go running out into the snow.

After getting changed out of my swimsuit, I go into the kitchen where everyone is taking shots. Christmas was hard. Will being away was hard. Life is just hard and I want to stop feeling so much. And so does Scout. We deserve it.

I take one shot.

And another.

And another.

Before I know it, I'm drunk. Really drunk. I've probably never been this drunk.

Everyone starts dancing to loud party music and Scout and I join in.

Then when it's almost midnight, Scout and I go hunting for a boy for me to kiss. Scout points at Matt who is playing pool with another guy.

"No, he's with Lucy. And I love Lucy." I stop walking and laugh hysterically at myself. "I Love Lucy. I used to love watching that show with my grandma."

How is nobody else laughing? I'm so funny.

Scout drags me across the room and points to Ardyn who's sitting on the couch alone.

"No, he doesn't like kissing me," I say loud enough for him to hear.

"What about Rafe?" she points at Rafe who is dancing with Lucy.

"Yes! Rafe... Can I kiss you at midnight?"

He has a shit eating grin on his face. "I thought you'd never ask, baby," he jokes.

At midnight we give each other a friendly peck on the lips.

Sometime after that, I suddenly feel really sad. My heart is aching for Will. Drinking was a very bad idea. I walk outside to get some space from the party. I'm still drunk but I just need a minute to myself. I look up at the stars.

I'm back at Boulder Beach with Will. We can't see the fireworks from here so we make our way down closer to the water. The water is kind of cold but I sit down in it anyway. I lay my head back into the sand.

"Will, I'm cold."

He picks me up and he's carrying me. His body feels so warm and he smells so incredible so I cuddle into him. I don't know where he's taking me but I feel safe. He's going up the stairs to my room. He puts me in my bed and I try to pull him in it with me but he won't let me.

The next morning I wake up hungover.

"My head hurts," I mumble to myself as I sit up.

Scout's still asleep so I go downstairs to find any sort of caffeine. I see Matt in the kitchen making coffee and go help him.

"How was your night Matt?" I ask.

"It was good. You really let loose didn't you? I've never seen a drunk Harper before."

I laugh, feeling slightly embarrassed. "Yeah, it doesn't happen very often but I had fun. Gosh I don't remember even going to bed."

Matt finishes putting coffee, fruit, and toast on a tray and says, "I'm glad you had fun. I'm going to take this to Lucy."

"You're so sweet to make her breakfast in bed. Thanks for letting us stay."

"You bet. Thanks for coming." He turns and goes.

How do I not remember going to bed? I'm never drinking that much again.

"Ughhh," I lay my head down on my arms. My head is killing me.

I go back upstairs to wake Scout.

We're walking out to the car when I look at the snow and I suddenly remember laying in it last night. I thought I was at Boulder Beach with Will. I could have frozen to death.

How could I be so stupid?

"Scout, did you help me to bed last night?" I ask her.

Scout groans as she's climbing into the passenger seat of my car, "I don't even remember how I got to my own bed last night."

I remember thinking Will was carrying me. I wonder if I somehow managed to get to bed myself.

Chapter Twenty-Three

Harper

Rafe walks into the coffee shop right as I'm finishing up my shift for the day.

"Hey Rafe!" I'm arranging some of the fresh muffins Tracy baked early this morning into the glass display cases for the customers to see. We sell a lot more when they can be tempted by how delicious they look.

"Hey, are you still coming to the movies with Scout and me tonight?" he asks.

"Yes, I'll be there." I smile.

"Okay you can ride with me. Scout's meeting us there at seven when she gets off work. For now, can I get a coffee with caramel and one of these scrumptious looking muffins?" he asks.

"Yeah, which kind?"

"Can I actually get a box of them?" he asks.

"Of course."

After Rafe finally decides on eight muffins, I box them up for him.

"Shoot. I just realized I don't have time to drop these off at home," Rafe says. "Can I come get them after class?"

"I'll take them home with me then you can just stop at my apartment," I tell him. "Do you want to take one now?"

"Yes! Thank you. I'll see you tonight," he says, grabbing a muffin and darting out the door.

I realized Rafe probably beat me home when he got out of class since he never picked up his muffins. I knock on his door around six thirty. "Hey!" Rafe says after he opens the door.

"Hey. Here are your muffins," I say, handing them over.

"I completely forgot! Thanks for bringing them. I'm going to go change then we can head out."

I nod and look around his apartment. "It's really clean in here," I say as he walks back to his bedroom.

I hear him laugh and yell back, "Yeah we like to keep it clean. Yours is too." I sit down at the kitchen bar.

I pick up a newspaper in front of me. There's an article about Afghanistan and I read about four soldiers who were killed in action and push it away after making sure Will's name wasn't there. If anything happens, Jameson will let me know. I won't have to read about it in a newspaper. I hear Rafe walk back out but I'm still focused on what I just read. I can't handle stuff like that. It makes me worry even more.

I smell Rafe's cologne as he walks behind me and it's heavenly.

"You smell amazing. Are you ready?" I ask Rafe as I turn my head toward him. Except it's not Rafe.

It's Ardyn.

He's looking back at me and his icy blue eyes look so intense, I have to glance down. My face is on fire.

"Sorry. I thought you were Rafe," I say, feeling embarrassed. He steps closer to me. I can really smell his perfect amount of tangy and sweet cologne now. I could sit here and smell him all night long and it'd be better than the movie we're about to go see.

I look up and I feel like he can see right through me. Ardyn's face is so ruggedly handsome and the way he's looking at me is making my face warm. He gets even closer. Then he puts his hand behind me on the kitchen counter and leans forward over me, reaching with his other arm. He's not touching me but I feel the heat coming off of him.

What is he doing? I don't even care. I like being this close to him. I like smelling him. Holy shit it's hot in here. He makes me feel like I'm on fire.

I can't help but notice how familiar he smells. That cologne. I know I've smelled it before.

On Will? No. Who I thought was Will. At the New Year's Eve party. Whoever carried me was wearing this cologne.

Was it you?

Ardyn grabs his keys from the counter. He looks at me one more time and pushes himself away. That was the weirdest, most seductive interaction I've ever had. Still feeling embarrassed, turned on, and confused, Ardyn opens the front door and walks out. He never said a word but somehow I feel like he just flirted with me big time. He didn't have to lean over me like that to get his keys. He *wanted* to be close to me.

"Ugh!" I say burying my face into my hands.

"Are you okay?" Rafe asks as he enters the room.

"Yeah I'm fine. I just hate the newspaper. And cologne. I hate cologne."

He smells himself. "Is it too strong?" he asks.

"No, you smell great. Let's go," I say, still feeling annoyed with myself for letting Ardyn get to me. But maybe he doesn't hate me after all.

Who are you Ardyn?

I ask Rafe as we get into his car to leave, "Did you help me to bed at the party on New Year's Eve?"

Maybe he borrowed Ardyn's cologne that night. That would explain it.

"No. I was honestly too drunk. Why?" he asks as he turns the key in the ignition.

I put the seatbelt across my shoulder and say, "I just remember somebody carrying me to bed but I have no idea who it was."

But really I do have an idea.

"I don't know. Maybe it was Matt or Jake," Rafe says as we pull away.

I don't think so.

Chapter Twenty-Four

Harper

My first semester of college is officially finished. I've passed all of my classes with flying colors. So did Scout. To celebrate the new semester, we make a plan to go to the Bar and Grill for dinner. I told her I'd meet her there. She'd been spending the day with a boy she likes named Vince. Everyone must have the same idea of celebrating the end of the semester tonight because when I get there, it's full of college students.

I see Scout and Vince sitting at a booth. I order a soda and sit down next to Scout as Vince gets up and kisses her on the cheek. She's been seeing him for a couple of weeks now.

"Later," he says before he leaves.

"Vince is actually really sweet," I say to Scout.

"He's fun to hang out with," she says.

Both of our phones ping. I look down to see a text from Rafe.

Weather is supposed to be great tomorrow! Want to go hiking?

"Rafe text you too?" I ask Scout.

"Yeah. That sounds like fun. Do you want to go?"

"Sure."

After we each let Rafe know we'll be there tomorrow, Scout grins then pulls me to the dance floor.

"How are you doing?" she asks as we are dancing.

"I'm fine. I couldn't have gotten through the semester without you," I tell her when suddenly I spot someone looking at me. A very familiar face stares back at me. I stop dancing as I realize who it is.

So many emotions flood over me at once.

It's Jameson Karter, Will's brother. I feel my heart sink all the way to my stomach, and I immediately think the worst. Did something happen to Will? Did he come here to tell me horrible news?

When I remember how my legs work, I walk over to him and he gives me a hug and says, "You look good, Harper."

"Jameson, what are you doing here? Is Will okay?"

"Yes, he wrote to me last week. He's fine," he says and I'm immediately relieved.

"Thank God. You scared me," I say, pulling him in for another hug because I could barely remember the first one he gave me.

"I didn't mean to do that," he replies. "I live here now. I'm working for the Police Department full time. I come here with my buddy sometimes. The food is great and there are always hot college chicks on the dance floor."

"You graduated from the Academy?" I ask enthusiastical-ly.

A pleased smile appears on Jameson's face. "I'm officially a police officer."

"That's amazing! I'm so happy for you," I say, realizing he's not even looking at me. He's looking behind me. His eyes are glued to someone else. I turn around and see Scout.

"Who's your friend?" he asks me.

I smile. "Let me introduce you."

I wave Scout over to meet Jameson. She makes her way to us and she's out of breath from dancing.

"Hi, I'm Scout."

"Jameson," he says, never taking his eyes off of her.

They continue talking some more and Jameson asks her to dance.

"I'm going to head home," I tell them as they make their way to the dance floor.

"Already? Are you okay?" Scout asks.

"Yeah, I'm just really tired. I'll catch a cab."

Jameson looks a lot like Will with his thick blond hair, except he has blue eyes instead of brown. And he's a little taller. Their faces are different but they look similar. From far away, when I first saw Jameson, for a split second I thought it was Will. Something always reminds me of him.

I couldn't get a cab so I start walking back to the apartment. I don't like walking alone in the dark anymore. But I don't want to go back to the bar either. I just want to be alone. I wipe my wet eyes with my sleeve.

Ardyn

Being near Harper brings a comfort I can't explain. Seeing her *live*. Sometimes I imagine this is how *Casey's* life would be like. Instead she fell in love with me and I destroyed it.

I know I shouldn't risk that again. But Harper is as tempting as this bottle of whiskey sitting next to me. Sometimes I think I should keep my distance. Because I don't know how much longer I can help myself.

My phone vibrates.

Rafe: Weather is supposed to be great tomorrow! Want to go hiking?

Who will be there? I text back.

Scout, Harper, Lucy and Matt.

I'll be there.

My phone vibrates again.

I open the text from my sister,

We thought about it and I don't think tonight would be a very good night. Graham has to go to bed soon anyway. We know today is hard for you. We miss her too. Come see him next weekend. Love ya.

I get out of my truck because if I don't I'm going to drink the whiskey that's waiting for me on the front seat. I never should've bought it in the first place but today is the hardest day of the year.

You don't need it. You don't fucking need it.

I've lost everything anyway. I hit the hood of my truck just as I realize that I do need it.

Just before I open the door and ruin a year of sobriety, I hear my name.

Harper

I make my way through the apartment parking lot when I see Ardyn hit the hood of his truck with his hands. He keeps them there with his arms extended and drops his head. He looks upset when he goes to open the door to his truck.

"Ardyn," I say as I'm walking by. "Are you alright?"

He looks over at me and I can see his worried eyes.

"Are you walking alone in the dark?" he asks sternly.

"I couldn't get a cab from the Bar and Grill so I had to walk."

He glares at me, "Try harder next time."

Who does he think he is? Telling me what to do?

I roll my eyes and start walking away feeling annoyed when he says, "Today marks the day two years ago that I lost someone. Her name was Casey." He closes his eyes.

I stop walking and turn to him.

"Ardyn, I'm so sorry," I say quietly. I feel a heavy amount of empathy toward him. I can't imagine losing someone I love.

"I keep finding myself trying to bring her back," Ardyn says.

I can tell he's serious but I'm not sure exactly what he means by that.

"Not literally of course. But in my mind. I'm still adjusting," he says.

"I can't imagine what that must be like." *It's not fair.*

"Now it's your turn to tell me why you always seem a little sad," he says.

"I always seem sad?"

"Not always. But there are moments you don't look happy. Like tonight. You look like you've been crying."

I sigh because I don't know what to say exactly. But Ardyn seems genuine tonight so I guess I'll open up a little.

"My best friend is in Afghanistan," I tell him. "He's been there for six months now. It's been hard.

"Will is your best friend?"

I'm shocked to hear Ardyn say Will's name.

"How did you know my best friend's name is Will?"

He looks like he regrets what he just said. "I heard you talking about him once at the New Year's Eve party."

I never talked about Will at the party. But I remember laying in the snow, saying Will's name when I was cold. I *knew it.*

"It was *you.* You're the one who helped me to bed that night. I called you Will didn't I?"

He runs his hands through his hair. "I saw you wander off and figured I'd better check on you after you were outside for a while. I saw you laying in the snow and couldn't let you freeze to death."

"I wouldn't have frozen to death. I wasn't even that cold. I'm sure I would've gotten myself back into the house eventually. You didn't *have* to help me, Ardyn."

Then he says, "Did you know a person who is drinking alcohol is more likely to develop hypothermia than a person who hasn't been drinking alcohol? The alcohol in your body basically tricks you into thinking that you're warm when you're really not. It's a fact."

I laugh. "Okay, thank you for helping me. And that's actually an interesting fact."

"I know a lot of interesting facts," he flirts.

"Okay tell me another one."

"Kissing burns calories," he says.

I laugh. "Basically everything we do burns calories."

"It's still a fact." He pauses. "Please don't walk by yourself alone at night Harper."

He's acting all protective, like he actually cares about me.

"You don't even know me. You don't have to pretend like you care. You've avoided me ever since that night in the bathroom."

"I avoid you for a reason," he says sharply.

"And what reason is that?" I ask, feeling irritated.

"You're the kind of woman that I would want to stick with. And I don't need sticky in my life right now. The more I'm around you, the more I have to have you."

"You can't be serious," I say, not knowing whether to take that as a compliment or an insult. "Is that why you're always with so many different women? You can't handle commitment?" *I know the type.*

"I was in a serious relationship once. Let's just say, she kind of fucked me up. I guess I found a way to cope with it. I haven't been with a single woman in a whole month though, thank you very much. My turn to ask a question."

"Okay."

"I don't think I've ever seen you with a guy. Well. besides Jake, but you don't seem that interested in him. How is that even possible?"

"Let's just say someone kinda fucked me up too."

Ardyn touches my chin and looks at me as though he's trying to discover my face, "How could anyone ever do that to *you*?" I feel my cheeks go hot and have to take a step back.

"God, why do you have to blush like that Harper?" Ardyn demands and I'm struggling to stay on my feet. He gets even closer to me now, "You've got to stop. Stop being so extraordinary so I can stop thinking about you," he says, his eyes never leaving mine.

Feeling completely dumbfounded, I whisper, "You don't want to commit to anything and I don't want to risk getting hurt again. We're just going to have to walk away from each other. Before we get stuck."

My heart is racing and butterflies are swarming my stomach. He's begging me to kiss him with his eyes and I feel every nerve in my body pleading me to give in. Ardyn's hands grip the back of my head and he leans his whole body into mine. Chills shoot up my spine when I feel his mouth against my ear. Then he says, "You're going to have to be the one to walk away Harper, because I can't."

I don't want to walk away either but somehow I pull away from him. As I'm walking backward, still facing him I say,

"Thanks for explaining why you avoid me. I thought maybe you didn't like me."

He smiles and says, "Quite the opposite. Have a good night Harper."

"Coffee drinkers live longer than non-coffee drinkers!" I shout.

"What?" he asks.

"An interesting fact," I smile before turning around.

Chapter Twenty-Five

Harper

"My head hurts," Scout groans, lying on the couch the next morning.

"That's because you drank too much." I hand her a glass of water. "Finish this. So how was your night?"

"Jameson's taking me out on a date next weekend," she says, now sitting up as she drinks her water. "He's really sweet."

I like the thought of them being together.

"So, is Will as hot as Jameson?" Scout asks with a grin.

"Jameson has always been like a brother to me," I say. "He's definitely good looking though. He and Will look a lot alike."

Scout groans and lays her head back down.

"You're going to have to pull yourself together if you plan on going hiking today," I tell her.

"Ugh, I forgot about that. I'm going to need some caffeine," she says getting up off the couch.

My cell phone rings.

"Hi dad."

"Hi Harper," my dad says.

My dad's upset voice has me on alert. "What's wrong?" I ask.

"Grandma Pearson is in the hospital. She's had a stroke."

"What? Is she going to be okay?" I ask, feeling worried.

"The doctors will let us know more soon. We'll keep you updated."

"No. I'm coming home. I have to work at the coffee shop tomorrow morning but I'll call Tracy. She'll understand."

"Harper, there's nothing you can do. If anything serious happens, we'll call you."

"Are you sure?"

"I promise. Right now your grandma needs a blood transfusion. Lucky for her, I'm her blood type. I'll call you in a couple of hours with an update. I love you."

"Love you dad."

I hang up and Scout asks, "Is everything okay?"

"My grandma had a stroke. Since we probably won't have service hiking, I'm going to stay here today just in case they call and I have to drive home. Will you tell Rafe I'm sorry I can't make it?"

Scout gives me a big hug, "I'm sorry Harper. Want some company?"

"No, don't change your plans for me. I have homework to do anyway. Thanks though."

After finishing all my homework and cleaning the apartment I get a call from my dad again. He said that my grandma is doing okay and the doctors said it might take some time for her to recover. They'll keep her in the hospital for at least a week. I feel relieved but am still going to stay home today just in case. I'd never forgive myself if something happened and I didn't get to say goodbye.

I'm sitting here bored out of my mind when I hear a knock on the door. I open it and am completely shocked when I see Ardyn standing there.

"Hey. Scout told us about your grandma. She said you're staying home today so I brought you some things." He hands me a grocery bag and two different books. "Comfort food and something to read. Scout told me you like historical fiction and romance so that's what I got from the library. I could go back and get you some different ones though."

I can't help but smile. "Thanks, Ardyn. I was just thinking how I wish I had a good book to lose myself in."

"I hope your grandma is okay."

I glance down at Ardyn's hiking boots.

"Are you going hiking?" I ask.

"Yeah I told them I'd catch up."

This guy has just done a complete turnaround and I feel dizzy. "I appreciate it."

"Bye Harper."

"Bye." I shut the door and cup my hand over my smile.

When I open one of the books Ardyn brought, a piece of paper falls out on the floor. It has something written on it. I pick it up and read it.

Fact: Reading books keeps you out of prison.

I laugh and keep the fact for a bookmark.

Later that evening, I call my parents to check on Grandma. My mom and dad say she's doing well but it might take her a while to do anything on her own again, so she will be moving in with my parents. At least for now.

When I'm at work on Monday, I see Ardyn walk in with a bunch of men I don't recognize. Some of them are wearing hard hats, some are in work overalls, and all of them are wearing boots. Ardyn's messy hair, dusty blue jeans and tight black shirt are making it difficult to want to look at anything else. He gets more attractive to me every time I see him. Ardyn gives me a small smile. But he still doesn't say anything to me. I hate that I'm disappointed when he gets on Tracy's line to place his order. I guess he's back to trying to avoid me. I ask Tracy if I can write something on his cup before she hands him his coffee.

Chapter Twenty-Six

Will

I miss Harper. I miss everything about her. I've thought about writing to her a million times. I want to let her know I'm okay. But I can't do that to her. I know I hurt her and I don't even feel like I deserve her right now. Holding her back from having a good time in college is definitely not something that I want to do. So instead I wrote James and asked him to check in on her, but without letting her know. Jameson wrote me back saying that Harper is doing great, and that he likes Harper's roommate. He said he's taking her on a date. I'm happy for Jameson.

We're on another night patrol. There are about eight of us marching along the berm quietly when Private Morris says, "I could really use a beer right now."

"I could really use a woman," says Evans.

There's quiet laughter.

"I need both," Morris says.

"If you could only choose one right now, which would it be?" Evans asks Morris.

"Without a doubt, I'd choose a woman."

Everyone laughs when the corporal stops and says, "Quiet, I think I see something in the distance."

Everyone gets low while the Corporal takes a look with his night vision goggles.

"They're just over there. There are way too many of them. We've got to lay low and stay quiet for a bit," he whispers.

We all lay down quietly on the other side of the berm to hide. My eyes are feeling heavy as I lay here.

Noel nudges me. "Don't fall asleep. Your snoring will get us all killed," he whispers.

"You're hilarious," I say with sarcasm. "How's Laura?"

"I miss her like crazy. I'm thinking of proposing when I get back home to Pennsylvania. Maybe for Christmas. But for now, I'm here. I'm focused on that."

"That's awesome. I better be invited to the wedding."

"You better be my best man. And I better be yours one day."

I laugh quietly. "What makes you think I'll get married?"

"Good point," he says.

We're silent for a moment when I ask, "Are you afraid of dying out here?"

Noel shakes his head no. "When I die, I'll know it's my time to go because I lived my life exactly how I wanted to. Instead of living day to day, I live second to second."

"What do you mean?" I ask.

"It keeps me in the moment. So I never have to worry about tomorrow, or dying. Or dwell on yesterday. Seconds add up and eventually those seconds are your whole lifetime. It makes you understand just how valuable each second is."

"Don't you have regrets?" I ask.

"No. That doesn't mean I haven't made any mistakes. Because I have. A lot of them. But I don't waste my time regretting them. Not a single second."

"Wow."

I find myself thinking about my mistakes. Especially the one I made with Harper the night before we said goodbye. We went way too far. Everything we did were some of my favorite seconds. My favorite mistakes. I have never felt like that with anyone else. I always think about that night. It lives inside of me. It weakens me. It gives me strength. It tortures me. It heals me. It tears me down. It keeps me moving forward.

"What's going on in your head?" Noel asks.

"Just thinking about that night I told you about with Harper. I don't regret that either. But it was definitely a mistake. How could I be so stupid Noel? I fucked everything up by almost sleeping with her."

"It may have been a mistake," Noel says, "but if you ask me, a mistake made out of love can never really be a mistake."

"I've already told you it's not like that between us."

"If you keep telling yourself that, you might lose her."

"I'm making sure that won't happen, trust me."

Suddenly Corporal Hoffman stands up and motions for us to move.

As we get up, Noel says, "I've had some amazing seconds in my life Will. Nobody knows when they'll die. So I make every second of my life matter before I run out of them. I suggest you do the same."

Chapter Twenty-Seven

Harper

It's finally the weekend and I just feel like having a lazy night in. Tonight Scout's going on a date with Jameson. I'm sitting on the couch reading one of the books that Ardyn brought me when Scout walks out from her bedroom looking incredible. She has tight leather pants on, showing off the muscles in her legs, high heeled combat boots and a white coat.

"You look great. Are you excited?" I ask her.

We hear a knock on the door and she says, "So excited and nervous. Wish me luck."

"Good luck."

When Scout leaves, I continue to read.

I wake up on the couch when I hear Scout come back in from her date. She has disappointment written all over her face and I assume it didn't go as well as she'd hoped.

She tosses her purse and phone onto the counter before walking toward her bedroom.

"How'd it go?" I ask her.

"I don't know. I'll tell you after I change," she says.

When I get up off the couch to get a drink of water, Scout's phone vibrates the counter with a phone call.

"Scout, Jameson is calling you," I say loud enough for her to hear me through her half-open door.

"Will you answer it? I'm still trying to squeeze out of these pants!"

I swipe the screen to answer the call.

"Hey James, it's Harper. Scout's struggling."

"Hey Harp. Will you tell Scout she forgot something?" he asks.

"What did she forget?" I ask.

"I'll be right there," he says before hanging up.

Scout runs out in a tank top and sweats.

"What did Jameson say?" she asks, out of breath.

"He told me to tell you that you forgot something. He's bringing it now."

She looks confused when we hear a knock on the door.

Scout opens the door and Jameson grabs her by the waist, pulls her into him and kisses her. She throws her arms around him and kisses him back.

Whoa. I was not expecting that.

Jameson grins at her before backing away. Scout shuts the door and I've never seen her smile so big as she mouths the words, "Oh my gosh," to me.

"That was the sweetest thing I've ever seen."

"I was so disappointed that he didn't kiss me after our date."

"So you like him then?" I ask.

She bites her lip and nods excitedly, "So freaking much."

Chapter Twenty-Eight

Harper

It's Saturday, March twenty-first and I have no idea what I'm going to do tonight.

After doing homework, my stomach grumbles. I guess I could order some pasta or something and stay in for dinner. I crawl off my bed and go where I left my phone on the counter in the kitchen. I have an unread text.

Mom: Doing anything fun tonight?

Scout walks into the apartment before I can text my mom back.

"Harper! I got all kinds of things from the store. Nail polish, hydrating face masks, self-tanner, although that's for me since your tan ass doesn't need it, some lip gloss, and lots of other makeup. Let's do makeovers and dress up for dinner tonight. I'm taking you out," Scout says, setting all of her Target plastic bags on the counter.

I text my mom back.

Yep! Girls' night with Scout.

Scout loaned me a dress to wear to dinner. It's pink with a long sleeve on one arm and the other is strapless, exposing my shoulder. I also let Scout run her straightener through my hair, making it look longer. I'm wearing more make-up than I normally do and high heels which I never wear.

I'm waiting for Scout to finish getting ready when Tracy calls my cell.

"Hi Harper. I think I left the center espresso machine on. We had a customer come in right as we were closing and I completely forgot to shut it off before I left. Is there any chance you could swing by the shop and shut it off? I'm already clear across town and my apprehensive brain is screaming fire hazard."

"I can do that. I was just getting ready to go out to dinner so I'll stop on my way," I tell her.

"Harper, you're a lifesaver! Thank you," she says before saying goodbye and hanging up.

After driving my car to the coffee shop, Scout and I get out.

"This will only take a second," I say, digging the key out of my purse.

I unlock the door and we walk in.

"Happy birthday Harper!" A crowd of familiar, friendly faces jump out and the lights come on. I see Rafe, Tracy, Jake, Lucy, Matt, and Jameson scattered about at the birthday decorated coffee shop. There are balloons, streamers, and music is playing. I was not expecting this. I didn't realize anyone knew today was even my birthday. I turn and look at Scout.

"Something tells me you had everything to do with this," I say, giving her a hug.

"The boy I'm dating is your best friend's brother. And now your birthday is burned into my brain for life." She winks.

I look at Jameson. "You're the snitch?" I tease.

He laughs before giving me a hug. "Happy birthday."

I dance with all my friends and eat too much cake.

Ardyn

I'm getting into my truck to head out for Harper's birthday party Scout invited me to when I receive a text from my sister.

Hey! We're in the city. Graham is asking for uncle Ardyn. Meet you for ice cream at Smiley's in 10?

I sigh as I start up my truck and head to Smiley's instead of Steamin' Mugs.

I saw the look on Harper's face two weeks ago in the coffee shop when I ordered from the other barista. She was disappointed. I liked it. And she wrote the most random fact that dolphin's sleep with one eye open on my coffee cup. That made me want to jump over the counter and kiss her right there.

I'm getting to her. Women are funny. The less you give them, the more they want you. It's probably a good thing I'm not going to her party.

Harper

I feel so happy that I have so many people in my life who love me. After telling everyone goodbye, I leave the coffee shop with Rafe. He definitely needs assistance getting home.

We're driving back to the apartment building when Rafe looks around the car. "Oh no! We forgot Scout. Quick, turn around." He panics.

"You told Scout goodbye, remember? She's going to Jameson's."

Rafe laughs hysterically. "I'm so happy for her."

After helping Rafe up the stairs we get to his door when he starts laughing again.

"I remember why I was so panicked about Scout not being with us in the car. She has my keys."

"Why does she have your keys?"

"I gave them to her."

Probably the responsible thing to do.

Rafe tries to open his door and it's locked, of course.

"Call Ardyn. He has a key."

"Why don't you call him? I don't have his number."

I'm puzzled when Rafe says his phone is dead and gives me Ardyn's number.

"You memorized his phone number?" I ask.

He shrugs. "I have photographic memory."

Yet, you forgot Scout had your keys.

As Rafe repeats Ardyn's phone number, I dial it into my phone. I'm kind of hoping he doesn't answer but he does on the second ring.

"Hello?"

I'm suddenly at a loss of words. *Where are my words?*

"Hello?" Ardyn repeats.

"Hi. It's Harper. I'm trying to get Rafe into your apartment but he doesn't have his key. Could you come unlock it?"

"Sup Roomie!" Rafe screams into my ear so Ardyn can hear him.

Ardyn says, "I'll be right there."

I tell him thank you and hang up.

Rafe is slumped down next to the door falling asleep when Ardyn shows up with a key.

"Hey," he says, scanning me over with his eyes. He clears his throat, "I see Rafe had a good time at your party."

As Ardyn unlocks the door I say, "Yeah he lost big time to some drinking game he and Matt were playing."

Rafe speaks up from the ground. "No, I won!"

Ardyn and I look at each other and laugh.

"I'll get him to bed," Ardyn says.

"Thanks. Bye Rafe."

"Bye bye," he says as Ardyn helps him up off the floor.

As I'm walking down the stairs I realize that's the first time Ardyn's talked to me since he brought me the library books.

I get to my floor and as I walk down the hall to my apartment, a familiar form comes bursting through the staircase door. Butterflies swarm my stomach.

"Ardyn?"

"I'm ready to stop avoiding you now."

My heart is beating fast as he walks toward me.

He's observing me with his seriously intense eyes when he says, "Harper. Let me help you forget that guy that hurt you."

I'm speechless. As soon as I nod my head, he grabs the back of my thighs and picks me up, wrapping my legs around him. I put my arms around the back of his neck and instead of him kissing me right away, he just looks at me like I'm the most important thing he's ever seen.

"You look absolutely incredible tonight," he growls. "So incredible in fact that I had to come down here and kiss you. Do you want me to kiss you, Harper?"

"Yes." I breathe.

Still holding me up, he pushes me against the wall. Anyone could walk down the hallway and see us but he obviously doesn't care. He slides his hands up my body and he locks them in mine and pins them above my head while he continues to admire me. I close my eyes waiting for him to kiss me.

"Not yet," he whispers right in my ear that sends a tingling sensation down my spine.

I want him to kiss me so bad right now. The anticipation is torturing me. He smiles slyly. He wants me to feel this way. Does he want me to beg him? Because I'm about to. I close my eyes as he slowly brings his mouth to mine.

My lips are melting into his.

He pulls away just to say, "You taste like frosting." He groans before kissing me again. Like he can't get enough. He slowly puts me down and has a grin on his face. "Happy birthday Harper."

I still can't talk. All I can do is smile as Ardyn walks back up the stairs.

This birthday is the best.

Ever.

When I finally get into my apartment, I'm changing out of my dress when I hear Scout come in. That's weird. I wasn't expecting her home so soon. I walk out of my bedroom and see Jameson and Scout are both in the kitchen.

"I feel like an idiot that I forgot to give you these. From Will," Jameson says as he hands me a Twinkie, a 7up, and a little piece of cardboard that says, *Happy birthday Harper! Love, Will.*

Tears blur my vision as Jameson says, "As soon as I realized I forgot, I told Scout we had to turn around. He told me I had to give it to you right on your birthday. Sometimes he can't get paper so he cuts pieces of cardboard off the ration boxes. That explains the birthday card."

A huge ball of guilt churns in my stomach. Here I am kissing Arydn and Will remembers my birthday. He can't even get paper but finds a way to make a card anyway. Out of cardboard. And then he sent it early just so that I can get it right on my birthday.

I tell James thank you and go back to my room.

I curl up in my bed, and cry.

The next morning, I pull out my "DO NOT SEND" box out of my closet and start another letter to Will.

Dear Will,

This is my first time writing you a fake letter since you've left for Afghanistan. I still miss you like crazy. Yesterday was my birthday and Jameson made sure to get me that Twinkie and 7up. But the cardboard note that said Happy Birthday meant more to me than anything. It means you're thinking about me. That you remembered my birthday. In Afghanistan, in the middle of war. Gosh, just when I think I'm almost over you, I realize I'm not. I'm trying so damn hard Will. How is my heart still with you even though you don't want it? You told me you don't want to risk losing me. So you just push me away. You're a thousand miles away and somehow I still feel you pushing me.

I kissed someone last night and it was almost as good as kissing you. This man is trying to take my heart from you. If you had any idea, I think you'd let him. You don't want it. So I'm going to try Will. I'm going to try and give my heart to somebody else now. I can't wait to see you. I'm on my knees every single night praying that I'll get to see you again soon.

I know I'm not supposed to. I know I'm not allowed to. I know you don't want me to. But I'll always love you.

Love, Harper

When I put the box back into my closet, I plug my dead phone into the charger because I forgot to last night.

I'm getting dressed after showering when my phone vibrates. It's a random number.

Fact: Cotton candy was invented by a dentist.

Right away I realize it's Ardyn. I never saved his number after calling him last night. But I do now. After adding my new contact, I google interesting facts and text him back.

Fact: Children of identical twins aren't just cousins. They're genetically siblings.

He texts back.

Fact: I like kissing Harper.

I'm smiling ear to ear when I text back. **Not a fact ;).**

Chapter Twenty-Nine

Harper

Jameson is sitting next to me on our living room sofa as Scout gets ready for their date. We've been talking about childhood memories and how we used to play hide and seek in my backyard. One time Will hid in the shed attic and Jameson and I started to worry about him when we couldn't find him.

"We looked for hours," Jameson says.

"I almost went inside to tell my mom to call the police," I say and we laugh.

Jameson gets quiet for a moment. He looks like he's thinking hard about something. Then he whispers, "What's Scout's story? I really like her but she seems closed off at times."

I whisper back, "Scout's amazing. She's a tough nut to crack. But she likes you too. She'll eventually open up."

"What are you two whispering about?" Scout asks, appearing in the living room.

Jameson's eyes widen and he stands up, "You look beautiful, Scout."

Scout's smile is so affectionate towards Jameson, I almost don't even recognize her.

"You two have fun on your date," I tell them as they're leaving.

I haven't seen Ardyn since we kissed. He hasn't been to the coffee shop all week. He sent me a random fact on Wednesday and I sent one back but I haven't heard from him since. But it's been almost a week now, and I just want to break the ice and see him.

I knock on Ardyn's door.

Rafe answers. *I don't know why I'm so relieved but I am. Confronting Ardyn is nerve-racking.*

"Oh hey," I say.

"Harper! What's up?"

I know if I ask for Ardyn, Rafe will ask questions. So I just play it cool and say, "Oh nothing. What are you up to tonight?"

"I was just headed to the market to get a few things. Would you like to join me?"

I could use a few things from the store and I love hanging out with Rafe so I say, "Sure. I'll drive."

When Rafe and I get back from the store, as we are carrying our groceries, he asks, "When are you going to admit who you actually came knocking on my door for?" he asks as he smiles playfully.

"What are you talking about?" I ask, even though now I know that he knows.

"You wanted Ardyn to answer the door."

"How did you know?" I ask.

"I could tell by the look on your face when it was me at the door. And I felt the tension between you two the other night when Ardyn had to come rescue us. I notice these things. So, tell me everything. What's going on between the two of you and how long has it been happening?"

I guess we've been caught. "I don't even know what it is. We just kissed."

"You kissed? So you're the reason he hasn't been bringing any more women home?" He grins.

"I guess so," I say.

After saying goodbye to Rafe at my door, as I'm putting my groceries away I realize I left the apples in the car. I go back out to grab them and I suddenly feel anxious. I don't know if it's because it's dark or because my instincts are trying to tell me something. After getting the apples from the car, I quickly look around the dark parking lot to make sure nobody is there. When I hear a thump, I bolt back inside the building. I'm running down the hall when I trip and fall. My apples fly everywhere. As I compose myself on the floor, I throw my hands over my face and laugh. *I'm such a scared-y cat.*

Ardyn

I was disappointed when Harper came to the apartment tonight to hang out with Rafe. I was hoping she came for me. When they left for the store, I went out to my truck to think. I can't stop thinking about her. Now I'm watching Harper carry in groceries in trying to decide when to ask her out. I tried to keep my distance but dammit, I can't anymore. I want her. I hit the dash and she looks around. I duck my head down.

I sit back up and Harper is already inside.

Here goes nothing.

I wasn't planning on kissing Harper on her birthday. But when I saw her, she took my breath away. As soon as I put Rafe's drunk ass to bed I ran to her. I had to kiss her. She looked so good in that dress. And her hair was straight. Just like Casey always wore hers. I went downstairs to kiss *her*, but ended up feeling guilty that I was actually kissing Harper. I've felt guilty about it all week. *I miss her so much it hurts.* But I know I've got to stop feeling guilty about it. I want Casey back so bad and this is the closest I'll ever get. Being near Harper isn't enough anymore. I need more of *her.*

Harper

"Harper, are you okay?" Ardyn asks.

I slowly uncover my face with my hands. Ardyn is standing over me looking concerned.

"I tripped."

"I can see that," he says as he picks up some apples and puts them back in the grocery bag.

"Thanks," I say after he sits down next to me on the floor. We lean our backs up against the wall. "Were you going somewhere?" I ask.

He smiles and says, "I was coming to find you."

There's those butterflies swarming in my guts again.

"Oh yeah?"

"Do you want to go get some dinner?" he asks.

"Yeah. Let me go put these apples away then I'll meet you outside."

Ardyn stands up and offers his hand to help me up.

I unlock my door as Ardyn goes walking down the hall. I put the apples away and throw on some perfume and lip gloss.

I spot Ardyn outside leaning up against his truck. Waiting for *me*.

"What's your favorite food?" he asks as I make my way over to him.

When I tell Ardyn pasta and he says he knows the perfect place, and it's close by.

"When did you graduate high school?" I ask him on our way to the Italian restaurant.

"Four years ago. I'm studying business and finance."

"Do you plan on having your own business one day?"

"I've been working at my dad's construction business. Right now we're partners, but he's wanting me to take over on my own one day. So I figured it'd be good to have a degree," he says.

"Wait. So you're running a business *and* going to school?"

He nods and my eyes widen.

"Impressive," I tell him as we enter the restaurant.

We are seated in a booth sitting across from each other. It smells like heaven in here as I inhale the combination of roasted basil and garlic.

After the waiter takes our order, Ardyn says, "I heard you telling someone once that you're majoring in Social Work. I could tell how passionate you are about it. It's one of the many things that draw me towards you."

"Oh really?" I ask, trying to hide how easily he makes me smile.

"Yeah, that. And many, many other things," he flirts.

I feel my face grow hot and he groans. "You've got to stop blushing Harper. Or else I'm going to kiss you before our food even gets here."

"I can't help it," I say, covering my face with my hands.

"It drives me crazy when you blush. Especially that time at Matt's cabin when Rafe and I caught you in the kitchen wearing your bathing suit."

I laugh and say, "That was embarrassing. Especially when I ran into you trying to get up the stairs."

He laughs. "It took everything I had to move out of your way. When you ran into me I wanted to kiss you right then and there."

I drop my mouth open. "You seemed so irritated with me. I thought for sure you hated me. Do you realize how intimidating you can be?"

He stops laughing. "Trust me Harper. Staying away from you is the hardest thing I've ever done in my life."

"Well, I'm glad you're not staying away anymore."

"Me too."

We're finishing up our dinner when Ardyn asks, "Do you want to go hiking tomorrow? We can go up to the waterfall. There's even a small watering hole you can swim in. You can bring that white bikini of yours." He grins.

"That sounds like fun."

After dinner, we are walking through the parking lot when Ardyn says, "Want to hear some of the other things about you that made me give up and accept the fact that I want you?"

He wants me. I want to take in all his words and trap this feeling inside me forever.

"Of course I do," I tell him as I feel his hand brush up against mine. I hold it and feel the roughness of his palm.

We are holding hands and walking as he says, "You have the prettiest eyes I've ever seen. I like the way you scrunch your nose and bite your tongue sometimes when you laugh. Gosh, even the sound of your laugh is sexy as hell. We've established already what it does to me when you blush. The way you smile at literally everyone, and your lips... the way they're shaped, the way they feel..."

He stops walking and I turn around to look at him. Ardyn is staring at my mouth as he gently runs his fingers up my jawline and over my lips.

"Do you have any idea what your lips did to me the other night Harper?"

I catch my breath as he pulls my bottom lip down with his thumb. "You have completely destroyed my ability to resist you," he says.

"Ardyn," I breathe out. "I thought you didn't want sticky."

"I changed my mind," he says before colliding his mouth with mine. He's backing me up as he's kissing me, gripping the back of my hair. I don't know where he's taking me but I'll go anywhere as long as he keeps kissing me like this. Someone whistles and we laugh and pull away. We get into his truck and drive home.

"Goodnight Hazey," he says when we get back to my apartment.

I'm completely caught off guard that he called me a different name.

He must see the confusion in my expression because he immediately says, "Hazey. Your hazel eyes. It's a nickname. A dumb nickname. I like giving nicknames. It's weird," he says.

He's totally embarrassed and adorable right now.

"Hazey. I like it." I smile. I actually love it. He grabs me again and kisses me way harder this time.

"Hazey," he says again before walking away.

Scout is sitting on the sofa eating ice cream when I walk in.

"How was your night with Jameson?" I ask.

"I like him a lot. He's so mature and we have so much in common. We made out in his squad car tonight," she says with a smile.

"I kind of kissed Ardyn again too. The night of my birthday and then tonight," I confess.

Scout jumps up. "What?! Tell me everything," she says.

I tell her about our date tonight and how upfront and vocal he is about how he feels about me. "He literally leaves me speechless."

"He sounds so sweet," Scout says.

"But I know that I have to be cautious."

Thinking about how things could end makes me want to deadbolt my door and never let Ardyn in here again.

"You deserve to be happy, Harper. If you like him, don't hold back because of Will. I know you have feelings for him but he told you he just wants to be friends. That most likely won't change when he gets home. Remember that."

When did Will's name alone cause me pain? I hate it. As difficult as it is to hear again, I know Scout's right. I'm not going to hold back because of Will but I am going to try and take things slow with Ardyn.

"Ardyn is taking me hiking tomorrow. Any idea what I should wear?"

Then Scout drags me to her room to find me a cute hiking outfit.

Chapter Thirty

Ardyn

Mornings used to be my favorite time of day. Now I hate them. Actually, I dread them. Waking up in my bed alone is pure torture. It never gets fucking easier. Opening my eyes to Casey every morning was something I took for granted. That's when she looked the most beautiful to me. Before the day even started, I would make love to her. God, I miss her so much. Since she's been gone, I've been with dozens of women to help numb the pain but I've never let them stay. Mornings will always be *hers*.

She had the biggest heart. And so does Harper. Every time I see her I want more. After swinging by the coffee shop, I knock on Harper's door. She answers and I hand over her coffee.

"Morning. Rafe told me you like vanilla creamer."

"Thanks. I never imagined you handing me a coffee. It's always the other way around," she says.

Harper is driving me nuts in those shorts she has on today. And she's wearing blue. My favorite. That's the color she was wearing the first time I saw her. I was buying a suit that I knew I was just going to burn after the funeral. I never wanted anything to remind me of that day.

That day at the store, there were young highschoolers around every corner trying to find a prom dress. It forced me to think about the night I took Casey to prom. I thought to myself how I'd do anything to see her in that blue dress again.

That's the exact moment I saw Harper. She walked out of the fitting room in a blue prom dress. It was the Exact. Same. Blue. Everything about this person was familiar. Her skin, her long hair, and when she looked my way I couldn't believe what I was seeing. Her hazel eyes took my breath away. *Again.*

Her mom called her Harper but I was looking at Casey.

Harper

Today feels like spring. The sun is shining and all the snow has melted. A perfect day for a hike.

We're quiet in the truck. Ardyn seems to really be thinking hard about something on the drive. He lets out a sigh before turning the wheel.

"What are you thinking about?"

"How good you look in blue," he says with a flirty smile.

I smile at him as we drive down a bumpy road and bonk my head against the passenger window.

"Ouch." I grab my head and laugh.

Falling down the hallway and scattering apples down the floor wasn't embarrassing enough apparently.

"Come sit closer to me, it's bumpy."

I slide into him and he rubs my head.

"You okay?" he asks.

"Yeah. I just love making a fool out of myself in front of you."

Ardyn laughs. "Well you're a damn cute fool."

He stops the truck. "We'll start hiking from here. I just have to grab my stuff out of the back."

We start up the rocky trail to the waterfall and Ardyn asks, "How's your grandma?"

"She's doing okay. She's living at home with my parents because she can't talk or eat or really do anything on her own anymore. What's your family like?" I ask.

"I have two younger brothers and an older sister. We all get along pretty well. My sister and I are really close. She's married and lives near my parents. I have a nephew."

He stops walking and pulls out a picture from his wallet and hands it to me. The picture is of a little boy with blond hair and blue eyes.

"Oh my gosh, he's adorable. What's his name?"

"Graham. He's four now," he says looking down at the photo in my hand. It's so sweet how much he loves his nephew.

We start hiking again and I can hear the waterfall in the distance. When we finally see it, it takes my breath away. It's absolutely beautiful. The water is running over a rocky edge down into a clear pool of water. Nobody is here and I can feel the cool mist spraying on my skin from the falling water.

"This is amazing, Ardyn."

"Isn't it great?" he asks, handing me a water bottle.

I admire the view for a moment when Ardyn asks, "Have you ever been underneath a waterfall before?"

"No," I say, before he grabs my hand.

After we take off our shoes and jackets, he leads me into the cold pool of water. As soon as my feet submerge, it feels like melted ice.

"It's freezing!" I yell.

"It's worth it, trust me," he says, looking back at me with a gentle smile. I can't feel my feet anymore and I'm glad the water only comes up to our knees. But the waterfall is splashing us as we're trying to work our way around it. I'm laughing as we finally make it underneath. We are both soaking wet. Ardyn is looking intently at me with his eyes. Sometimes it's hard to focus on anything but his blue eyes when he looks at me. They are beautiful. I am completely lost in them right now. His wet dark hair and wet face make this moment better. He's wearing a white T-shirt and I can see right through it. He's so physically fit. I find his blue eyes again and he's staring into mine.

It's even louder underneath the waterfall but there is something so relaxing and exhilarating about it. I close my eyes for a moment to take it all in. I feel Ardyn behind me as he wraps his arms around me. His hands feel warm on my arms.

"You're incredible Harper," he says into my ear.

I lean back into his body. We're being splashed from the waterfall but I don't even care. *It feels so good.* I don't know if my chills are from him or the waterfall. Something inside is holding me back and screaming at me not to get too attached to him. But he's making it so hard. I can feel his hot breath on my neck as I tilt my head toward him. He gets his mouth close to mine, but doesn't kiss me. He's tormenting me again. I feel his hands move from my arms and they make their way down to my waist. I gasp when his hands touch my bare stomach and I realize the water must have pulled my shirt up. Then as he holds one arm around me, he brings his other hand up and touches my face. He presses his forehead against me and I know if I turn my head just a little bit further our lips will touch.

"Ardyn," I say loudly so he can hear me under the roar of water. He lets me know he's listening to me by sliding his thumb across my cheek. His forehead still pressed against the side of my face.

"I've been thinking a lot about this," I say. This thing we have. I don't even know what to call it. I think we need to slow things down a bit. We hardly know each other but we can't seem to stop kissing."

He skims his warm mouth up to my ear. "I know you more than you think Harper. But we can slow down," he says. He presses his lips to the side of my head as he continues to hold me from behind.

"Is this too much?" he asks.

I shake my head because it feels too good to be in his arms like this.

I run my fingers through his wet hair. He brings his mouth close to mine, never kissing me. I let out a small breath and he smiles. I turn around so that I'm facing him. I know if I don't make us leave right here, right now, I'm going to end up giving into his warm mouth. I need to take a breath and figure out my emotions before we let the physical stuff get the best of us.

"I could be with you under a waterfall all day," I say, "but I'm freezing."

He laughs and we walk out from under the waterfall and toward Ardyn's backpack. I put my shoes and jacket on as Ardyn pulls out some towels.

"Here," Ardyn says, wrapping a towel around my shoulders.

I'm towel drying my hair when we get back to the truck. March in Ohio is usually pretty cold but today is warmer than usual and the sunshine feels so good, even though I can't stop shivering from our swim.

After getting into Ardyn's truck and before pulling away he turns around and grabs a black hoodie from the back seat of his truck. "Here. Put this on. You still look cold."

"Thanks," I say. I take off my now soaking wet jacket and pull the thick hoodie over my head.

When we get home, I take off his hoodie. I hand it over to him and he shakes his head.

"No, you keep it. It looks way better on you." I scrunch my nose and smile.

"I had so much fun. Thanks Ardyn," I tell him as we stand in front of my front door.

"Do you want to come over later?" he asks.

There is no way I am even a little ready for that. I told him I want to take things slow.

"Just for dinner," he says quickly. "I want to make you dinner. I promise that's all I meant. I know you don't want to move things too fast. I'll stay at your pace. I promise."

I love that he says this. I kiss him on the cheek. "I'll be there for dinner," I say before walking into my apartment.

I'm startled when I see Scout and Jameson making out on the couch. Jameson is on top of her. I shut the door and clear my throat. Jameson jumps up and Scout throws her shirt back on.

"Hey Harper." Scout laughs.

"Hey guys. Pretend I'm not here. I just have to get out of my wet clothes," I tell them.

I walk quickly to my room and shut the door. My stomach growls as I change. I put Ardyn's hoodie back on. It smells like him.

"Can I open my eyes?" I tease Scout and Jameson as I head back to the living room. "We're decent. Sorry about that," Jameson says.

In the kitchen, I make a quick sandwich and take it to my room to finish homework. I feel exhausted from both the hike and from fighting the side of my brain that always wants to kiss Ardyn. Homework can wait. Sleep first. I crawl under my sheets, lay my head down into my soft pillow and quickly drift off.

After my nap, I finish homework then hop up to go shower and get ready for dinner.

When Ardyn opens his door, he smells like he just got out of the shower. He hugs me and I get a faint whiff of his fresh body wash. His hair is still wet and he's now wearing a dry white t-shirt.

Ardyn looks so good.

"Hey I was just about to start cooking dinner. Come in," he says.

I walk in and look around. "Is Rafe home?" I ask him.

"He went to see his family this weekend. How do you like your steak?" he asks as he makes his way down the hall. He walks into his bedroom.

I feel a little nervous that we are in his apartment alone. I'm about ready to bolt to the door and crawl back into my bed.

I have got to get my nerves under control.

"Medium," I say as my voice cracks.

I don't know why I followed him to his room. But he doesn't seem weird about it so I just lean against the door-frame and watch him.

He pulls a flannel button-up shirt off a hanger in his closet and puts it on. I skim my eyes over his bedroom.

"Your bed is made so perfectly," I say.

He laughs. "It bugs me if it isn't. I'm sort of a neat freak."

I spot another picture of his nephew on his dresser. I walk into his room and pick up the frame. "Your nephew looks a lot like you. He has your blue eyes."

"Yeah, people say that a lot," he says.

Then he takes the picture out of my hand, sets it back down on the dresser and we go back into the living room.

He tells me to sit and make myself comfortable and gives me a quick kiss. Then he turns the TV on and hands me the remote.

"What do you want to drink?" he asks. "I have soda. Or water?"

"I'll take a soda."

He brings me a coke then heads back into the kitchen to start dinner. I get up and follow him. "What can I help with?"

"Nothing. Sit down and relax," he says with a grin.

"I'm not going to sit down and relax while you work in the kitchen. I can help."

"If you don't go sit down right now I'm going to have to make you," he teases.

"You wouldn't dare."

Then Ardyn scoops me up into his arms, carries me to the living room, and drops me on the couch.

I'm laughing when Ardyn says, "Stay put and let me make you dinner."

I'm watching the cooking channel when the smell of sizzling, seasoned steak makes my mouth water.

I hear Ardyn come up behind me as he says, "Come and eat, Hazey."

"It smells amazing."

We sit down at the kitchen table and eat our steak dinner.

It feels so casual. I finally feel a little more relaxed being here alone with him.

"That was delicious. Thank you Ardyn," I tell him.

I take our plates to the sink and start washing the dishes.

"Thanks for coming with me today. You're the only woman I know that actually enjoys that hike as much as I do."

Am I just another date to him?

"Do you take all your girlfriends underneath the waterfall?" I ask, half joking. But realize now that I kinda sound like a jealous, angry person.

"All my girlfriends?" he says and turns me around to face him. "Harper, I told you how much I like you. You're not just another random date to me. I want *you*."

He rubs his forehead in frustration and shuts off the running water. "I haven't cared about anyone like this in a long time. I don't think you realize how much I want you. I want you all of the time. I can't help it. I never stop thinking about you."

I'm scared to admit that I want him back. I sigh. I don't know what to do.

He obviously sees my doubt because he's not done trying to convince me.

"My God Harper, do you have any idea what you're doing to me?"

His words tug at my heart.

He grips the kitchen sink behind me, blocking me in. A thrill surges through me at the way he looks at me. He gently brushes my hair out of my face. Then he grabs me by the waist and presses his lips softly against my neck. I tilt my head back, wanting more. I breathe wildly as he continues to kiss my neck.

"Are we moving too fast Harper?" he asks as he brings his hands up my ribcage.

"No," I whisper.

I suddenly forgot why I ever wanted him to stop kissing me. When I can't take it anymore, I grab his face and press my mouth to his. This makes him groan and he picks me up and sets me on the counter.

"I can't get enough of you," he says. "We better stop before I invite you to my bedroom."

"Yeah, I wouldn't want to mess up your bed," I tease.

"You can mess up my bed anytime you want," he says playfully.

I jump off the counter and he follows me to the living room. He's letting me set the pace.

While we sit on the couch, I ask him what kind of kid he was in high school.

"I don't know. I had a lot of friends and I played tennis. I didn't take high school very seriously. But my parents pushed me to keep my grades up. What kind of girl were you? Let me guess. A cheerleader?"

I shake my head and laugh. "Definitely not. I'm not co-ordinated enough for that. But I did have a couple friends who were cheerleaders."

"How close were you and Will?" he asks and I feel a little uncomfortable.

Closer than anyone will ever know.

"We were really close. We grew up together. He was in the grade above me but that never stopped us from being best friends."

"I bet every single guy in school wanted to date you." He smiles.

I scrunch my nose and say, "Absolutely not."

We sit in silence for a moment when Ardyn says, "You seem guarded with me at times and I get that. But I just want you to know I'll always be honest with how I feel about you."

"I appreciate that. I like that you're so straightforward and honest. I want to keep getting to know you," I tell him.

"Good." He smiles.

"I better get going. Thanks for dinner Ardyn." I kiss him quickly on the lips and get up to walk away.

He grabs my hand and pulls me down on his lap and gives me a way better kiss. We make out for ten more minutes before I have to pull away or I'll never leave.

"Goodnight," I say before shutting his door.

Chapter Thirty-One

Harper

The next few days Ardyn and I are both busy finishing up the last semester of school that we hardly see each other. On Thursday, the line is so long at the coffee shop. I'm pouring more water into the espresso machine when I look up and see him. He's the last customer in line. He's watching me. We smile at each other and when I finish helping the three customers ahead of him, it's finally his turn.

"What can I get you sir?" I say and lean over the counter to give him a quick kiss.

"More of that please," he says with a grin on his face.

"Just the usual. I've hardly seen you all week. Let me take you out tonight. I know a good drive-in burger spot," he says.

"That sounds fun. Is seven o'clock okay?" I ask. "I'm going to donate blood today after class. Then I really have to do homework."

"You astonish me every day," he says as I hand him his coffee.

I'm doing homework in my room tonight and trying really hard to focus on my school work. It would help if I was at the library. But I know I can't go there because that's where Ardyn likes to study. He's too much of a distraction. Last week I was minding my own business doing homework in the library when I felt a ball of paper hit me right in the face. Startled, I looked up and saw Ardyn in front of me, sitting at a nearby table.

He laughed quietly and mouthed the words, "I'm so sorry. I didn't mean to hit you in the face."

I stuck my tongue out at him and smiled. He made a funny face and I laughed, probably a little too loud for the library. I put my finger up to my mouth and said, "Shh."

I tried my best to focus on my work in front of me but had to get Ardyn back, so I took a piece of paper out of my notebook and wadded it up into a ball. When I made sure his head was down I chucked the wad at him. Someone was walking right in between our tables just when I threw the ball of paper and it hit the him in the leg. The stranger looked at me and glared. Ardyn laughed so hard I thought they were going to kick us out.

So I decided if I wanted to get any homework done tonight, I better work on it in my room. But clearly, it's not the solution to my problem.

I've thought about writing Will a *real* letter to tell him about Ardyn. I used to tell my best friend everything, but that was before I realized I was in love with him. I'm *still* in love with him. I'm trying to move on and I want him to know that but I just can't bring myself to tell him yet. I throw my head back onto my bed and sigh.

There's a knock on my bedroom door.

"Come in," I say as I sit up.

When the door opens, it's Ardyn.

"Hey I'm a little early," he says.

I'm such a mess. After my shower, I threw my hair up on the top of my head into a sloppy bun. I'm even more embarrassed when I realize I'm wearing the Snoopy Christmas pajama bottoms that my parents got me years ago. They don't even fit right anymore. They're too short but I love how comfortable and soft they are.

"Hey, I'll go get ready so we can go," I say, scrambling around my room to find different clothes. Anything but my damn Snoopy pajamas.

"Take your time," he says.

After grabbing a shirt off a hanger and some jeans off the floor, I head for the bathroom.

"Wait here. I'll hurry," I say.

On my way out the bedroom door I stumble over Ardyn's foot and he grabs me by the arm before I hit the ground.

"Whoa, you okay?" he asks.

"Yeah I'm good," I say feeling so flustered I can't even look at him.

"You're quiet tonight," Ardyn says, sitting in his parked truck at the drive-inn.

We already ate our food and there are no other vehicles here. It's nice being alone with Ardyn, but my mind is still preoccupied.

"What's wrong?" he asks, tucking some stray hair behind my ear.

"Nothing" I lie. "How was your day?"

"Busy," he says. "We poured the foundation for a new house going up this summer. Then I was late for class and the professor locked me out so I missed it. That's why I was early. How was donating blood?"

"It was good," I say, massaging my sore arm.

"What made you want to donate?"

"There are wounded men in Afghanistan right now who need it. I know that I won't know how my blood will be used, but it makes me feel like I'm doing something to help."

"So, for Will?"

"Sort of, I guess."

He nods as he looks out the window.

Feeling a little awkward, I change the subject. "I can't believe it's almost the end of the second semester. It went by so fast."

"Are you staying here for the summer or going back home?" Ardyn asks.

"I'm staying. I'm actually going to take a couple classes. I figured I might as well since I'm planning on keeping my job and working. Tracy is giving me a couple more shifts this summer, too. So I'll be busy. What about you?"

"I'm going to hang around too. I'm not planning on taking any classes but Bennett Builds has so many houses going up here this summer, it wouldn't make sense to go back home and have to drive back every day. Summer is definitely the busiest time of year for construction."

I can't help but smile knowing that we will both still be here.

"Good," I say, "I'm happy I get to spend the summer with you."

"Me too," he says. "Is Scout sticking around too?"

"Oh definitely. I think she's probably here for good. Speaking of Scout, she's throwing a birthday party at our apartment next Saturday for her boyfriend Jameson. You should come."

He nods and I slide over closer to him.

He pulls me onto his lap and we kiss until dark.

Chapter Thirty-Two

Harper

It's Saturday and Ardyn said he'd be back sometime tonight. He went home to visit his family this weekend. He was excited to get to spend time with his nephew Graham.

I'm comfortable on the couch when I get a text from him.

On my way home. Do you feel like doing anything tonight? Rafe invited me to a party up Green Canyon if you want to go.

Scout told me about the party before she left. I text back.

Sure, sounds like fun.

Ardyn and I make it up to Green Canyon and there are even more people here now than there were in October. It's just starting to get dark. There's a fire going so we make our way over to it when I spot Scout sitting between Jameson's legs. She smiles enthusiastically when she sees me.

"Hey guys," I say plopping down next to them.

Ardyn sits down too.

"Hey! I'm so glad you made it," Scout says.

"Do all these party animals know you're a police officer, James?" I wink at him.

He laughs. "No, probably not. I decided to leave my squad car at home."

"We rode up with Matt and Lucy," Scout says.

Ardyn reaches across me and offers his hand over to Jameson.

"I'm Ardyn. I don't believe we've met yet but apparently I'm coming to your birthday party next weekend."

Jameson takes his hand and shakes it. "I'm Jameson. It's nice to meet you man."

Ardyn gives him a friendly nod.

"Hey guys!" Rafe says, handing me a beer.

"Hey Rafe," I say. "No beer for me. I'll let Ardyn drink tonight and I'll drive."

Rafe shakes his head. "Ardyn doesn't drink, so you can have all you want." He hands me the beer and without realizing it, I take it. I'm a little caught off guard.

I look over at Ardyn."You don't drink?"

"No," he says.

"But what about that night I first met you in the bar? You were drinking."

"It was soda."

"I'm not much of a drinker either. But is there a reason you don't?" I ask.

"I just don't anymore," he says looking into the fire.

I want to know everything about him.

"Ardyn!" yells a girl I don't recognize. She comes walking up to him.

"Hey," he says looking at the really pretty redhead.

"What have you been up to?" she asks. "I haven't seen you in a while."

She sits down next to him. A little too close.

"Just school and work," he tells her.

Then she whispers something in his ear, touching his knee.

Feeling super uncomfortable, I stand up and go talk to Matt and Jake.

"Hey you two."

"Harper. I didn't know you were coming." Jake hugs me.

I feel Ardyn's eyes on us.

"I heard you and Ardyn are a thing now," Jake says.

"Yeah. Sort of."

"He's a lucky guy."

"That's awesome," Matt says. Jake walks off.

"Don't worry about him," Matt says.

"Is he mad at me?" I ask.

I feel bad I sort of turned him down months ago. I wonder if he's upset that I'm seeing Ardyn.

"No," Matt says, "a little jealous maybe."

Lucy appears at that moment and gives me a hug.

After talking with them a little more, when I see the girl that was all over Ardyn is gone, I go back to where he's sitting. He looks at me and smiles.

"Sorry about Britney. Were you just trying to make me jealous? Hugging Jake over there?" he asks.

"What? No, I just felt uncomfortable sitting by you with Britney basically kissing your ear with her hands all over you."

He smiles again. "You were jealous."

"I was not!"

He tilts his head with a smirk on his face. Like he's waiting for me to tell the truth.

"Fine, maybe a little," I admit.

He has a very pleased grin on his face now.

"But I saw you watching me talk to Jake," I say.

He shakes his head. "I know you're not into Jake."

I kind of love that he doesn't seem jealous. His confidence is very attractive.

"What did Britney want anyway?" I ask.

"Do you really want to know?"

"Yeah, I really do."

"She asked me if I wanted to come over later."

I'm sure he's slept with her before. I know about his past and I've already accepted it. So I try not to let it get to me.

I don't say anything so Ardyn says, "Harper. She meant nothing to me. You are the only girl I think about."

I smile. "I know."

I hold his hand and lay my head down on his shoulder while I sip on the beer Rafe gave me. Being here with Ardyn makes me happy. I love that he's so mature. I'm still leaning against him when I notice someone looking at us in the distance. I squint my eyes and see that it's Jake. He immediately looks away.

"I remember seeing you here and you pretended you didn't know me."

He looks at me. "I did not want to get involved with the perfect Harper," he says.

"Yeah you made that clear in the women's restroom at the Bar and Grill," I tease him.

"I'm sorry. I just knew that we couldn't go that far. I could almost tell you didn't really want to either. You were with me but you definitely seemed somewhere else."

In my own broken head. "Yeah you were right about one thing that night. When you said that wasn't me. I'm honestly glad you stopped us. If you hadn't, we wouldn't be here now."

"You're right. But then when I saw you here, I regretted it so much."

I roll my eyes playfully. And he grips onto my waist making me laugh.

"It's true. I tried so hard to keep my eyes off of you but I couldn't help it. You looked so good I thought about asking *you* out into the trees."

I laugh. "I thought you were such a jerk. But I did catch you looking at me a few times. If you would've asked me to go out with you to the trees then, I would've said hell no."

He stands up off the ground and offers me his hand.

"What if I ask you now?"

I take his hand as he pulls me up.

"Sure. I want to see what all the fuss is about."

The fire gets smaller and it gets quiet as we make our way out into the forest. It's so dark I can barely see anything at all.

"This is eerie. It's so dark." I say.

Ardyn grabs me by the hips and pushes me up against a tree. "That means nobody can see us."

He kisses me on the lips, then my neck and his hands are *all over me*. Okay. *This is fun.* He told me I could set the pace but I'm kinda liking his pace instead. After running his hand up my chest and feeling my bra on the outside of my shirt, he unclasps the hook. I have no idea how he knew that it was a front-clasp bra. *This obviously isn't his first time.* After getting his feel through my shirt, his hands slide into the pockets of my jeans. Then he brings them back up my bare back and down again. His finger hooks the string of my panties.

"Are these what I think they are?"

"A thong?" I ask.

He groans. "Dammit Harper. I can't handle you."

His hand stays where it is, touching me softly as he kisses me again. I'm taking deep breaths because it feels good and I'm a little nervous he's going to try and go further.

With his hands still on my bare waist he asks, "Are these little bumps I feel on your skin from me or are you cold?" he asks.

"Both," I admit.

"Should we go back to the fire?" he asks.

"Yeah," I say. Even though I don't want to, we definitely should.

Once there, I sit between Ardyn's legs and lean my head back into his chest.

"Are you tired?" he whispers into my hair.

"Yeah, I feel like I could fall asleep right here."

"Let's get you home," he says.

I find Scout and Jameson still cuddled up around the fire. They're laughing together.

"Hey. We're going to head home," I tell them.

"Can we come with you?" she asks.

"Of course."

"I'm going to let Matt know we don't need a ride," Scout says before walking away.

I look over at Jameson. "You guys look so good together."

He smiles. "Really?"

"Definitely. I've never seen Scout this happy."

Ardyn is driving my car, Jameson and Scout are sitting in the back and I'm in the passenger seat.

"So how did you two meet?" Ardyn asks them.

Scout says, "Harper introduced us."

I look at Ardyn. "Jameson is Will's brother," I explain.

"Oh. I didn't know that. Are you older or younger?" Ardyn asks Jameson.

"I'm older," Jameson says.

"Oh man, that's rough. How's he doing?"

"He's doing well. I don't hear from him too often. He got hit by shrapnel his first day out there though. Twice."

"Wait what?" I ask Jameson.

This is the first I've heard about this. I'm so glad I'm not the one driving or we would be off the road.

"Why didn't I hear about this?" I ask James, looking back at him. I'm horrified.

"Shit. I drank too much tonight. I wasn't supposed to tell you. Will didn't want you to worry."

"Well you should have told me anyway," I snap at him.

I feel sick to my stomach that Will was shot. What if he gets hit again? He's in danger all of the time while he's there. I want to believe he's safe but I know he's not. It's the worst feeling in the world.

"I'm sorry Harper," Jameson says. "They made him sleep in an ambulance his first night there and some mortars went off. He was in the hospital for a few weeks. He's okay though. He's been awarded the purple heart."

I can't even say anything. I'm mad at Will for making Jameson keep something like that from me and feel petrified that Will had to go through that. I hate this and wish he would let me be there for him. I wish he would reach out to me.

I'm trying to stop myself from crying. I look out the window so nobody sees and wipe my tears away with the sleeve of my jacket. We pull up to the apartment and I jerk the passenger door open and run inside. I don't even care what anyone thinks right now. I just need a minute alone. I'll explain everything to Ardyn tomorrow.

I drop onto my bed and instantly cry into my pillow. I scream out of frustration and chuck the pillow across the room. I feel so many emotions all at once: fear, anger, and devastation. Someone knocks on my bedroom door.

Scout asks, "Harper? It's me. Can I come in?"

I sit up and wipe my eyes. "Yeah."

She closes the door behind her and rushes over to hug me. "I'm so sorry, Harper. That had to have been hard for you to hear about Will. What do you need?"

She hugs me tight as I say, "My best friend back."

Scout hugs me tighter.

"I just can't imagine how scared Will must've been. If I'm his best friend why wouldn't he tell me he got hurt? He could have died and he didn't even tell me about it. He told me he didn't want to lose me by risking our friendship. But I feel like I've already lost him. He's gone. I don't mean just at war."

Scout grabs my hands. "Maybe he really just doesn't want you to worry. It had to have been scary for him and I know it hurts you that he kept it from you. But, he obviously cares much more about you than he does himself."

"What? How?" I ask.

"Think about it. He probably wanted to come to you more than anyone. I know without a doubt he did. But he chose not to, so that you didn't have to feel scared too. So that you didn't have to worry about him," she says.

I don't know if that's true but I hug Scout tight for saying it.

"Thank you," I say.

Scout smiles. "I'm here for you, always. Jameson feels really bad that he ruined your night. Ardyn drove him home and said he was going to stop by and check on you on his way back. Can I send him in when he gets here or do you still want time alone?"

"Yeah, it's fine if he comes to see me."

She walks out and I get up and toss my pillow back on my bed and change into comfortable shorts and a tank top, making sure to keep my bra on knowing Ardyn will be here, even though he was trying to get me out of it an hour ago. I go to the bathroom and wash my face and brush my teeth. When I get back to my bedroom, I shut off the light, turn on my lamp and crawl under my cool sheets.

I left my door open for Ardyn. After I hear Scout let him in, he stands in my doorway with his hands in his pockets.

We make eye contact when he says, "Hey, are you okay?"

He looks unsure if he should be here, but I love that he is.

I smile at him. "What are you doing clear over there? Get over here," I say.

Ardyn sits down on my bed.

"I'm fine. I'm sorry about that," I say.

"You don't need to be sorry. I'm just glad you're okay," he says, and gives me a peck on my cheek.

"Thanks for checking on me."

He scoots back on the bed, leaning up against my head-board.

"Come here," he says and I sit in between his legs.

He rubs my shoulders.

"Thanks."

He kisses my head and continues massaging me.

"Jameson's a nice guy," Ardyn says.

"Yeah he's great. I hope he doesn't feel too bad."

"He did feel bad but that's not on you," he says.

I nod.

"Do you always sleep in such sexy pajamas Harper?" Ardyn asks as I feel his thumbs doing circles on my back.

He makes me blush and I'm relieved he can't see my face right now.

Then he says, "They're almost as sexy as your Snoopy PJ's."

I laugh. "I would say I'm burning those but they're too comfortable. Even though they're too hot to sleep in."

"I get hot at night too. I sleep in my underwear," he says.

"Me too sometimes," I tease and look back at him.

He's grinning. "You can't say stuff like that when I'm in your bed Harper."

I laugh and crawl away.

"Your turn. Lay on your stomach," I tell him.

He happily flips over and I sit down on his lower back while I massage his shoulders.

"That feels too good," he says.

My fingers caress the muscles on his back. Ardyn's hands are down by his sides as I feel them touch my legs. Giving me chills. *Good thing I shaved today.*

"What do you do for fun Harper?" he asks.

"I like riding horses, doing anything outdoors, swimming, dancing even though I'm terrible at it, and reading. What do you like to do?" I ask.

"I like fishing, I also like anything outdoors, building things, watching sports, working out, and tennis. It's cool that you like horseback riding. Do you have horses back home?"

"Yeah. I have a horse named Taffy."

"I've never had a horse but I had a dog once who I loved. His name was Cricket. I was devastated when he got old and died when I was fourteen."

"That's sad. I love animals."

We sit in silence for a moment when I remember seeing Ardyn for the first time. "I just realized something."

"What's that?" he asks.

"You weren't even living at the apartments yet when you held the door open for me when I was moving in. Why were you here?"

His back tenses.

"Oh God, I don't want to know do I? You were with a girl."

He sighs. "I'm sorry."

I laugh. "Am I crushing you yet?"

"Not at all but I am getting tired. You're about to put me to sleep," he says.

I roll off of him and lay down. "I don't want you to leave yet."

"Good because I don't want to leave yet," he says, laying on his side so he's facing me.

Ardyn's eyes glance down at my cleavage.

I saw that.

"What are you doing tomorrow?" he asks.

"Probably homework. Maybe take a nap. I read a lot on Sunday. It's my lazy day."

"Yeah, lazy Sundays are the best. But maybe when you're done with homework we could go hiking again. Or we could rent bikes and ride around town. Unless you're committed to being lazy tomorrow. I'll be lazy with you."

I love that he wants to spend the day together tomorrow.

"Let's rent some bikes. That sounds fun."

I roll over and scoot closer to him so he's spooning me. It's so comfortable I wouldn't care if we stayed like this all night. My eyes get heavy as I drift off to sleep.

Chapter Thirty-Three

Harper

Ardyn isn't in bed with me in the morning. When did he leave? I woke up in the night and felt him sleeping behind me. After crawling out of bed, I smell coffee. There's no way Scout is awake at eight o'clock on a Sunday. This is the only day she doesn't get up early to run.

I open my bedroom door just as Ardyn is about to walk in. He hands me a mug.

"I made coffee. Sorry I stayed over last night. I almost left when I felt myself falling asleep but your bed just felt too comfortable. It didn't help that I was lying next to you either. Don't worry. I didn't sleep in my underwear."

I sip on my coffee and taste the vanilla creamer. He remembered.

"You slept in your clothes? That would drive me crazy."

He shrugs and walks back into the kitchen. "I thought about making breakfast but I wasn't sure what to cook."

I open up my fridge, find some eggs and pull them out.

"It's my turn. Make yourself comfortable." I smile at him.

After preparing French toast, we eat it at the kitchen bar together.

Ardyn leaves before Scout is even awake. I'm cleaning the breakfast mess when Scout drags herself into the kitchen.

"I made French toast if you want some."

Her expression changes from tired to delighted just from the words French and toast.

"Yes, please! How did last night go?" she asks.

"It was good. Ardyn stayed the night."

Her eyes go wide as she pours syrup on her plate.

"Nothing happened. We just talked for a while and dozed off. We're renting bikes later. What are you up to today?" I ask.

"Jameson has to work so I'll be able to get some homework done. He's been so distracting. It's hard to focus on anything else but him."

"Oh, I'm going to get him a birthday present today while I'm downtown. Any ideas?" I ask.

After Scout swallows her huge bite of sticky bread she says, "I got him a really nice set of sheets and a comforter for his bed, two shirts and cologne. So anything but those things."

"That's a lot of presents."

"Well the sheets and comforter are mostly for me." She winks.

"Oh?"

"We haven't slept together yet but it's going to happen soon. I want to make sure we're ready. I want to do it for different reasons this time. Sleeping with Jameson won't be just sex. He's not just another guy. I kind of want him to be *the* guy. But, I don't know if a girl like me gets to keep someone like him," she says.

How does she not feel good enough for him?

"What do you mean someone like you Scout? You're incredible."

"My baggage is with me for good. It comes with me. It'll always stay with me. He doesn't deserve someone that can never be fixed. He probably deserves someone better."

"No Scout. Your baggage, your flaws, everything that comes with you is good enough. It makes you who you are. Jameson sees that. I know he doesn't want to fix a thing. He's so lucky to have found you. I see the way he looks at you. You're not just a broken girl to him Scout, I promise."

Scout hugs me. "Thanks Harper. I hope you're right. I'm going to go pretend I'm doing homework and paint my toes. Breakfast was delicious," she says as she leaves the kitchen.

Ardyn and I decided to rent a side by side tandem bike with two seats. Neither one of us has ever been on one so it takes a minute to get the hang of it.

After successfully stopping our bike, we step into a gift shop.

I'm looking through the card games when Ardyn says, "Look at these fuzzy handcuffs. How funny would that be to get Jameson and Scout these?"

I laugh. "I'm sure he has plenty of handcuffs."

"Yeah but not fuzzy ones," he says, making me laugh again.

"These whiskey glasses are nice. Does he like whiskey?" Ardyn asks.

"That's a good question. I don't really know if he drinks much. His dad was an alcoholic and it made him an absolute nightmare of a father. He and Will always promised each other they'd be really careful when it came to drinking. It was actually a little surprising that he was even indulging last night."

Ardyn nods with a pained expression on his face.

"Are you okay? Did I say something wrong?" I ask him.

"Oh no. I was just looking at the prices on these," he says holding up some coasters.

They have a really cool wooden finish and I love them.

"Okay I'm getting him these," I say, taking them from him.

"They're really cool. I think he'll like them," Ardyn says.

After buying the wooden coaster set and a trivia card game, Ardyn asks if I want ice cream.

"I'd love some."

We're sitting on our bike eating our ice cream cones.

"I've never even heard of pistachio ice cream. Is it good?" he asks.

"Try it," I say, holding my cone up to his mouth.

He licks it and says, "Wow. That's actually really good. Want to try mine?"

After licking the rocky road ice cream cone I say, "Bubblegum ice cream was my favorite flavor when I was a kid. Now I can't even stand the thought of eating it."

"I used to love that kind too. I think I swallowed all the bubblegum. No wonder it always made me sick."

We finish our dessert and ride our bikes down by the river, both of us feeling glad we finally got the hang of it.

"I have a super busy week between school and work," Ardyn begins, "now that it's getting warmer we'll be building more houses. So I apologize in advance for not being able to see you much this week. That's why I wanted to be with you today. Sundays might be the only day of the week we can spend the whole day together. But I promise next time we can relax."

"Sounds good. I'll be pretty busy this week too, with finals coming up."

He nods.

"I love your hair straight like that. It looked like that on your birthday, when I first kissed you."

I smile at him before he kisses me now.

"I really like you Harper," he says when our lips come apart.

"I really like you too, Ardyn."

Chapter Thirty-Four

Harper

M onday morning on my walk to work, I think that I see Robby's Camaro driving toward me. I don't even know if that's him for sure, plenty of people own that same car. But I still don't like knowing it could be him, seeing me walk alone. Not wanting him to stop to try and talk to me, I rush to the coffee shop door, just in case.

My shift is almost over and there are no customers in here when Jameson walks in wearing his police uniform.

"Hey, Officer Karter. I've never seen you in here before. What can I get you?" I say cheerfully.

"I've never been here but it looks great. Scout told me I'd find you here. I want to apologize for the other night. I'm sorry you had to find out like that," he says.

"James, I'm not even mad at you. It just shook me up. I worry about him."

"Will is doing fine, Harper. They call him the Kid because he looks so young."

I smile at the thought of him having a nickname there.

"The Kid. I like it."

"I'll take one of those double chocolate muffins and a caramel frappuccino please," he says.

After Jameson pays for his very sweet breakfast he says, "I'll see you this weekend. Thanks, Harper."

Chapter Thirty-Five

Will

Our unit is on a helicopter getting ready to get dropped off in a hot landing zone, which seems to be normal around here. There comes a time in war when you adapt to *everything*. The killings. The atrocities. Being away from home. One of the things I have the hardest time with is when I'm trying to save someone and they're bleeding all over me. There is so much blood that I know they probably won't make it. I hate it when I see a picture of their family in their pocket or see a ring on their left finger. Their family has no idea that they are dying at that moment. Then I have to move on to the next casualty. So much death. That's what is going to haunt me forever.

"We're going in. Get ready to make contact," Corporal Hoffman says as the helicopter lands.

As soon as we disembark, the shooting begins. "Get low!" I hear someone shout.

Dropping down low, I watch Corporal Hoffman get hit in the head with a bullet and I run to him. I try to save him but he's already gone.

I look up to see the Chief Corpsman, Shaun, helping someone in the distance who is screaming in pain.

"Corpsman up!" I hear someone yell.

"I'll cover fire!" yells Noel as he sees me making my way over to the injured soldiers.

My bootlace comes untied and I trip just as one the Taliban soldiers opens up on me with an automatic weapon. As I'm falling the bullets are going straight past me. Noel comes running up to me.

"I'm fine, I wasn't hit," I tell him.

"You lucky bastard," Noel says before crawling away toward an injured marine.

I stay down and start crawling like a snake making sure to keep the berm in between me and the enemy so they can't see me. I see a marine lying on the ground and crawl up to him and check his pulse. He's dead. I take the canteen of water off his belt and take a drink.

Then I see Noel running over to me. We suddenly hear three shots coming from an abandoned building clear out in the distance.

"Holy shit. Is that a sniper?" Noel whispers as he lies next to me.

"It sure as shit sounded like it."

"Damn. I have to take a piss. How the hell am I supposed to do that with a sniper shooting at us?" he asks.

"Better to piss your pants than stand up and get yourself killed."

Private Batra jumps up on the berm squatting down low, about twenty feet behind us.

"Get down!" I say loudly.

"Doc, do you need any help?" he asks.

He didn't hear me. I immediately think about the picture of his wife he showed me.

"Batra, get your ass down! We got snipers right in front of us!" I yell louder, as the sniper shoots him right between the eyes.

I can tell he's dead, but Noel jumps up to help him.

"Noel! He's dead." I try to stop him.

The sniper shoots Noel right through the back.

He looks at me terrified and says, "I'm hit."

"Fuck!" I cry out.

All of these men who have become like brothers are being killed all around me. I can't let Noel die.

I run to him before dropping down next to him and quickly wet down a gauze pad with my canteen water with shaky hands. I put it around his waist to control the bleeding.

I'm doing everything I can to save him. "You're going to make it, Noel. You have to. Stay with me."

His eyes look tired as he begins slowly shutting them. I grab his face. "Don't you dare fucking close your eyes. You have to stay awake."

I'm covered in my friend's blood as he looks at me and smiles weakly.

"Will, you're worthy of love. You have to tell her," he says before shutting his eyes.

"No, buddy come on. I need you to open your eyes," I beg before starting CPR.

"Breathe. Come on Noel. Breathe. I need you to fucking breathe," I cry to him as I push down hard on his chest.

Shaun crawls up next to us and checks Noel's pulse. "He's gone Kid. Stay low. There's still sniper fire here," he says.

I ignore him as I push down harder onto Noel's chest. I have never felt so desperate during compressions before. "He's going to be okay," I crack.

"Will! Stop! He's gone."

I stop and stare down at Noel's lifeless body.

Noel ran out of seconds.

I spot another body lying on the ground in the distance. He has grenades attached to his web belt. Fuck it. I quickly make my way over to him and take off his belt to get a grenade.

"Will! What are you doing?" Shaun asks.

Once I get the grenade off, I stand up. I don't even care if I die anymore. Just as I'm on my feet getting ready to throw it, something bright on the ground shines into my eyes.

I drop back down and crawl over to where I was earlier by Noel's body.

"Are you trying to get yourself killed?" Shaun yells over to me. I pretend not to hear him as I look for the shiny item that on the ground. I pick up Harper's hair clip. It must have fallen out of my pocket. I told her I would make it back to her. After tucking it safely away, I set the grenade down.

Knowing I'll never get to see Noel again, I force myself to look over at him one last time. Then I do the hardest thing I've ever had to do and leave my friend behind.

After we make it back to base at dark, I lay down on the hard ground with the rest of the unit. Today was a nightmare. When you come this close to death every day, the things that matter most start to become clear. Noel's dying words are stuck with me. I've been lying to myself for too long. I look up at the stars. I hate that I didn't tell her. I hate that I might have ruined ever getting a chance to tell her how I actually feel. Looking up at the stars at this second, all I see is Harper.

I'll tell her, Noel. I promise.

Chapter Thirty-Six

Harper

On Thursday after class, Scout talks me into going into the gym to lift weights with her. She shows me some dumbbell exercises when I spot Ardyn doing pull-ups.

It just got extremely hot in here.

He's still going. He's had to have lifted himself up on the bar at least fifty times now.

He doesn't see me checking him out. But Scout does.

"Harper. I know your man looks good but you have to focus. Do three sets of twenty," she demands.

Oops.

"How's track going?" I ask Scout, while trying my best to focus on my own workout.

"It's good. First home meet is next Wednesday," she says.

"I'll be there."

After our workout, I set the weights down and look around for Ardyn when I see him smiling at me from across the gym. I wave and he takes a drink from his water bottle, never taking his eyes off me. Then Scout drags me to the locker room.

When I come back out, Ardyn is gone.

"I'll see you after track practice," Scout says.

When I get back from the gym, my phone vibrates in the pocket of my hoodie.

Ardyn: I'm picking you up at eight for dinner. By the way, I loved watching you work out at the gym today. But watching you sweat like that was very distracting. I could hardly finish my own workout.

I'm happy he can't see just how much I'm blushing right now.

I can't wait. I text back.

Ardyn and I are driving up a steep road when a huge, secluded, unfinished house appears at the top of the hill.

"Is this one of the houses your family's company is building?" I ask.

"Yeah. It's my favorite one. I call it the sunset house. It should be finished by the end of August."

When we reach the front door, Ardyn says, "Let me blindfold you."

I turn around and he ties a bandana to my head, making sure to cover my eyes. He leads me into the house and I breathe in a new wood and fresh paint smell throughout the house. A small breeze gently cools my face when Ardyn takes off my blindfold.

After opening my eyes, I see we're on a balcony behind the house. There are lit candles surrounding a blanket Ardyn has put down. The view is absolutely incredible. The sun is setting and it shines a beautiful shade of pink and orange light on the horizon. It reminds me of home.

"Ardyn, this is beautiful."

We sit down on the blanket and he opens a basket and pulls out some sandwiches and fruit.

"A picnic and a sunset. I love it."

"Isn't the view great?" he asks.

"It's breathtaking."

"Sunset has always been my favorite time of day."

"I know," Ardyn says. I don't know how he could possibly know this but before I can ask him how he says, "I mean I don't know that it's your favorite. But it's mine too."

I say, "Back at home, during the summer I'd sit outside and watch it almost every time."

"Really?" he asks.

"Yeah, it just feels different from the rest of the chaos of the day. Calm I guess."

Ardyn is looking at me with his watchful eyes.

"Who do you get your eye color from?" I ask him as I feel myself getting lost in them again.

"My dad has blue eyes. Where do you get your hazel eyes?"

"From my mom. I hope you never make me mad because all you'll have to do is look at me with your blue eyes and you'll be forgiven," I joke.

A sheepish grin crosses his face. "Thanks. I'll definitely remember that."

We finish eating and enjoy the view some more.

Ardyn's truck warms us up after he starts it and cranks the heat.

"Should we go?" he asks as music is playing quietly in the background.

"No," I say, scooting closer to him.

It's not quite dark yet so I can still see him. My hand touches the side of his handsome face. He caresses my hand and looks over at me.

"I think I might be falling for you Hazey," he says, waking up every fiber of my being.

I know my feelings are getting strong and I think I might be falling for him too. But I don't tell him yet. I kiss him instead. The way he kisses me proves what he's just said.

"I've been waiting for this all day," I admit to him in between kisses.

He kisses me harder as he lays me down on the bench seat. I love that we can lie down and make out in his truck like this. His hand slides up my shirt and stops at my belly button. Pulling away from my lips, he looks down at me.

"Is this okay?" he asks.

It's *more* than okay so I kiss him again and move his hand up higher. Ardyn stops kissing me and his hand moves up to my bra as he continues watching me.

"Your skin is just as soft as I remember it, Hazey," he says.

I assume he means when we were in the trees at the bonfire but I don't ask questions because I can't speak with him doing this to me.

I try to turn my head so he can't look at my red face but he doesn't let me. He turns it back to him.

"Stop doing that. I want to look at you."

I don't want him to stop touching me like this. I kiss him deeper, letting him know I want more. We continue kissing when I feel his fingers run down my stomach. When he unbuttons my shorts, I gasp.

"I want to touch you."

Desperately wanting him to keep going, I nod my head. He slowly slides his hand down under my panties, stopping my breath. I arch my back, wanting more.

"Do you like that Harper?" He whispers.

"Yes."

He's making me forget.

Ardyn's phone begins ringing and I'm relieved that he ignores it. He kisses me deeper and his phone goes off again.

"Sorry," he says, climbing off of me. He looks down at his phone and opens up the driver's door. "I have to take this," he says before getting out, the door slamming shut behind him.

I quickly button my shorts back up and look out at Ardyn as he paces outside.

It must be important.

Ardyn is quiet when he gets back in the truck. I'm a little surprised when he throws back the gear shift and pulls out of the driveway. He seems upset.

"Everything okay?" I ask.

"Fine. It's getting late."

"You seem upset. Who called you?"

"Just someone trying to take everything else away from me," he mumbles under his breath.

"What do you mean?" I ask.

"It's nothing," Ardyn says.

Even though I can tell it's obviously something. He clearly doesn't want to talk to me so I drop it. It stung a little that he picked up his phone and it hurts even more now that he's being so closed off.

When Ardyn kisses me at my apartment door, I look away. This is exactly what I don't want. I need honesty. And I feel like he's hiding something.

"Goodnight Ardyn," I say before closing the door.

Chapter Thirty-Seven

Harper

"Wow. Our apartment has never looked so festive," I say to Scout after we spent the day decorating it for Jameson's birthday party.

There are streamers and balloons everywhere and a banner in the living room that says "Happy Birthday."

I change into my spaghetti strap black dress and I let my wavy hair fall down over my shoulders.

After getting ready, I pull out some of the bags of chips and party snacks we picked up from the store. I'm laying them out on the kitchen counter when Scout walks out of her bedroom.

"You look amazing, I like your outfit," I tell her and she does a spin in her new skirt.

"Think Jameson will too?" she asks.

"He'll love it."

"If you think he'll love this, you should see the black lingerie set I have under it," she says with a grin. "And you look gorgeous too, by the way."

We hear a knock and Scout opens the front door. It's Rafe, Jake, a blonde girl, Matt and Lucy. Jake introduces us to his cute blonde friend. Her name is Katie.

"I'm so glad you guys are here," Scout tells them.

I don't know whether to expect Ardyn to show up tonight. If he's anything like he was last night, I don't think he'll be in a party mood.

I realize we forgot the music so after telling everyone hi I go back to my room to find my speaker.

I'm reaching up in the closet when I feel someone looking at me. I turn my head to see Ardyn in my door with his eyes all over me.

Feeling flustered, I try to push a big box out of my way and it comes crashing down, everything spilling everywhere.

He grabs me by the waist from behind and flips me around and kisses me on the mouth, pushing me into the closet but stopping me from falling with his arm holding me up as his other hand grips the wall.

"Ardyn," I whisper when he pulls away.

"I'm sorry about last night," he says.

"What aren't you telling me?"

"I don't want to explain everything now. But I will after you meet my family Let's have fun tonight."

I wish he could let me in, but I'm glad he showed up and that he's sorry.

"It's okay. Will you help me get the speaker?" I point up at the closet.

He reaches up and gets it down as I bend down to start picking up the mess I made. That's when my eyes spot the roller skates on the floor.

I pick them up and my mind is back on that bench. With Will. Something inside of me is throbbing when I feel his hand holding my foot. When I see the way he looks at me.

"What's wrong?" Ardyn asks, bringing me back to the present. With *him.*

"Oh nothing," I say, throwing the roller skates into the box. "We better go out and join the party."

I see Jameson talking with Scout and two other men I've never seen before.

"Happy birthday Jameson," I tell him and give him a hug.

"Thanks. Meet my friends from work. This is Cam and Dean."

I shake both of their hands.

Music is playing as everyone mingles and eats the party snacks.

After I give Jameson his gift we decide to play the trivia card game I got him. We're all sitting in the middle of the living room floor with the men on one side and the women on the other. There are definitely more guys than gals so we make Rafe join our team and he agrees. After a very competitive battle of trivia, the women win by one point.

We all jump up with excitement and the men pout. Scout runs to the kitchen and lights candles on the chocolate layered cake she spent hours making.

"This cake looks amazing," Jameson says after blowing out the candles. Hugging Scout from behind, he whispers in her ear and she smiles.

After our guests leave, I decide to give Jameson and Scout some alone time considering she has on lingerie tonight. I go up to Rafe and Ardyn's apartment for a while.

"I'm going to bed. Goodnight," Rafe says as he opens his bedroom door.

"Night Rafe," I say.

"How are you?" I ask Ardyn who is now looking at me with his striking blue eyes.

"I'm good. How are you?" he asks, pulling me into his chest.

"Good. Especially after kicking your ass at that trivia game."

He laughs. "You did win fair and square."

Ardyn leans down and kisses me softly. "I'd invite you to my bed but I told you that we're doing things on your terms," he says bluntly and I blush.

"Want to go on a night walk?" I ask him.

"Sure."

We stroll along in silence for a bit and then he abruptly asks, "There's a summer carnival near home that Graham loves. I take him every year. Do you want to come? My family is dying to meet you."

I'm surprised he already wants me to meet his family but it makes me happy.

I say, "I'd love to."

Chapter Thirty-Eight

Harper

I'm walking over to the track meet before it starts to wish Scout good luck. My phone vibrates in my pocket and I pull it out.

Ardyn: Do I get to see you tonight?

I stop walking and text back. **Do you want to go to Scout's track meet with me? I'm on my way there now.**

Ardyn: Yeah. But I'll be late just finishing up at work. I'll meet you there.

Okay, see you there. I text back.

Scout is running around the track warming up when I get there. Everyone on the team is dressed in the same red uniform. I wave at her from the fence and she runs over to me.

"Hey, I'm glad you made it. Jameson is sitting down in the bleachers if you want to find him," she says, breathing hard.

"Good luck Scout!" I say as she runs back to her team.

I find Jameson sitting in the front row of the bleachers.

"Hey," I say sitting next to him.

"Hey Harp," he says back.

"I wonder if Scout's even nervous."

James says, "She said she was a little bit, but she sure doesn't seem nervous."

I watch Scout as she stretches in the middle of the field with some other track members. She's laughing.

"I got a letter from Will yesterday. He's saved so many marines and done such good work as a Corpsman they told him he'd be getting plenty of awards."

I smile because I feel so proud of him.

"I knew he'd be great," I say.

"He said he misses you and he should be home in a few months."

I feel the nerves churning in my stomach just thinking about Will coming home.

"I can't wait. What's he planning on doing when he gets back?" I ask.

"He's going to move in with me. Try and find a job. And if the military helps with tuition, he'll go to school. He'll have to finish up his enlistment with the Navy of course but he thinks he can do that from the base here in Columbus. He mentioned something about working at the Naval hospital."

"That's great. I wonder what he'll want to do first when he finally gets back to civilization." I smile at the thought of it.

"He'll probably come find you before he even gets in the shower," Jameson says.

We laugh. I sigh because I miss Will so damn much.

"Don't worry. He's going to make it home. I know it."

Jameson's hope is refreshing. I'm daydreaming about Will getting home and how hugging him again will feel. I imagine what Will's touch alone does to me.

Jameson interrupts my thoughts and says, "I told him about Scout and Ardyn."

I'm shocked. "He knows I'm dating someone?" I ask.

He looks confused. "Yeah. Is that okay?" he asks.

"Oh yeah. That's fine. I-uh-"

I see Ardyn walking toward the bleachers with his hands in his front pockets. I feel so much guilt for feeling such strong feelings for two people. What is it going to be like when Will gets home? What will it be like introducing him to Ardyn? I can't imagine how awkward it's going to be. I look back at Jameson. He has a look on his face like he's waiting for me to say something.

"I just didn't expect him to know is all. But that's great. I can't wait for them to meet," I lie.

I wave over at Ardyn so he can see where we're sitting. My heartstrings are being pulled in two directions. Even though Will already cut his side. That makes things easier I guess.

"Hey man," Ardyn tells Jameson.

He sits next to me and kisses me on the cheek.

"Did I miss anything?" he asks.

"Nope, they're just barely starting. Scout told me last night the mile run is right after the medley."

I look down at the paper I picked up from the table near the entrance. "We have a while. There are four events in front of the women's mile race."

Matt and Jake are warming up with the guys on the field.

"What events are Matt and Jake in?"

I'm looking on the paper but can't find their names.

"I'm not sure," James answers.

The announcer comes on and starts the first event. Ardyn and I decide to go to the concessions and get nachos.

We are walking back to the bleachers when I see Rafe standing in a crowd of college students one section over.

"There's Rafe," I say to Ardyn.

We wave at him and he whistles at us. He's decked out in school colors and has red paint on his face. I hear people cheering loudly as we sit down.

"Matt ran the 100 meter dash. He came in third," Jameson tells us as we sit down.

"That's awesome," I say.

Scout looks like she's warming up again.

After the medley, the announcer calls out that it's time for the woman's mile so the runners are lining up on the track.

"You've got this Scout!" I yell out and Jameson whistles.

The starting gun goes off and they begin the race. Scout is about three people behind the leader as she makes her first lap. She runs by us and Jameson yells, "Go Scout!"

She's running so fast it blows my mind that she has to run three more laps.

Out of twelve runners, Scout is in fourth place as she ends her second lap. By the third lap, she catches the front of the pack and her legs speed up as she runs past us to start her fourth lap. All of us cheer her on.

"One more time around, baby!" Jameson yells.

She's now in second place.

The racer in front wearing purple speeds up as they turn the corner. They're about 200 meters away from the finish line when Scout runs so fast she passes the leader. Jameson stands up. The woman in purple catches up to Scout and they are running side by side until just yards away from the finish line. Then Scout sprints harder when she crosses the white tape, taking first place. The crowd goes wild. She's so strong and it's beautiful to watch.

Ardyn and I jump up next to Jameson and I scream, "She won!"

Ardyn and Jameson whistle as we clap. The student section is cheering hard for Scout. The announcer comes on the speaker and says that Scout won and that she's only a freshman. My ears are ringing from the noise as the crowd gets even louder.

When the track meet finishes, Jameson rushes over to the gate to see Scout. I watch her run to him and he picks her up and spins her around. She looks so happy. They're both happy.

Ardyn and I make our way over to them.

Hugging Scout, I say, "I'm so proud of you."

Ardyn says, "Good job."

"Thanks. There's a pool party later. The whole team will be there. You guys should come."

"Shoot me a text with the details. We'll meet you there," I say.

Ardyn and I show up to the crowded pool party just before dark. Loud music is playing outside and bright colored lights shine in the pool.

Scout comes running up to us in her red bikini.

"Hey Speedy, do you ever slow down?" Ardyn teases her.

Then Jameson walks up behind her. "I can't seem to keep up with her," he says.

"Nobody can," I say proudly.

We all laugh and Scout says, "As much as I love this, enough about me. I want to get in the water."

She and Jameson go swimming while Ardyn and I sit on some beach chairs on the side of the pool.

"How's work going?" I ask him.

Ardyn is hunched over with his elbows resting on his knees, staring at the ground. He's completely zoned out.

My hand touches his back and he looks at me with tired eyes.

"You okay?" I ask him.

"Sorry it's been a long day. Somebody broke into the sunset house. They didn't do too much damage but it has the owners all worried."

"Should they be?"

"No, I think it was probably just some teenagers. It's not the first time it's happened to a house we're building."

"That's frustrating. Hopefully it doesn't happen again."

Scout waves at us from the pool to come over.

"Do you want to swim?" I ask him.

"I'd love to watch *you* swim," he says.

"Are you sure?" I ask.

"Yeah, I'm just a little tired tonight is all."

After taking off my shorts and t-shirt, I turn around and see that Ardyn has a grin on his face as he's watching me walk away.

I sit down on the side of the pool and stick my feet in near Scout and Jameson. It's surprisingly warm. Jameson is having a conversation with some other guys.

Scout swims up to me and hangs on the edge of the pool with her head resting in her folded arms. "Ardyn totally just glared down a guy for checking you out," she says.

I shake my head and laugh. I already know Ardyn isn't the jealous type. Scout just doesn't know he's not in the best mood right now because of work.

"Jameson!" somebody yells. I recognize the voice and grimace.

"Hi Robby," Jameson mumbles as Robby stands over him on the side of the pool.

Robby leans down and says, "I haven't seen you since your last fight. You really got your ass kicked. Is that why you gave it up and became a cop?" He smiles wickedly.

"Go away Robby," I say, feeling annoyed that he always has to be such a jerk.

Robby glares at me.

"Hey, Harper. Does Will know you dumped him for a new boyfriend while he's fighting in Afghanistan?"

Ardyn appears just then and looks mad. Really mad.

"I'm Ardyn," he says, giving him a look that might kill him. "You must be Robby. I've heard a lot about you."

Robby's face reddens. He didn't know Ardyn was here. Jameson stands up next to them.

"You have anything more to say? Or are we done here?" Jameson asks Robby.

He glares at them and walks off to find his friends on the other side of the pool.

Ardyn turns away and I stand up to follow after him.

"Ardyn," I say, as he sits back down in the chair.

"Sorry. I just need to cool off for a minute, before I beat the shit out of Robby."

I sit down next to him.

"I think I'm going to take off. You should stay with Scout," he says.

"Okay. I'll get a ride with her. Are you sure you don't want me to come with you?"

"Don't worry about me Harper. Have fun."

Ardyn kisses me on the forehead before leaving.

Chapter Thirty-Nine

Will

Dear Will,

Remember Harper's roommate, Scout? The one I took on a date? Well, we've been on way more dates now and she's officially my girlfriend. Holy hell man, she's the real deal. There is just something about her. I can't even believe I met somebody like her, let alone get to be with somebody like her. She's different. In a good way. Not to mention she's a fucking smoke show. You won't believe she's with me when you see how amazing she is. Her heart is made of gold. And she's a runner. A really good runner. She's on the school's track team. She works so hard. She hasn't had an easy life. She's been through some things she won't talk about. But I've been able to open up to her. Scout understands me more than anyone ever has. I can't wait for you to meet her. She and Harper threw me a birthday party at their apartment last weekend. Speaking of my birthday, where was my Twinkie and 7up? When everyone else left the party and Scout and I were left alone in the apartment, I realized nobody has ever thrown *me a birthday party before. Hell, nobody has ever made me a cake since mom died. I've never felt like this with a girl before.*

By the way, Harper is doing really well. She's dating a guy named Ardyn. She seems happy. He's a good guy. I think you'll like him. I'm sorry man, but when I met Ardyn he asked about you and I had a few drinks in me. I slipped up and told him right in front of Harper that you were hit on your first night there. Harper was so upset. I felt terrible. I went into the coffee shop where she works to apologize to her this morning. She misses you. A lot. And I miss you too, brother. I'm so damn proud of you. Be safe out there. Remember there are people at home who love you.

Love, Jameson

I'm sitting on the ground with nothing to lean up against and the heat is getting to me today. And this letter really got to me. I rip off my helmet and throw it on the ground harder than I meant to. I can't help but feel pissed off. Not at Harper. But at myself. It's all my fault somebody else is kissing her right now. I kind of wish Jameson never told me about this guy. But it's good I know now so I can be prepared to see her with somebody else. It's going to hurt like hell. It already hurts like hell just imagining it. I have to be happy for her no matter how bad it kills me. I'm the one that let her go. I'm the one that hurt her. I deserve this.

But if Noel were here right now he'd be telling me, "Don't let this Ardyn guy get in your way. I see it on your face when you talk about this girl. You love her."

I can't count the times he told me I loved Harper.

Wiping the sweat away from my forehead, I think about how I wish I was more like Noel. He made his life matter. He didn't waste any time.

Harper is moving on.

I won't let anything stop me this time. I'm still going to tell her how I feel. How I've always felt.

Chapter Forty

Harper

Since I don't have work on Saturday I decided to go home for the weekend. I almost invited Ardyn but I haven't even told my parents I'm dating anyone yet.

We're sitting down at the dinner table on Friday when I decide to rip off the band aid.

"I'm seeing someone. His name is Ardyn," I blurt out.

They both look surprised.

"Really?" My mom finally speaks. "That's wonderful. When can we meet him?" she asks.

"I don't know. Soon. It's still pretty new."

My dad nods. "We're happy for you."

I smile at them but I know by the looks they are giving me what they're really thinking. They're wondering about Will. They saw us together. They saw the way we looked at each other when he was here. I'm relieved they don't ask about him. After talking with my parents for a while I decide to go for a walk. It's May and rain is pouring down but I don't care. I need air. After telling my parents about Ardyn it all seems so real.

Before I realize it, I'm at Boulder beach. It's a little over-whelming just how much I feel him here.

Will's hands are in my hair, I hear his laugh, he's picking me up off the rock and throwing me over his shoulder, he's splashing me in the water, he's staring up at the stars with me. I feel his mouth on mine, I feel his strong chest and dog tags pressed up against me. I feel everything.

I wish I didn't feel this way.

My heart is aching as tears fall down my cheeks. I shouldn't have come here. My feelings are getting stronger for Ardyn. How can I turn off my feelings for Will? I won't come here again. I can't. Every emotion comes rushing back to me again, reminding me how much I love Will. It's too much. I feel him too much. *It hurts.* I curl my knees up to my chest and lay my head down and cry. I stand up off the rock and walk near the water. The wind blows my hair making it stick to my wet cheeks. I close my eyes again and feel him one more time. My eyes open and I take one more look around at Boulder Beach. Our spot. Mine and Will's. I look down at my feet and pick up a rock. Just like my heart feels, it's heavy. I watch it disappear when I throw it out into the water. *It's time to let go.*

After spending the day with my parents grilling out on the patio on Saturday, I decided to come back to the apartment. I was planning on staying until Sunday but it's hard being home when everything reminds me of Will. I texted Ardyn and told him I was headed back and he invited me over. Ardyn answers his apartment door and pulls me in. He immediately starts kissing me and I melt right into him. I don't want him to stop but he pulls away.

"I missed you," he says.

"I missed you too. What did you do while I was gone?" I ask.

"I went to work yesterday, then Rafe invited me to a party tonight. But as you can see, I didn't go."

"You weren't in the party mood?" I ask.

"No. My girlfriend was out of town and she's who I wanted to see."

I smile and he kisses me on the cheek. "Your girlfriend?" I ask.

"That's up to you. That was my way of asking," he says, still smiling down at me.

The hopeful look on his face is adorable.

"What do you want to do, boyfriend?" I ask. "That was my way of saying yes."

He kisses me again on the lips. "Good. We could watch a movie?"

I stay put on Ardyn's chest as we lay cuddled up on the couch after the movie is over.

"Do you like movies or books better?" I ask him.

"Definitely movies. I'm not much of a reader. I take it you like books more?" he asks.

"Definitely books," I say, "there is just so much more detail in a book. And you get to read the character's thoughts. That's what I like most. In the movies, you don't get to. You don't see as much in the movie as in the book as ironic as that sounds. It's just not the same."

After my way of trying to explain why books are better, I look at him to see if he thinks I'm crazy. He's smiling at me.

"Well that makes sense I guess. If you were a book, I'd read the shit out of you," he says playing with my hair.

"Oh yeah? You want to see my thoughts?" I tease.

"Absolutely. That'd be the best book ever," he says, making me laugh.

"Well, you're pretty much an open book when it comes to your feelings toward me. You just say whatever you're thinking out loud so you're basically a novel, Ardyn."

"Trust me. You do not hear all of my thoughts out loud," he says looking serious.

"What don't I hear?" I ask playfully.

"Well for one, I don't tell you how bad I want to do things to you. Things that will make you scream my name."

I drop my jaw and laugh. "Ardyn!" I yell and I feel so hot in the face right now that I bury it into his chest.

"Just like that. Say it again, but louder." He laughs.

"I have a book for you to read," I say, crawling off him. "I'll be right back!"

I make my way downstairs to my apartment. Scout isn't home so I assume she's at the same party that Rafe's attending.

I grab the book out of my room and run back upstairs to Ardyn's apartment. He's still on the couch but he's sitting up now when I walk in. I take a seat down next to him.

"Here you go. It's a romance novel. It has lots of descriptions. Lots of dirty thoughts. You'll love it."

He laughs and says, "Thanks. But none of the thoughts will be as dirty as mine. Trust me."

I say, "Prove it to me. What's something you're thinking right now?"

"I'm thinking how bad I want to bend you over this couch right here and fuck you."

My thighs clench together at the throb between my legs. I'm so on fire. I cover my face with my hand and he grabs my wrist.

"I wish you'd stop doing that," he says, still staring at me intently.

I love when he looks at me like this, but it makes me feel nervous.

I whisper, "What are you thinking now?"

"How much I like making you nervous," he says mischievously. "I'm wondering how else I can make you blush."

I shake my head. "I bet you can't do it," I say competitively. Even though I know damn well that he can. I just want him to keep going. To keep making me feel this way.

"Is that a challenge?" he asks.

I nod and bite down on the inside of my cheek as he reaches over me and grabs the side of the couch with one arm while he stands up in front of me, keeping his other hand on the other side of me. Never taking his eyes off of me, he has me trapped.

"Now I'm thinking about how badly I want to touch you again," he says.

He's so close to me, he probably hears my pulse hammering away.

Then he scoops me up off the couch and wraps my legs around him. Just like he did when he kissed me on my birthday. He walks us to his bedroom then he drops me down on the bed.

"Wait," I tease. "We're going to mess up your perfectly made bed."

He laughs. "Good. I hope we do."

I throw the covers down and crawl into them. He's still standing, just watching me with his intense blue eyes.

"What are you thinking now?" I ask him.

"I'm thinking I never want you to leave my bed," he says.

I smile at my mischievous idea. I want to make *him* nervous. I sit up and remove my bra underneath my shirt and fling it at him, trying not to laugh. He does not look nervous at all, but he smiles.

"That was hot," he says and starts to lay down next to me when I stop him.

"Nope. You can't get in yet."

He likes this game. He leans against the wall, folds his arms, and watches me while I take off my jean shorts and throw them across the room, still staying under the covers. The way he's looking at me makes my toes curl.

"What are you thinking now?" I ask.

"I'm thinking how bad I want in my bed right now."

I bite down on my lip as I take off my shirt and throw it at him, being careful not to let the sheets slip down, exposing me to his gaze.

Then I watch him as I reach down and pull off my panties, still keeping my naked body hiding underneath the sheets to his bed. I throw my panties across the room. He looks down at them and he arches his eyebrow. I don't think he was expecting me to get completely naked.

"Holy shit Harper."

His gaze now looks desperate. He wants in his bed so bad right now, it's written all over his face.

"What are you thinking?" I ask less playfully.

"There are way too many thoughts going through my mind right now, Harper."

I want him to get in bed with me. "Come here."

He isn't sure I'm serious as he gives me a questionable look.

"Do you still want to?" I ask.

"Is that even a question?"

"What are you waiting for?" I ask.

"I need to know you want me too," he says.

"I want you Ardyn."

Ardyn walks over to me and slowly slips under the covers, never taking his blue eyes off of mine. Then he kisses me with so much passion I can hardly breathe. My naked body is pressed up against his fully clothed body as he looks down at me with a gentle expression now.

"Are you sure?" he asks.

"I'm more than sure. I'm ready," I tell him.

I kiss him again while I unbutton his jeans and he helps me undress him. When he takes off everything else, his naked body up against mine makes me *need* him. He stops kissing me for a moment as he lifts the covers to look at me.

"You're beautiful."

He crawls on top of me kissing me deeper. He stops and opens his nightstand drawer and my eyes fall shut. I hear the sound of him opening the condom and my head is spinning but I want this. I open my eyes and Ardyn is looking down at me.

Those blue eyes.

"Are you sure?" he asks.

"Yes."

He lowers himself on top of me and I give myself to Ardyn.

All of me.

And then we do it again.

Chapter Forty-One

Harper

Final's week was insane. The coffee shop was even busier than usual and I made sure to study hard every night for each test. Ardyn and I decide it's probably best to stay away from each other this week. We tend to distract one another. Especially when there's a bed involved. But today was my last exam and I smile as I walk down the hall to my apartment knowing I made it through my first year of college. I see Ardyn's anticipation as he's standing by my front door waiting for me.

"I passed!" I yell.

He looks up at me and smiles.

"Me too," he says.

We kiss in front of my door.

"Let's celebrate tonight. What do you want to do?" he asks.

"Scout is staying at Jameson's tonight. How about we order take out and you can stay over?" I ask.

He smiles and I lean into him and whisper in his ear, "You can even sleep naked this time."

The way Ardyn looks at me still gives me butterflies.

"I will if you will," he says, picking me up.

He sets me down inside the apartment.

"Do you want Chinese food?" I ask.

"Yeah, that sounds good."

I call in an order and we cuddle up on the couch and wait for it.

"Have I ever told you how good you smell all the time?" I ask, taking in the familiar scent of him.

"You told me I smelled amazing once when you thought I was Rafe." He laughs.

"That was so embarrassing. That was the moment I realized just how attracted I am to you," I admit.

"Oh yeah? That was the moment I knew just how badly I hated staying away from you."

"I kind of wanted you to kiss me," I confess.

"I *really* wanted to kiss you. I remember you looked upset about something. You were reading the newspaper and I saw you push it away. I almost asked you what was wrong. What was it that you were upset about?" he asks, running his fingertips lightly over my arm.

"I read something about Afghanistan. Some soldiers were killed and I examined all the names to make sure it wasn't Will. It made it feel more real to see something like that. I haven't picked up a newspaper since."

He nods. "When will Will get to come home?" he asks.

"James said that he'll be home in September."

I feel a ball of stress form in my chest from the thought of seeing Will, but I try and stop worrying about it so much.

"Are you excited?" Ardyn asks, and I sit up suddenly feeling really uncomfortable.

I walk into the bathroom and shut the door. I close my eyes tight as I crouch down next to the wall. What am I going to do? What if my feelings for Will never go away? I need them to go away.

I hear a knock on my front door and Ardyn opens it and pays for our food.

"Harper?" Ardyn knocks on the bathroom door. "Are you okay?"

"Yeah, I'm fine. Just freshening up. I'll be right out."

I try and rub the stress off my face and look at myself in the mirror.

You'll never be with Will when he gets home. He only wants to be friends. He'll never explain why he kisses you and looks at you the way he does. He'll never want to be with you. He doesn't love you. Get over him. You're with Ardyn. Go be with Ardyn. Be happy.

I put a smile on my face and walk out to Ardyn setting food on plates for us.

"You sure you're okay?" he asks.

"Yeah."

I know I should tell Ardyn about Will, but what if he doesn't understand? What if he thinks as soon as Will comes home I'll leave him? I can't let him think that. I can't tell him yet. I'll tell him someday but not before Will comes home. Not before he even meets Will. I sit down next to Ardyn on the couch and we eat our food in silence.

Chapter Forty-Two

Harper

We pull up to Ardyn's childhood home on Thursday afternoon and it's beautiful. We both took tomorrow off from work so that we can spend the weekend with his family. My hometown is at least two hours south of here. The huge white house sits in a secluded area thirty miles outside of Columbus. They have no neighbors for miles and a giant front yard with giant landscape rocks and blooming flowers.

"Wow. This place is incredible. This is where you grew up?" I ask.

"Yeah. My dad thought about selling it and building us a new house but my mom is in love with this one. And you can't beat this location. Wait until you see the backyard. There are so many oak trees, my siblings and I called it a forest."

I smile at the thought of Ardyn being a kid. "I can't wait to see pictures of you as a little boy."

He laughs.

I feel nervous to meet his family as we get out of the truck.

His mom and dad are waiting on the front porch, ready to greet us.

"Hello. You must be the one and only Harper we've heard so much about," his mom says.

I smell cherries and almonds as she gives me a huge hug. Then with a grip on my arms she pushes me out to get a better look at me.

"You are stunning. Oh my goodness," she says as I feel like she's examining my soul.

I'm dating her son so I can't blame her.

But I have no idea what her hard expression means. She's really studying me and I don't know how to react. I feel a little uncomfortable.

She says, "You remind me of someone."

Ardyn laughs. "Jesus mom. Give her some space."

I smile at Ardyn's mom when she lets go of me and shakes her head. Like she's coming out of some kind of trance. "Sorry, you are just the prettiest thing. I'm Mary. This is my husband Daniel."

"Thank you Mrs. Bennett. It's lovely to meet you both."

"No, no, no. You call me Mary or mama. Not Mrs. Bennett." She smiles.

I shake Ardyn's dad, Daniel's hand. "I'm Harper."

He smiles shyly. "It's so nice to finally meet you. Ardyn has told us a lot about you. I almost feel like I already know you."

I take a look around outside this beautiful home again when Ardyn's mom says, "come in. Let's show you the guest bedroom. Unless you and Ardyn are staying together. He hasn't told me how serious you are yet."

I laugh at how open his mom is as we walk into the house.

"We'll both stay in the guest bedroom mom. Thanks," Ardyn says, walking up behind me.

"Your house is absolutely beautiful," I tell the Bennetts as they give me a tour. I stop in front of some photos.

Ardyn and his dad are talking about the construction business as I continue looking at family photos.

We walk up some stairs and into a bedroom.

"Here you are," Mary says.

I look around the guest suite with its attached bathroom. It's beautifully decorated in sunflowers. I set my bags down and Ardyn's mom and dad leave us to unpack.

Ardyn shuts the door and looks at me the way he does when he wants me. I laugh.

"Not here. Not right now."

He steps closer to me and kisses me on the side of the head.

"Okay, I can wait until tonight I guess," he says.

"How about we take a break from that while we stay here?" I suggest.

"How am I supposed to sleep with you for two nights without making love to you Harper?" he asks into my ear.

I look into his blue eyes and kiss him. I kiss him deeper and deeper and realize we are on the bed having a full on make out session and we've only been here for fifteen minutes.

"Ardyn we've got to stop." I laugh.

He groans. "Fine." He looks at me and tilts his head. "You only have one earring in."

"Oh shoot I probably lost it in the bed."

We look all over but can't find it. Ardyn is scrummaging through the pillows when I crawl to the edge of the mattress and bend over to look underneath the bed. Maybe it fell off on the floor.

"Gah. It's gone," I say, still bent over the bed with the blood rushing to my head.

"I kind of hope you never do," Ardyn says.

I laugh when I realize what he means. I sit up and feel the blood rush back down to my body where it's supposed to be.

Ardyn is grinning when he says, "I found it just as you were bending over Hazey. But the view was so nice, I just didn't want to tell you yet." He winks.

I shake my head and grab my earring from him and put it back in.

"We better go downstairs."

Ardyn's mom is making dinner in the kitchen.

"What can I help you with Mary?"

She puts me right to work cutting vegetables and talks my ear off while Ardyn sets the dining room table.

I hear the front door to the Bennett's house open and a little boy's voice shout, "Uncle Ardyn!"

I walk out to see the cutest blond boy with bright blue eyes hugging Ardyn tightly around the neck.

"I missed you bud," Ardyn says.

"I missed you too," he says with the sweetest high pitched voice. My heart might just burst.

"Hi. I'm Emily," says a younger looking version of Mary, except Emily has blonde hair. She shakes my hand and right away I notice she's more shy and reserved like her dad. But she's looking at me just like her mom did. That same hard expression that I have difficulty reading.

"I'm Harper." I smile.

"I'm Tyson, Emily's husband," says a handsome man with jet black hair and brown eyes.

"And this is Graham," Emily says, touching her son's shoulders. Her son is now standing in front of her.

He grins up at me. "Are you Uncle Ardyn's girlfriend?" he asks, and everyone laughs.

"I am. My name is Harper. And you have the coolest toy fire truck I've ever seen," I say looking down at the toy he has in his hand.

"Thanks," he says with a serious look and pushes the button that makes a siren noise.

Then he takes off running with it.

I hear Mary greeting her grandson in the kitchen.

Ardyn told me he and his sister are close but the hug between them seems tense. Ardyn pulls away quickly without saying a word. Emily appears to be nervous. But I don't know her that well so maybe she's always this timid.

"Can we talk?" Emily asks her brother.

Ardyn nods and tells me he'll be back before walking outside with Emily and Tyson.

I go back to the kitchen to help Mary finish dinner where Graham is begging her for a snack.

"Dinner is almost ready. Why don't you go play for a while?"

He continues to whine and I remember seeing a box full of toys in the family room.

"Graham," I say, "do you want to show me some more toys?"

"I want to play with Uncle Ardyn," Graham pouts.

"He's busy right now but I'd love to play with you," I tell him.

He giggles and takes off running toward the family room so I go to follow him.

"Thank you Harper," Mary says.

Graham is splitting up two groups of dinosaurs on the floor while I watch.

He points to one of the piles and says, "These are the herbivores." He points to the other pile. "And these are the carb-ivores."

I know he meant carnivores but I laugh picturing the meat eaters eating bread.

"Hey, what's so funny?" he asks.

"I'm just delighted with how smart you are," I tell him.

"Rawr!" Graham yells with a T-rex in his hand.

I hear Ardyn's laugh and look up to see him leaning against the wall, watching us.

"How long have you been there?" I ask him.

Before Ardyn can answer, Graham squeals when he sees his uncle.

"Dinner is ready. Let's go wash those germs off your hands," Ardyn tells Graham.

Everyone's sitting at the dining room table eating dinner. Ardyn is sitting next to Graham and I'm on the other side of Ardyn.

Emily and Tyson are talking quietly with Ardyn's dad Daniel.

"No toys at the dinner table. Eat up so you can be big and strong," Ardyn tells his nephew.

Graham puts the fire truck down on the floor.

"Like you Uncle Ardyn? Will I get as big and strong as you if I eat?" he asks.

"Yeah, buddy."

Graham digs into his mashed potatoes.

His mom looks at me across the table and says, "I'm sure Ardyn has told you that his brother Clayton lives in West Virginia."

Ardyn drops his fork onto his plate, startling me. I look at him expecting him to be upset but he's not. He smiles at me as he stands up. Then he kisses me on the head and asks if he could refill my glass for me.

I give it to him and look back at Mary. "Ardyn did mention that. Does he like it there?" I ask.

Mary's telling me about how Ardyn's brother works for a coal company when Ardyn comes back in with my drink. He loudly pulls his chair out from under the table and he shakes his head at his mom.

Odd. What was that about?

After helping clear off the dinner table, I walk into the family room to see Ardyn and Graham playing on the floor.

"How about if I play with the blue truck this time?" Ardyn says laying down on his side, picking up the blue truck.

"No," Graham whines. "You get the green tractor."

Ardyn laughs. "Alright, alright. I'll play with the tractor."

I leave them alone to play some more and head back into the kitchen to continue helping clean up when I hear Emily tell Mary, "He's upset now that he knows we might move four hours away. I'm worried he won't-"

Mary coughs when she sees me and Emily turns around and looks at me.

I feel embarrassed for walking in on a very obvious private conversation.

It sounds like Emily, Tyson, and Graham might be moving. I bet that's what they were talking to Ardyn about.

"How can I help clean up?" I ask.

"We've got it covered. Thank you Harper," Mary says.

"Are you going to the carnival with Ardyn and Graham?" Emily asks with a friendly smile.

I say, "Of course."

I smell Ardyn's cologne as he appears behind me and wraps me up in an embrace.

"Are you ready to go?" he asks.

"Yep."

I turn around and Graham is of course right next to his favorite Uncle Ardyn.

"What about you, cutie? Are you ready to go have some fun at the carnival?" I ask and he grins.

"Yes! Let's go, let's go!" He tugs on my hand.

"Wait Graham, don't forget your jacket. Be really good for Uncle Ardyn okay?" his mom says.

After Graham's parents hug him goodbye, the three of us go to the Summer Days festival. A lot of people are there enjoying the carnival rides, playing games, and waiting in long lines. The smell of fried food lingers in the air and the sound of roller coasters and children's laughter is ringing in my ears. Ardyn and I are standing back, watching Graham play a fishing game, trying to win an actual goldfish in a bowl. I tell Ardyn that I like his parents.

"Your mom is straightforward, like you. I can see where you get that now. I didn't even know what to say when she basically asked me if I was going to marry you."

We both laugh and Ardyn says, "Yeah, sorry about that."

Then I say, "But you look a lot like your dad. With his dark hair and blue eyes. They are both so sweet."

"Yeah, I'm glad you got to meet them. I can tell they already love you."

"And you are the best uncle to Graham. It's an extremely attractive feature," I admit, making him smile.

I'm about to ask him why he shook his head at his mom at the dinner table when she brought up his brother Clayton's job, but Graham walks back over to us, looking defeated.

"I lost again, Uncle Ardyn," he pouts.

"Let's get you some cotton candy to take on the Ferris wheel," Ardyn says, instantly cheering Graham up.

We order Graham cotton candy at a food booth and I get myself a caramel apple.

We eat our treats while we wait in line for the Ferris wheel. Ardyn takes a bite of my apple and a strand of caramel lands on his lip. Graham bursts out laughing at Ardyn's messy face. Ardyn puckers his lips and pretends like he's about to kiss Graham and he giggles. I love watching the two of them together. Ardyn is so good with kids.

We hop on the Ferris wheel and they stop us at the top.

"Wahoo!" Ardyn yells and Graham puts his little arms up in the air.

"Wahoo!" Graham yells and we all laugh as the Ferris wheel moves again.

"That tickles my tummy!" Graham squeals through continued laughter.

He is the cutest little guy ever.

After the Ferris wheel, Graham wants to ride the teacups.

"I'm going to sit out on this one," I tell them and sit down on a bench nearby.

A man with a Yankees baseball cap stands next to me with a little girl by his side as I watch Ardyn and Graham load up on the ride.

"Are you here with Ardyn Bennett?" the man asks me.

"Yeah. Do you know him?" I ask, watching Ardyn and Graham go round and round on their blue teacup. Graham is squealing and laughing hysterically.

"I used to," the man says. "I'd be careful if I were you. You know he killed his wife, right?"

Feeling completely caught off guard and like I've been punched in the gut, I see Ardyn and Graham climb off the stopped teacup. I turn to look at the man with the red baseball cap but he's already gone. Dammit. I want to know what he's talking about.

I'm scanning the crowd for him when I hear Ardyn say, "Looking for something?"

"No. You guys, I guess." I force a smile and swallow the lump stuck in my throat.

What did that guy mean Ardyn killed his wife? He was married?

I have so many questions for Ardyn but I have to wait until we're not with Graham.

"Harper? You okay? I asked if you're ready to go back to my parent's house now?" Ardyn asks.

"Oh yeah. Yeah, I'm ready if you are."

Graham groans. "I have a tummy ache."

I rub his head. "Let's get you to your mom, sweet boy."

Ardyn picks Graham up and puts him on his shoulders as we make our way to the parking lot.

Back at the Bennett's, I'm in the shower connected to the guest bedroom. I can't stop thinking about what that man said to me at the festival. I can't imagine Ardyn would hide the fact that he was married. And he'd never hurt anybody, let alone kill someone. I take my time in the shower before getting out. The heat in the bathroom is making me nauseous so I crack open the window for fresh air. It's dark outside now. I hear Ardyn's voice coming from the yard. He sounds angry.

"No. I already told them, I'm not signing the papers. Not yet. I still haven't decided what I want to do."

I get closer to the window to listen to the conversation more clearly when I hear his mom say, "Honey. You know what's best for him. Graham will always be your son. But all he's ever known is Emily and Tyson. They're his parents for as long as he can remember. You can't take him away from them now, and you know that. You've already come to an agreement with them."

What? Graham is his son?

Ardyn says, "I've been sober for over a year now. Please understand where I'm coming from. I'll hardly see him if he moves away. It's not fair. I don't want to talk about this anymore. Not right now. I haven't even told Harper yet."

Sober? Is that why he doesn't drink? He's an alcoholic.

I'm shocked that he has kept so much from me. I quickly get dressed.

Ardyn walks into the room as I'm packing my bags with shaky hands. He looks worried.

"Harper, what's wrong?" Ardyn asks behind me.

I turn around and say, "Take me home."

"Why? Is something wrong?"

"You lied to me, Ardyn. How could you keep so much from me? I heard the conversation you were having with your parents. I heard everything and I want to leave right now."

He rushes over to me and says, "Whoa. Slow down. Let's go for a ride and I'll explain everything. If you still want to go home, I'll take you."

I agree.

When we get into Ardyn's truck he sighs. He brings his hands to his face. I've never seen him look so stressed.

"Start with your wife. You were married Ardyn?" I ask.

He looks at me confused. "How did you know I was married? My parents and I didn't talk about that," he says.

"Some man at the festival wearing a Yankees baseball cap came up to me and told me to be careful because you killed your wife. You'd better start explaining."

I see the heaviness in his eyes after telling him this.

"Was it Casey? The person you told me you lost? Was she your wife?" I ask.

He nods yes. "I'm so sorry I haven't told you. I promise that I was going to tell you. It's just a lot. I was worried I would scare you off. I married Casey five years ago. I was only nineteen. We eloped behind our parents' backs. We dated in high school and we were young and in love. I loved her so much but I couldn't save her."

He drops his face back into his hands in devastation. "It's all my fucking fault the mother of my child is dead."

It's heartbreaking to see him like this. But I'm still mad at him for not telling me.

I hate to ask but I have to. "What happened?"

Ardyn can't even look at me. He's staring out the windshield in front of him. "We found out Casey was pregnant right before we got married. We lived happily in a two bedroom house while I worked for my dad. We were the picture perfect family. One November night when Graham was two years old, I had a couple friends over and we had been drinking before the power went out. Graham was scared, so we lit some candles in the family room. After they left, Graham, Casey and I played games. We made shadow animals out of our hands. It was the perfect night. Then Graham got tired so he and Casey snuggled up on the couch and fell asleep. I carried Graham to his room and left Casey on the couch. I didn't want to wake her. She was the type of person that wanted to be left alone wherever she was sleeping. I blew out all the candles and went to bed. At least I thought I blew out all the candles. I think I drank too much. That's the only explanation I can think of. How did I not blow out all the damn candles?" he asks this as though it's a question he asks himself every day. He continues after rubbing his forehead. "I woke up to the smell of smoke and immediately ran across the hall to grab Graham from his crib then into the family room where Casey was still sleeping."

He takes a deep breath. This is so hard for him to talk about.

"The flames were so high. The family room was full of smoke. I quickly called 911 and they said the fire department was on their way. I couldn't see so I screamed Casey's name. She wasn't answering me and I knew I had to get Graham outside to safety. After I got Graham out of there, I was praying to God she got herself out. But she didn't. So I tried to run back in and save her but a couple of firefighters held me back and wouldn't let me. They held me down and told me they were doing everything they could to get her out. But they didn't. It was too late."

"Ardyn. I'm so sorry. That's devastating."

He continues, "After Casey's death, things got bad. Especially for Graham. I drank and drank to take the pain away. Two months later, I was a raging alcoholic, unable to take care of my own son. That's when I asked my sister, Emily to take Graham. She and Tyson had just gotten married and she loved Graham like her own and I knew he'd be better off with them. After a few more months I finally hit rock bottom and after Graham's third birthday, my parents finally convinced me to get the help I needed. And I knew I had to change if I ever wanted to be a fit parent for Graham. I checked into a rehab center for three months and I've been clean ever since. I haven't touched a drink for over a year."

I can't believe what he's been through. My heart is aching for him.

I touch his shoulder and say, "You've been through so much. This can't be easy for you to talk about. I'm glad that you're clean now and doing the best that you can. That's all that matters."

I scoot over next to him and hug him tightly.

"Your sister wants to adopt Graham?" I ask.

"Yeah. I agreed to it while I was in rehab. It's the only life he knows. That he remembers. He doesn't even know I'm his real dad. So it's probably for the best. But sometimes I feel like I'm giving him up by signing the papers."

"Ardyn. You're not giving up by signing the papers. You're doing what's best for him. That makes you an amazing father. Would they let you and Graham visit each other often?" I ask.

"Yeah they told me I can see him whenever I want. And as long as I stay sober he can come stay with me often if he wants to. But they told me tonight that Tyson got a job with my brother Clayton in West Virginia. The pay is a lot better so they might move out there. Now I feel like I'll never see Graham. I know that I have to do what's best for him. I just need a little more time to decide."

I'm so proud of him for doing what he thinks is best for Graham. I find myself thinking of Will's father and how I wish more than anything he would have been more like Ardyn and let his boys live with somebody else. But he was too greedy. Ardyn is not. He's a better man. A better father.

"Thanks for opening up to me. I can't even imagine how you must feel. I'm here, Ardyn. I'll be here through it all."

He smiles at me appreciatively.

"So who was the guy at the carnival in the Yankees hat?" I ask.

"I honestly don't know. Her family blames me for her death. A lot of people that know them and even people we went to high school with think I did it on purpose. Especially when they heard that I went to rehab. After the fire, I told Casey's family what happened. I understand why they blame me, but they don't even want anything to do with Graham. It's just too hard on them. They haven't seen him since her death."

I shake my head. Life is so cruel and unfair.

"I'll take you home now," he says.

"No. Thanks for being honest. I want to stay with you now."

Everyone is already in bed when we sneak into the Bennett's house. I see Graham sleeping on the couch in the living room with a teddy bear in his arm.

"Aww," I whisper.

Ardyn walks over to the couch and kneels down. He kisses Graham on the head and this image might just crush me. A father, not getting to be a father because he's too good of a person to keep his child. He knows what he has to do and it's so hard to watch him go through it.

I walk into the guest room to give Ardyn privacy with his son.

Ardyn walks into the room with slouched shoulders and a painful expression. He's so sad. I hate it so much.

Everything about Ardyn makes so much more sense now. Why he and Graham are so close, why he tried so hard to avoid another serious relationship, and why he was probably upset the other night when he got a phone call.

"I'm going to shower quick. I'll leave the door unlocked if you need in," Ardyn says before walking into the attached bathroom.

After finding my toothbrush, I brush my teeth and then I move the shower curtain and see Ardyn's arm up on the wall, with his head slumped down. He's in so much pain. I wish I could take it away. He's lost so much. I don't even take off my clothes before I get it with him. He needs me. When I touch his back, he turns around and looks down at me. I can't tell if he's crying or if it's the water from the shower running down his face. Probably both. I lean into him and we're holding each other tight, letting the hot water fall on us.

His body is slippery but he still manages to pick me up and press me against the wall.

He closes his eyes and rests his head on my chest. I feel him shake. He's crying. Ardyn is crying and it's killing me.

"I'm so sorry Ardyn," I whisper.

He squeezes me tighter. Then he looks up at me. "I love you Hazey."

The intensity in his watery eyes holds my gaze for a moment as he sets me down. He starts removing my wet clothes. I help him as he takes my top off then my pants. Then he quickly unclasps my bra and tugs down my panties. He takes a step back and I watch him take in my body. I fold my arms over my chest even though he's already seen me naked. But standing here in front of him like this is making me a little self-conscious.

Ardyn takes my arms and puts them down. "Christ Harper, look at you."

Then he steps forward, bringing his hand between my legs and crashes his wet mouth to mine, making it hard to stand.

"Ardyn," I whisper in between the kisses, "Let's go to bed."

He backs me up so I'm leaning up against the shower wall, his hand still moving between my legs and says, "Not until you finish."

I never want him to stop doing this. I can't even kiss him anymore because I can't focus on anything else besides what he's doing with his fingers moving in and out of me.

I start to shake. "That's my good girl. I love watching you come on my hand." I cry out and tilt my head back as he keeps going. I'm losing control over what's happening but I never want it to end. He continues until my whole body tightens and I have to grip his back to hold myself up.

After wrapping up in a towel, Ardyn is carrying me into the bedroom, still kissing me wildly. Like he's afraid he might lose me too.

Before I get a chance to dry myself off, Ardyn is ripping the towel off me. His eyes are on me again as he flips me around and holds me from behind.

His fingers intertwine with mine as he bends me over the bed. "You're mine, baby. Only *mine*."

My body is filled with pure pleasure as he pushes himself inside of me.

I know I can't keep quiet enough in this position so I reach out to grab a pillow and bite down on it. He's hitting that spot again that makes me want to scream out of pleasure.

He grips my hips tightly as he groans.

I'm still laying on my stomach when he's finished. Then my heart sinks. Ardyn climbs off of me and I stare up at him. By the look on his face right now I can tell we're both thinking the same thing.

"Ardyn? You didn't wear a condom. Why didn't you wear a condom?" I ask, standing up next to him.

Why have I not gotten on the pill?

He sits back down on the bed and drops his head. "I'm so sorry, Harper. I couldn't stop. I was completely in the moment. What is wrong with me?"

The pain is still there, clear as day, all over his face.

He's still hurting. I sit down next to him on the bed.

"Nothing is wrong with you. It's okay. I didn't even think about it either."

I bring my legs up on his lap and he lays his head down on my shoulder. I run my hand up and down his back, trying to give him comfort. Laying down on the bed, I pull him down with me. I can't believe we just had unprotected sex. I can't get pregnant. I'm getting on the pill as soon as possible.

"I'm so happy you're here," Ardyn whispers.

I feel closer to Ardyn than ever before. His breathing gets slower as I lay on his chest. I can tell he's asleep by the slow rhythm of his breath. He must be exhausted. I close my eyes and try not to think about the consequences of our actions.

I wake up in bed alone. Ardyn is gone. After I get up and quickly get dressed I go look for him. Ardyn is holding Graham on the couch, both of them still sleeping. I wonder when he came down here to be with him. They are adorable. Graham looks so much like Ardyn, especially right now, with their heads together. Although I know if they both had their bright blue eyes open they'd look even more alike.

After sneaking into the bathroom to get ready for the day, I walk back out and smell sausage and something sweet cooking in the kitchen.

"Good morning Mary. How can I help?" I ask, noticing the waffle iron heating up on the counter.

She smiles brightly. "I'm surprised to see you up so early, after that long night you had with Ardyn." She winks and I feel my face go hot.

Oh my gosh. She heard us.

She laughs. "It's okay. I get it. I was young once too. I think I've got breakfast ready if you want to go find the boys out back."

I see Ardyn and Graham outside on the grass with coloring books and crayons. They must have gotten up when I was getting ready. Ardyn's in gym shorts and a T-shirt and Graham is wearing 101 Dalmatian footie pajamas. I make my way over to them and sit down. I can picture kids playing hide and seek in all the trees out here and imagine how much fun that must have been.

"Morning," I say, taking a seat in the grass.

Ardyn looks at me and smiles. "Good morning." He kisses me on the cheek.

Graham is still drawing a picture intently. His tongue is hanging out the side of his mouth and he doesn't even notice me.

"Don't look yet," he says to Ardyn, completely focused on his drawing.

"I'm not looking," Ardyn reassures him.

"How was your night?" I ask.

"Well the shower was great but what happened in bed was even better," he whispers.

"Your mom heard us," I say and Ardyn tips his head back from laughing so hard.

"It's not funny! And when did you end up on the couch with Graham?" I ask.

"I heard him yelling for his mom so I rushed out there. He said he was scared so I slept next to him. I think it was like four in the morning. Emily and Tyson went back to their house last night. Usually when I come visit, Graham stays over with me and they go home."

I nod. I'm happy they have such a healthy way of sharing time with Graham. He's such a happy boy.

"Uncle Ardyn!" Graham yells. "Look what I drew for you."

Graham hands him the picture and Ardyn smiles. "That's you and me on the teacup ride," Ardyn says, nodding his head. "I love it buddy. You're a great artist," he tells him.

Ardyn hands me the drawing.

"Wow. Graham, it's so good. I love all of the colors," I say and Graham smiles cheerfully. "I think breakfast is just about ready. Should we go pig out on some yummy waffles?" I ask, and Graham takes off running inside.

We spent the rest of the day with Graham. The three of us played hide and seek in the trees, old maid and go fish, and we set up our dinner outside like a picnic at Graham's request. Then instead of Ardyn and I sleeping in the guest room, I asked if we could "camp out" in the living room. Ardyn and Graham were so excited about the idea. We built a huge blanket fort and watched "101 Dalmatians."

I can see how hard it is for Ardyn to tell Graham goodbye on Saturday.

He's quiet on the drive home.

"Are you okay?" I ask.

He smiles. "I'm more than okay, Harper. Thanks for everything. Graham loves you."

"I love Graham. He's such a sweet boy but I'm exhausted," I say and Ardyn laughs.

He says, "By the way, every year some of my high school friends and I get together on my dad's yacht. That's where I'll be tonight and I probably won't be home until late tomorrow."

"Your dad has a yacht?" I ask.

"Yeah, it's located at a lake about seventy miles from here."

"That's fun. What are these high school friends of yours like?"

"We definitely don't see each other as much as we used to. They drink a lot. So I try to keep my distance. But we still get together from time to time."

Now that I know about him and alcohol, I feel bad for ever having had a drink in front of him.

"Is it tempting for you to watch other people drink?"

"No. My willpower has gotten very strong. Except for when it comes to you." He winks and I laugh.

"Well good. You deserve a fun night with old friends."

Chapter Forty-Three

Ardyn

Life has been so good lately. I don't dread waking up anymore. All because of Harper. After seeing just how good she is with Graham I know for certain now that I'm in love with her. It felt so good to tell her everything the other night at my family's house. I'm glad she knows everything now. I really was planning on telling her about my past but it was terrifying. I'm just so damn scared of losing her. I'm just glad she took it well. She and Graham are everything to me. The only problem I worry about is Will. I can't stop thinking about those letters I saw in her closet the night of Jameson's party. I wasn't snooping, just happened to look down to find a box of DO NOT SEND letters to Will. I wanted to know what she wrote. Sometimes when I bring him up she gets this sadness about her that makes me wonder if she's not truly over him.

After seeing her with her mom the day she was getting her prom dress, I was curious so I followed her home. Then I realized how bad I needed to see her in that dress again. She looked so much like Casey. It didn't take long to find the high school in her small town. Once I broke into Wood Lake High, I was able to find out when prom was with all the posters hanging on the walls. *It was as if I was going to see Casey again.*

The next week I saw the way Harper and Will looked at each other at a gas station that night after the dance. She looked so much like Casey as she sat there flirting with another guy, I wanted to rip her away from him. I had to be near her but watching them together was hard. It was obvious to me that they were more than just friends. But she hasn't told me that and it makes me fear that she might choose him over me. But I'm figuring it all out.

After seeing Harper and Will together after prom, I couldn't stop drinking even when I got home. It was getting worse and worse with each trip I made to watch Harper. I was going crazy. After seeing the two of them kiss on the Fourth of July, I thought I was going to lose my goddamn mind. That's why I threw a rock out into the water. I had to make it stop. Then when I followed Harper home that night. I felt terrible when she saw me and crashed her bike. I almost got to her then, but she rode off fast. I just wanted to make sure she wasn't hurt. That's when I realized I've had to stop for a while. I was almost caught. My parents finally convinced me not long after that to go to rehab. With the intensive therapy I received there, I calmed down a bit. I wasn't going to go back and see her. It wasn't good for me. But then one morning I missed Casey so much, I had to see Harper. She was a senior in high school and about to graduate. I knew that Will was gone so I continued to go see her. I wasn't going crazy anymore because she was alone. Just being near her made me feel better. When I snuck into her graduation, I heard that she was going to Copper Hill University. That's the same day I enrolled. I knew I wasn't ready to stop being near her.

I miss Harper so much. I haven't been gone more than a few hours on this yacht and I can't stop thinking about her. Some chick keeps eyeing me. I told Harper that this would be a guys only evening, but I knew they would invite some women. I just didn't want her thinking of me differently after meeting my friends. They tend to get wild.

I told this chick I can't fuck her but she insisted on going down on me anyway.

I close my eyes and imagine it being *Harper* instead.

"Fuck Hazey," I moan.

She stops and looks up at me. "What the hell? I told you my name is Elana."

I'm not even mad that she stopped. All I want to do is get back to Harper. I have to know what's in those letters. I'm not going to lose her again.

Harper

I'm alone at Boulder Beach waiting for Will. When I hear a branch crack, I'm startled to look up and see someone watching me from a distance on the trail.

"Will?" I ask, squinting my eyes trying to clear my vision. It's too dark to make out who it is.

Silence.

My heart is hammering as I stand up off the rock.

"What do you want?" my voice cracks.

My eyes open wide when I hear a thud. I sit straight up as I try to steady my breath. I'm shivering as I run my hands over my chilled arms.

"Just a dream," I whisper to myself.

The noise that woke me must have been Scout getting home. I look at the clock and it's three AM. Then I remember Scout telling me she was staying at Jameson's tonight. That's weird. Maybe she ended up coming home after all. I sit and listen. When I don't hear anything, I get up and go check to see if Scout's here. That's when I realize my bedroom door is shut. I always sleep with it open and I know I didn't close it last night. But maybe for some reason Scout did if she's home. But Scout's not in her room or the bathroom.

She's not here.

I walk to the front door and look through the peephole. I don't see anything in the dimly lit hall. Grabbing the doorknob, I'm relieved that it's locked. I remember locking the door last night so it was probably just Scout coming in for something with her key. I drag my feet to bed and eventually fall back to sleep.

Just as I get up for the day, Scout walks in with a wide smile.

"Hey, Harper," she says.

"Hey," I say. "You look happy."

"Last night was amazing. Jameson and I stayed up all night just talking."

I smile at Scout who is now heading to her room.

"I'm going to take a nap," she says.

"Wait, did you come home last night at all?" I ask.

She turns around to face me and shakes her head.

"No, why?"

"Are you sure? I heard something last night. I know I did. And my bedroom door was shut."

"I was with James all night."

I'm covered in goosebumps when I remember my dream. Someone was watching me.

"Are you okay?" Scout asks.

"I'm fine. It's weird I don't remember shutting my door. The thud I heard must have been a dream," I say, trying to convince myself more than I am Scout.

"I'm sure it was," Scout says. "It's supposed to be really nice today. I'm going to lay out on the rooftop later. Want to come with me?"

"There's a rooftop?" I ask.

"Here? No. But there is at the dorm on campus. I laid out up there yesterday and nobody said a thing."

"I'll come with you, but if you get us both kicked out of school, I'm relying on you to win a gold medal at the Olympics and support us forever."

She laughs. "I'll do my best. Let's plan for two o'clock. Night," she says before shutting her door.

I plop myself down on the couch and wonder what the heck I'm going to do until two o'clock when I hear a knock. I hope it's Ardyn telling me his plans changed and he's back already. I'm being ridiculous.

Rafe has a grin on his face when I open the door. He pulls me in for a hug.

"Hey you. I've missed you," he says.

Rafe is so full of positive energy all the time. Everyone loves to be around him. It explains why he has so many friends.

"I've missed you!" I say. "How was your weekend?"

"Fantastic. How was yours?" he asks.

I'm overwhelmed when I think about Ardyn's past.

"Are you okay?" Rafe asks.

"Yeah. It was a great weekend. But I could definitely use a friend if you want to hang out."

"Let's go to Smiley's and play stupid arcade games or bowl or something," he says with a grin.

"That sounds perfect."

I look down at the tee shirt and leggings I have on today and run my hand down my long braided hair. I notice how dressed down I am compared to Rafe. He's wearing nice jeans, and some other expensive brand of clothing I don't even recognize.

"But maybe I should change. I look like a rat compared to you," I tell him.

"You look great," he says.

"How come you always dress so nicely?" I ask.

He shrugs. "This pretty boy has rich parents."

I roll my eyes and we head out the door.

After playing arcade games for an hour we pick out our silly prizes. I'm wearing my ten colorful beaded necklaces and a giant ring on each finger. Rafe is wearing huge, green sunglasses and a polka dot bow tie as we wait for our pizza at a booth in the food area at Smiley's.

"How are things going with Ardyn? Did you like his family?" Rafe asks.

"Good, I guess. I care a lot about him," I say, feeling kind of silly having such a serious conversation while wearing my jewelry prizes. "And I really liked his family."

"I can see why. He seems like the whole package. You guys are cute together," he says.

I smile.

"You're falling for him aren't you?" he asks.

"Maybe. But it's hard because I had such strong feelings for somebody else not that long ago. He's always still in the back of my mind."

"You can't just get over someone overnight," he says.

The waiter brings us our pizza and we thank him.

Rafe continues saying, "But give it time. I can tell Ardyn is really into you. A couple weeks ago I got home and I saw him reading a book, grinning ear to ear on the couch. I asked him when he picked up reading as a hobby and he said, 'Since Harper told me books are better. And she's right, I can't put this damn book down.'"

I laugh as I take a bite of greasy pizza.

"Happy to know I proved my point."

I notice the time and stand up. "I told Scout I'd meet her on the dorm rooftop at two o'clock to sunbathe."

Rafe grabs what's left of the pizza in the box and stands up. "I was over at my friend's dorm yesterday. You can see the rooftop from his balcony. I thought that was her laying out up there. I knew she couldn't see me so when I whistled at her, she flipped me off."

I laugh. "Sounds like Scout. Wanna come with?"

"I wish I could join but I have a hot date."

"Oh yeah? I can't wait to hear all about it. You were just the light I needed today, Rafe."

"Anytime," he says as we leave Smiley's.

⚶

"Are you on the pill?" I ask Scout as we lay flat on our backs on the dorm rooftop.

The warmth of the sun is so relaxing as I lay here in my swimsuit, I almost regret asking such a daunting question. I sit up on my forearms on the blanket we have laid out on the solid concrete floor. Scout stays laying down but turns her head toward me.

"Of course I am," she says, sliding her big sunglasses down to her nose to get a better look at me. "You are too, right?"

"No but I'm going into the clinic first thing tomorrow to get on it."

"It's really simple. I have tomorrow off so I can go with you if you want."

"Sure, thanks."

Scout sits up on her forearms too. "Jameson said he got a letter from Will," she says, as if Will's name has no effect on me. "His best friend from basic was killed in Afghanistan. Noel, I think, was his name."

I remember Will telling me about Noel and how much he loved him. I can't imagine how much he's hurting. A tear runs down my cheek as I feel the heaviness in my chest.

"It's not fair," I whimper.

Scout shakes her head. "Not at all."

After work on Monday, I met Scout at the clinic close to campus. Before giving me my birth control pills, the nurse took a blood test to check for pregnancy instead of a urine sample since it yields a faster result. Luckily, it was negative.

I'm walking into the entrance doors to the apartment when I hear Ardyn yell, "Hazey!"

I turn around to see him jumping out of his truck in the parking lot.

"Hey," I say with a giddy smile as he walks over to me.

"Hey," he says, hugging me tight.

"How was your trip?" I ask.

"It was fun, but I'm happy to see you," he says. I feel awkward as his eyes glance down at the brown paper bag full of three months' worth of birth control pills.

Not that it's awkward that I have them. But what happened between us the night that made me want to get on them.

Then Ardyn puts his arm around me as we walk into the entrance door.

Chapter Forty-Four

Ardyn

I miss my family so much it hurts. Every fucking molecule that makes up my body and soul, aches to have them back.

When Harper showed up at her apartment at Copper Hill that first day, as much as I knew I shouldn't, I had to get closer to her. To get a better look of those hazel eyes I miss so much. When I opened the door for her, I didn't think I'd ever actually try and pursue anything. I had to constantly remind myself that her name was Harper, not Casey. That's when I tried to get an apartment there and they told me it was full. But I was still watching from a distance. I couldn't stay away. Then after I was finally able to move in after paying off Rafe's old roommate, I was able to follow her to the bar the night we kissed. When she caught me staring across the room, I was scared that I was caught. I thought she was going to chew my shit. But I quickly understood that she actually wanted me. It was the hardest thing I've ever had to do, to take a step back from her. But I still knew that I couldn't ever be with her, as much fun as it was making out with her in the women's restroom. That's the furthest I was ever going to let it go.

Obviously, staying away from her got way too hard. The more I was around her, the more I wanted her. And I don't regret it at all.

I don't come here often. This isn't necessarily where I feel her. But before I do what I have to do next, I feel the need to tell Casey first. I kneel down next to the gravestone and read the name, *Casey Parken Bennett (Hazey). Loving mother, wife, daughter, sister, and friend.* I never meant to give Harper Casey's nickname. But the way her striking hazel eyes look just like Casey's made it impossible not to slip up eventually. Sometimes I look at Harper and only see Casey. Sometimes I look at her and only see Harper. That's when I feel guilty. Recently I've realized that I really love them both. I don't only see Casey or Harper anymore. I see both of them. I've fallen in love with my new Hazey.

When I broke into Harper's place and read those letters she wrote to Will, I couldn't believe it. It's worse than I thought. She's in love with him. I can't wait much longer. I can't wait for Will to come home before I do what I have to do. As messed up as it seems, I thought getting Harper pregnant would be enough. But I saw the brown paper bag. I know she's on birth control now so I guess I messed that plan up when I didn't wear a condom. But now that I think about it, I think I'd rather marry her first anyway. Then as a social worker, Hazey can help me get Graham back. Or at least partial custody so he can't ever move away. After that, we can have a baby. It will be perfect. I'll have my family back.

Chapter Forty-Five

Harper

Now that it's summer, I work more days and longer hours at the coffee shop. Which is good because that means more money and Ardyn works a lot anyway.

We finally both have the day off on the Fourth of July. After spending most of it hiking with Jameson, Scout and Rafe, Ardyn tells me he has a surprise. We make our way out to his truck. Warm summer evenings make me think of home. I have so many emotions going through me right now, being that it's the Fourth of July.

"Please tell me we're watching the fireworks from the sunset house," I say to Ardyn.

He opens the passenger door and says, "We would be if the owners weren't going to be there."

"Are they moving in already? I thought the house wasn't finished yet?"

"No. It's not. They just had the same idea of watching the fireworks from up there, I guess."

We pull up to a park and it's still light out. Ardyn tells me to stay in the truck for a minute and to not look back.

"What? Why?" I laugh.

"Just don't." He kisses me then shuts his door.

After a couple minutes, Ardyn opens the passenger door and I step out. Ardyn takes me by the hand and I can't help but gasp when I see how beautiful the back of his truck looks. Ardyn put down blankets and pillows down with candles and some snacks.

I smile. "This is amazing."

Ardyn picks me up from behind and lifts me up onto the tailgate. Trying not to step on candles, I make my way back to the pillows that are placed by the back window.

"It's so comfortable," I say snuggling into the cushions.

He's still at the bottom of the tailgate, watching me. He's absolutely amazing. I love how often he surprises me.

"I love this," I say as he jumps up and sits next to me. I cuddle into him. "Pringles or licorice?" he asks, holding out the options. I point to the red licorice and we sit back and eat our snacks while we wait for the fireworks.

I pick up the champagne bottle next to me. "You didn't have to get this just for me," I tell him.

"I'd do anything for you," he says.

I look out in front of me. "This park is cool. I've never been here before. I love the creek," I say.

"Me too. There's a running trail right over there." He points.

"I wonder if Scout ever runs over here. What's it called?"

"White Creek Park. Look, ducks." He points.

"How cute," I say as I watch them waddle into the trees.

It's starting to get dark out but I still listen to the sound of water running down next to us.

When I lean back and look up at the faint stars, I close my eyes as Will seeps into my head. The guilt I feel for missing him so much wrenches in my gut. I ignore my feelings and remember that I'm here with Ardyn.

"What's your family doing tonight?" I ask. I'm kind of surprised he didn't want to spend the day with them.

He shrugs.

I feel bad for bringing them up. Obviously, he doesn't want to talk about it. I know how stressed he's been about trying to decide about the adoption. I'm relieved to be interrupted by fireworks booming into the dark night. I look up and Ardyn pulls me into him. We cuddle and watch the colorful, loud sky. When the fireworks go off like crazy, I assume it's the finale. Ardyn gets up and I realize he must already want to start packing up to leave so I stand up to help him when Ardyn drops down on one knee and pulls out a small white box. I cover my mouth.

"Hazey. When I first laid my eyes on you, I knew I didn't want to let myself get involved with you. I felt myself being pulled toward you as I tried so hard to avoid you. But only because I knew I'd never want to let you go. I knew you would stick. We have only known each other for a short period of time but I feel like I've known you for so long. Getting to know you has been the best thing to ever happen to me. You're changing me. You've changed my life. I never thought I could love again. But then you came along and proved me wrong. You're the most extraordinary human

I've ever met. You see me for who I really am. You have such a kind and gentle heart. You put others before yourself and you are absolutely perfect for me. I know it's too soon, but take all the time you need. I'll be waiting for you. I have you Hazey. That will always be enough for me. I'm asking you to stick with me tomorrow, and the next day, and the next day after that. I'm asking you to stick with me for the rest of our days. Forever. Will you marry me?"

Ardyn opens up the box and a beautiful, round diamond ring glows in the dark night.

Chapter Forty-Six

Will

All of the Fifth Marine Regiment was ordered to support the Army's 101st Airborne. There are at least two thousand marines all strung out in one big line. Waiting.

It's getting dark out when I hear airplanes. I spot something clear out into the distance next to the mountains. Parachutes. 101st Airborne parachute soldiers. We were told the Taliban is located somewhere between us. I jump when I hear gunfire.

"We're being overrun!" someone yells out in the distance.

The parachutes must have pushed the enemy to run right toward us.

"Shit. Shit. Shit." I say to myself as I look around.

Explosions blast so loud I can't hear anything but ringing in my ears. I look around as soldiers start scattering everywhere. After attending to all of the wounded marines I could, I see another corpsman, Ed waving over to me.

"Over here! Hurry!" he yells out and I sprint as fast as I can toward him. He starts running and tells me to follow him. If I can keep up with him, there's no way anyone can catch us.

I see marines panicking everywhere as I sprint past them. Some are jumping over a berm to take cover, others tuck behind a string of humvees. Ed stops and he points at a tiny abandoned building made of brick.

I look inside to see a terrified old Afghan man and a little boy.

They look both scared and confused. "Are they lost?" I ask.

"No, he told me we could hide here. I think it's where they live," he says.

I nod and smile at them so they know they can trust me. And we hide.

The little boy doesn't look older than five or six years old. They're hiding behind us, none of us making a sound. Outside of our shelter, I can hear machine guns firing and people yelling. People are dying. I know if the Taliban looks in here, they'll shoot all of us. So being as quiet as possible, we stand ready with our rifles pointed at the small hole where there's a missing brick. My heart is racing but I don't make a sound.

I look out and see a Taliban soldier in the distance walking our way with a group of them coming up behind him. My heart rate speeds up. He's coming to look in here. Ed and I both look at each other like we know what's about to happen. They're going to kill us. We can't shoot and give up our position. That's too dangerous. There are too many of them.

I slowly take my dog tags and press my lips against them.

Chapter Forty-Seven

Harper

I'm staring at the ring back at my apartment. I feel like that's all I've been doing the past two days. I told Ardyn I need time and he kissed me and told me to take the ring and all the time I need. *He'll wait.* I'm starting to fall in love with Ardyn. I can see myself marrying him. I picture a wonderful life with him. With a beautiful home he built just for us and with two kids running around. Sometimes we could have Graham over to visit too. Maybe even for a whole summer. Ardyn would love that. I picture myself being Ardyn's wife. And I imagine Ardyn as my husband. But I can't shake the feeling I had when he proposed to me. When I saw him get down on one knee and look at me with a gorgeous diamond ring in his hand, all I could think of was Will. How I wish more than anything it was him on one knee instead.

I'm startled by a knock on my door. It's 11:30 PM. I walk to the door and see Jameson in the peephole. *That's weird.* Scout is staying at his house tonight. Why would he be here so late?

Then my heart races when I open the door and see that Jameson has been crying. His eyes are red and puffy.

"Harper," he says quietly, "Can I come in?"

No. No. No. No. No. *This can't be happening.*

"What is it? What happened?" I ask as I back away from the door to let him in.

I.

Can't.

Breathe.

Jameson can see that I'm afraid of what he's about to tell me. He wraps me in his arms and he cries.

"I'm so sorry Harper. Will is gone. He was killed in Afghanistan. I got the call an hour ago."

I fall to my knees. I'm crying harder than I ever have in my life. My chest hurts. My whole body hurts.

Will.

Isn't.

Coming.

Home.

Jameson is telling me something as I cry on my apartment floor. I have no idea what he's saying.

It hurts too much.

All I feel is pain. All I'm ever going to feel for the rest of my life is this horrible pain in my heart. My throat is aching. I want to scream. I think I am screaming now. Jameson reaches out his hand to help me up. I don't know when Scout walked in but she is putting me to bed. They're speaking to me, but I don't hear a word they're saying.

Why did you leave me, Will?

It hurts. I don't know how long I've been crying. I look at the clock and it's four in the morning. I hear someone move and I look down on my bedroom floor to see Scout laying there with a pillow and blanket. When did she get in here?

I can't believe Will is gone. I miss him so much it hurts. I question God in my head asking him how he could do this. *How could he do this?*

The light is shining through my window as I watch the sun come up. I think I've cried all my tears away because now all I can do is stare. Stare out my window. Hopefully I never have to go out there again, into the sad and cruel world. I think Scout said something to me but I still can't hear her. I'm still staring out the window when I hear some-one walk into my room. I don't know who it is. *I don't care.* I continue staring out my window. It's all I can do. I feel someone lay down next to me and feel them pull me into a warm, comforting embrace. It's Ardyn. I smell his fresh cologne and I feel at peace. I close my eyes.

Will is holding me now. Saying, "I'll make it back."

I'm crying again when I wake up.

"No. This can't be happening." I think I say those words out loud. I still feel Ardyn's arms around me. I feel so ex-hausted from crying. Everything hurts.

I wake up again and wish I hadn't. The pain and grief feels too much to bear. Looking out my window again, I feel Ardyn move and sit up to check on me.

"You're awake. Let me get you some food."

"I could use some water," I say.

Ardyn comes back with water and crackers and I sit up. I drink the water fast. Too fast.

I run to my bathroom and vomit in the toilet. Then I lay down and curl up on the bathroom floor.

Ardyn walks in and picks me up. I'm back in my bed and I'm crying again.

Looking out my window, I'm surprised to see that it's dark. Time no longer matters.

I'll never see Will again.

This morning, things are a little more clear. I didn't get any sleep last night but I've got to help Jameson with things I know he has to do alone. I've got to pull myself together. *For Will.* I move Ardyn's arms off of me while he's sleeping and go shower and brush my teeth. Scout must be at Jameson's because I don't see her anywhere in the apartment. When I come back into my room Ardyn is awake.

"I'm so sorry you're going through this," he says and wraps me in his arms again.

"I'm glad you're here. I need to go see Jameson. Can you take me?"

When we get to Jameson's house, Scout answers the door and pulls me into a tight hug.

"You're here," she says.

I force a smile and make my way to Jameson, who's sitting at the kitchen table looking at photos of Will. He's not crying anymore but he looks exhausted.

"Hey Harper. I'm just trying to figure out the dreaded funeral. My father obviously can't."

I hate that this is all on him. I won't let it be.

He looks up at me and says, "I'm not even going to ask how you're doing because I *know*."

I force the lump down my throat and ask, "How can I help?"

After hours of talking about memories of Will and going through photos, Jameson says, "Thanks, Harper. My Uncle Mike should be here any time now. You're more than welcome to stick around though."

I stand up. "No. That's okay. I'll come back tomorrow."

Ardyn is sitting on the couch waiting for me. He tries to comfort me with a smile and stands up.

"Oh before you guys leave. I have something for you Harper. From Will. Hold on, let me get it," Jameson says.

He goes into his bedroom and walks back out. He hands me an envelope and a little box.

"A letter he wrote you before he left for Afghanistan. Open the box after the letter. He told me to give it to you if he doesn't make it home. At first I refused to take it and told him he's going to make it home and give it to you himself," he chokes up and looks down.

Scout holds on to him. I'm staring at the envelope and little box. I can't open them *yet*. I give Jameson a hug and thank him. Scout gives me another hug and tells me she'll be home later. This has to be hard for her, comforting both her boyfriend and her best friend.

"It's okay, Scout. Jameson needs you. I have Ardyn."

We say goodbye and get back into Ardyn's truck. I suddenly want my mom and dad. I haven't even told them about Will yet.

And just like the universe heard my thoughts, we pull up and my mom and dad are outside my apartment waiting for me. *They know.*

I jump out and give them each a big hug. We're all crying. How have I cried so much?

"If I need you I'll call, I promise. I have my parents with me all night," I'm telling Ardyn as he's about to leave my apartment. He kisses me on the head.

"Whatever you need Harper," he says before shutting the front door to my apartment behind him.

My mom made me eat a grilled cheese sandwich and now she's tucking me into bed like I'm a little girl again. She and my dad are sleeping in the living room. My dad on the floor and my mom on the couch. I told them as they were laying down blankets in the living room after dinner that they didn't have to stay. They refused to leave and I feel grateful.

I look over at my night stand and notice my dead phone that's been sitting there for I don't know how long. I don't want to turn it on. Receiving texts and phone calls will make it too real. Next to my phone is the unopened envelope and box Jameson gave me earlier. *Will's letter.* I take a deep breath and I sit up in my bed. I open the envelope and close my eyes for a moment. I open my eyes again and begin reading.

Dear Harper,

If you're reading this letter it means I'm not coming home. It means I lied to you. I'm so sorry for lying to you Harper.

Tears burn my eyes and blur my vision but I wipe them away and continue reading.

But I'm sorry for a lot of things. I was never really fair to you. I know it's going to be hard for you, me not coming home. I know it hurts. I can't imagine losing you. But you're going to be okay Harper. I just know it. I'm at Jameson's right now writing this letter. I said goodbye to you yesterday and it was the hardest thing I've ever had to do. I'm so sorry I hurt you. I'm sorry for everything.

I'm sorry I hurt you by risking our strong friendship by kissing you the first time at Boulder Beach. I'm sorry for hurting you by possibly destroying everything that night we almost slept together. I'm sorry I couldn't tell you what you wanted to hear when we had to say goodbye. Our last goodbye.

Harper. I'm just so sorry. I'm sorry that was our goodbye. Please know that I'll always be here. Running the universe with you.

Love, Will

P.S. Open the box. I wanted to give it to you myself when I got home. I wanted to see the look on your face. I knew I had to go back and buy it for you by the way you were looking at it at the gift shop.

I'm crying hysterically as I open up the little box that Jameson gave me with the letter. I hear myself gasp. I'm laughing and crying at once. I pull out the extravagant, turquoise beaded bracelet, the one from the gift shop back home. I don't know how he knew I loved it so much. He'll never know how much this means to me.   Then I curl up with my bracelet and cry so hard yet I don't make a sound.

Chapter Forty-Eight

Harper

I want to wake up from this nightmare. It's got to be a nightmare.

I hardly got any sleep again last night. I would do anything to see Will just one more time. My heart is aching all over again this morning. I'm so mad that I'm awake and this isn't actually a bad dream. It's my tragedy. Even though Will never told me, I'll always remember the love he showed me. I'm so glad he wrote me that letter. His apology. I needed that.

I'm staring at the bracelet on my wrist when I hear a knock on my door. My dad's knock.

"Come in."

He brings me some scrambled eggs and orange juice on a tray.

"You used to love being sick when you were a little girl just so you got breakfast in bed." He smiles.

I try to smile back. "Thank you," I say as he hands me the breakfast tray.

I hear a knock on my front door and my mom answers it. It's Ardyn.

"Good morning. How's Harper doing today?" I hear him ask.

I hear my mom whisper but can't make out her words. I listen to their footsteps as they make their way to my room.

"Ardyn is here now. He said he'll bring you home tonight. Do you need anything before your father and I get going?" my mom asks.

"Nope. I'll see you tonight."

I thank them again and hug them goodbye.

After my shower, I decide I need to go out and get some fresh air. *Alone.*

"Hey," I say to Ardyn, who is sitting on the couch.

I sit next to him. "Thanks for being here. For everything. I need some air. I'm going for a walk."

"Do you want me to come with you?" he asks.

"No, that's okay. I'll be fine, I promise. I'm just going to White Creek park. It's not too far from here."

Ardyn looks concerned.

"Ardyn. I'm so grateful that you're here and that you've been helping me get through this. I'll be back soon," I assure him and he nods.

"Okay. I'll be here when you get back. I love you Harper."

I know you do. I smile and kiss him on the cheek.

When I get outside the apartment I spot Robby in his car staring at me. I feel pissed off. You've got to be kidding me. *Not today.* I storm up to his car and slam down hard on his hood.

"Stay away from me Robby! If you come back here, I'll call the police. Leave me alone!"

It feels good to scream at somebody. Especially the only person Will didn't really like.

I turn around a few times and make sure Robby's not following me on my walk to the park. It's so hot outside I wish I would have brought water. I lay down in the grass by the little creek. *I hear kids playing out on the playground and close my eyes. I picture the first day I saw Will sitting alone in the grass at recess. Then I picture him next to me on the haystack, handing me his shoes when I lost mine. I see his excitement as he shows me Boulder Beach for the first time. He's chasing me with a handful of flour as we laugh throughout my parents' house. I picture him pressed up against me as we slow dance. I feel us kissing on my bed where we almost made love. Why did you have to stop us Will? I loved you.*

You're not coming home.

I'm still sitting in the grass staring out at the running water when Ardyn calls my name.

"Harper. It's time to go to your parents' house. You've been here a long time. Are you okay?"

I look up and notice how red and heavy Ardyn's eyes are. I don't think he's had much sleep either.

"I'm so sorry. What time is it?" I ask, feeling numb.

"It's six o'clock," Ardyn says.

"Shoot, I lost track of time. I told James I'd help him today. I was supposed to be there hours ago."

Ardyn offers his hand and helps me stand up.

"I already told him you just needed time alone, that we were headed to your parents and you'd call him from there. Your parents are really worried about you. They've been calling every hour to check on you. I told them I'd come get you and we'd go straight there," he says.

"Okay. Yeah, we'd better go," I say as we walk toward Ardyn's parked truck.

"I packed a bag for you."

Ardyn kisses me on the head and opens the passenger door for me. There's a water bottle and granola bar for me on the seat.

I drink the water as we start our drive to my parent's house.

"You didn't happen to grab my phone did you?" I ask.

"Sorry, I didn't," he answers.

I honestly don't really care to have it. I'd still rather have it off anyway.

"I'll just call Jameson from your phone when we get there."

"Of course."

I lay my head down on the seat and try to forget about everything. My eyelids feel so heavy but I try to hold them open as I stare out the window, still feeling numb. I wonder when looking out a window will ever feel normal again. Will anything ever feel normal again?

Suddenly, the truck jerks to the right and I hear someone honk.

"What was that?" I ask, sitting up.

"Sorry," Ardyn says, "I thought I saw something in the road. You should sleep. You must be exhausted."

I lay back into the seat again and close my eyes this time. But they fly back open when I hear Ardyn swear.

"Shit," he says.

I feel the truck slow down on the highway.

"There's a car at the sunset house," he says.

I look over at him, feeling confused.

"The owners are out of town. After the break in a couple months ago, they asked me to keep a close eye on the property. I better check it out."

"Yeah, you'd better."

He turns into the driveway where a blue car is parked.

"It won't take long. I'll get you home soon, I promise."

Ardyn opens his door and says, "I don't know who it is, so you just stay in here okay? I'll hurry."

He shuts the door before I can say anything.

I'm glad these people are finally going to get caught. I remember him telling me someone was vandalizing the houses. Ardyn looks into the car then walks up to the porch, he peers in the window and slowly opens the door. He must have tripped as I see him stumble inside the house.

I wonder what's taking Ardyn so long. It's been at least ten minutes, I think. Time is still really off to me from the shock of Will being gone, so I could be wrong.

But I honk the horn anyway.

Nothing.

I honk the horn again, this time holding it down.

Nothing.

I'm beginning to feel really nervous that he's not back yet. It shouldn't be taking this long.

After stepping out of the truck, I walk up the steps to the front door of the house. When I look inside through the window, all I see is an empty front room.

Knocking on the window I yell, "Ardyn!"

Nothing.

When I try and open the door, it's locked. *That's weird.*

Maybe I should check the backdoor. But just as I turn around on the porch, I'm frozen in fear. In front of me is a person wearing all black and a black ski mask just at the bottom of the steps. Just standing there, staring at me. I'm flooded with terror. Once my instincts finally kick in, I whip around and pound on the front door. "Ardyn!" I scream.

Then I feel something hard hit the back of my head and everything goes black.

Chapter Forty-Nine

Harper

W ill is pushing me on the tire swing out back. He looks really scared.

"Harper, listen to me."

I try to hear what he's saying but I can't understand him.

"Will what is it? I can't hear you. Say it louder."

He's yelling at me now but I can't make out what it is he's saying. All I hear is loud ringing in my ears.

I open my eyes as I lay on the cold concrete floor. I slowly sit up immediately feeling panicked when I remember what happened. I run straight to the door. It's locked. I look around to see an empty room with no window and a dim light flickering on the ceiling. This must be the basement of the sunset house. What's happening? There's no way out. I bang on the door. "HELP!" I scream at the top of my lungs, feeling defeated. I cry out of frustration. "Ardyn!" I'm screaming. I hope he's okay.

I hear a door open and shut.

When I hear banging around and a man's voice, I press my ear to the wall to try and make out what he's saying.

"Please don't do this. Let her go," Ardyn says.

I hear a loud crash and Ardyn grunts.

"Ardyn!" I call out.

He grunts again.

"Stop hurting him!" I yell.

The beating stops and I hear footsteps coming toward my locked door. I step back so my back is against the far wall. As he begins to unlock the door, I'm frozen in fear when it opens. I can't move. I feel like I'm going to be sick. He's going to hit me now. Then the man in black just stands there for a moment before he slams the door shut and locks it behind him. I'm relieved when I hear him walking up the stairs.

"Ardyn!" I scream but he doesn't answer me.

Oh God. Please be alive, Ardyn. I sit down against the wall and bury my head into my folded arms. I've never felt so small, so weak. I hear someone outside the door.

"Ardyn! Is that you?"

He sounds like he's in pain.

"Hazey? Are you hurt?" he mumbles.

I say, "He knocked me out before he brought me down here. I heard him hitting you. Are you okay?"

"That son of a bitch. Are you sure you're okay?" he asks.

"I'm not hurt. Just scared. What happened?"

"When I walked into the house, a man dressed in black knocked me out too. Then he must have brought me down here and tied me up. I woke up to him and another guy talking outside my door. I heard you calling for help then obviously you heard them knock me out cold again."

"Wait, there are two of them?" I ask.

"Yeah. Goddammit this is all my fault. I'm so sorry. I can't believe this. I'm going to get us out of here Hazey I promise."

I'm so relieved to hear Ardyn's voice. I'm not alone and we're both alive.

"I'm so glad you're okay. I'm not tied up."

"They must not want me to fight back. Fucking cowards."

"Do you have your phone?" I ask.

"They took it."

I stand up and start pacing the floors when I remember Robby being parked outside my apartment. When I hit his car, I probably pissed him off.

"Ardyn. Robby was parked outside the apartment when I left for the park. I hit his car. Do you think it's him doing this?"

"No. He came upstairs to your apartment after you left and told me he saw you. He told me he was only there to apologize for what happened to Will. He seemed like he felt bad. Do you know a guy named Bert?"

I picture Will and the man with the gray beard at the gift shop back home. His name was Bert.

"Yeah, why?"

"Well when I heard them talking outside my door, I heard one of them call the other Bert. They said they're going to kill us, Harper. They know you. They were targeting *you*. Who the hell are they? Why would they want to kill you?"

"Bert is a friend of Will and Jameson's dad. He's dangerous. He seemed to have it out for Will. But I don't understand why he would be doing this. I'm so sorry, Ardyn."

"Don't be sorry. This isn't your fault. I'm going to get us out of here," he says.

I can tell in his voice he's scared too.

"Did you already check your door?" he asks.

"Yeah, it's locked."

I hear him grunting.

"Why did we put locks on the goddamn doors down here?" he mumbles.

"Do you have a window?" I ask.

"No. I hate this basement," he says.

I hear a loud bang. "Dammit!" Ardyn yells out. He must have hit or kicked the door.

I try to twist the door knob over and over again. I heard Ardyn doing the same thing but I think he gave up. We stop talking. I don't think we even know what to say to each other anymore.

When my hands are sore, I finally give up on the door. I close my eyes as I lay back down on the hard, cold ground.

My body is shivering when I wake up. It's freezing in here. And I'm so tired of feeling this scared. This hopeless. I run to my door and it's obviously still locked. I bang on it because I feel pissed off that I'm still down here. I curl up in a ball and cry. My parents must be so worried. Ardyn's family is probably worried. Surely, they're looking for us. They must know we're missing. Bennett Builds contractors are probably coming into work on this exact house on Monday. They're going to find us. They have got to find us. I say a prayer over and over again that they find us before something terrible happens.

I hear Ardyn moving.

"Harper, are you okay?" he asks.

"Not really. Are contractors going to be here on Monday?" I ask.

"Yeah. I thought of that too. They'll find us Harper. But I'm still going to try and get us out of here before then. Just hang tight a little bit longer okay? I love you," he says.

Ardyn and I haven't talked for hours. I have no idea what time it is. Is the sun shining outside? I have no clue.

"I wonder what time it is."

Ardyn doesn't answer me.

I don't want to think anymore so I lay down and try to get some sleep too.

My body jolts when I hear footsteps coming down the stairs. My heart is racing out of control when the man in black throws my door open and walks over to me.

I have to fight.

He tries to pick me up over his shoulder but I kick him hard between the legs and he drops me. I start crawling towards the door when he grabs my foot and slides me back aggressively across the floor.

"Let me go!" I yell out.

He flips me over on my back and climbs on top of me. I can smell alcohol on his breath. He's holding an open pocket knife.

Fight Harper.

You can't let him win. You can't let him kill you. I punch him hard in the chest but he doesn't budge. The sound of the knife dropping on the floor has me feeling relieved. But the man still has me pinned to the ground when he gets out some rope and starts tying my hands together. He rips off my turquoise bracelet and I hear the beads bounce and scatter everywhere.

"Please! Stop! Let me go!" I scream.

I'm kicking and screaming.

"What do you want?" I ask.

The man stops tying my hands and looks me in the eyes for the first time. Oh my gosh...

I know those eyes.

I love those blue eyes.

"Ardyn?"

He immediately backs off of me, stands up, and drops the rope. I get up off the ground and stare back at him.

When he takes off the mask I fall to my knees. He looks completely different to me now, but it's him. It's Ardyn.

I have never felt so betrayed in my life. I'm broken. I'm damaged.

Why did he do this to me?

"You're the man in black? You did all of this? You tried to kill me?" I ask.

"Oh Hazey no. Of course not," Ardyn says.

He steps toward me and I have to take a step back.

"I'm so sorry. I wasn't trying to kill you. I was trying to *rescue* you. I was trying to rescue you so that you'd choose me. I was trying to save our family. Don't you get it?" he asks. "We are going to be a family again Casey. I promise I'll make everything right."

Casey? He thinks I'm his dead wife?

"Casey? I'm not Casey. I'm Harper."

He looks puzzled as he runs his hands through his hair.

"Hazey," he corrects himself. "Come on. We have to go now. We're getting out of here."

Ardyn grabs me by the arm then begins dragging me out of the room. Sun is coming through the window in the unfinished basement. I look around and notice there is no other bedroom, just an open living area and a basement door that goes outside.

I can't believe this is happening. Ardyn pushes me forward toward the stairs. I smell whiskey on Ardyn's breath as he says, "We're going to be a family again. I'll save you this time."

Chills run up my arms as we walk up the stairs.

Ardyn is trying so hard to convince himself that I'm actually his wife. That I'm actually Casey right now.

"Ardyn? You're confused. You've been drinking. We have to get you help. You're not thinking straight. I'm Harper. Casey died in the house fire," I say as we walk out the front door.

This causes him to grab his ears and stop walking. Like it's so painful to hear, he can't even listen to me. He lets go of his head and he cries.

"Casey. Oh my gosh Casey. I'm so sorry. I tried to save you. I tried. I have to make it up to you."

He's scaring me. Not knowing what else to do, I begin running away from him.

"Hazey!" he yells and I hear him running up behind me.

I only made it down the porch steps when he grabs me by the waist and I lunge myself forward as he picks me up. I begin kicking and screaming for help.

"Stop!" he yells directly in my ear. He sets me down on the ground but has my arms pinned behind my back in a death grip.

"Let me go!" I scream at him.

"No. I'm never letting you go," he says softly. I can feel his breath in my hair as he continues to say, "We have to go get Graham so that we can be a family again. Let's go."

Ardyn pushes me forward, toward the truck.

He's obviously not in his right mind. He's not himself. He's different.

"Ardyn. Let me drive. You've been drinking."

"No, I'm fine Hazey," he says. "We have to get out of town. Before they kill us," he says.

Ardyn has even convinced himself that somebody is after us. Trying to kill us. Doesn't he realize it was him all along?

He opens the driver side door and my heart rate speeds up.

"No, Ardyn. Please listen to me. You're not thinking clearly. I'm Harper. You kidnapped me. You made me believe someone was trying to kill me. Trying to kill you. You were the one who was pretending to do it. You even gave yourself a black eye. Why are you doing this?" I ask.

"Get in," he demands.

"You're going to have to let me go, so I can move."

As soon as he loosens his grip, I lunge forward to the driver's seat and I'm flooded with disappointment when the keys aren't in the ignition.

Ardyn grabs me hard by the arm.

"What do you think you're doing?" he yells.

"I think I should drive. You've been drinking."

"I'm driving. Move over."

I slowly scoot over and slide across an empty bottle of whiskey. I have never felt this scared of a human I used to feel so safe with before.

Ardyn slams the door shut and starts the ignition.

When we begin driving, I can see him as he looks over at me. Folding my arms, I turn away. I don't want him to see me cry.

"I'm so sorry. I'm sorry I hurt you. I couldn't let you go, Hazey. I promise I'll never hurt you again. You know how much I love you."

I don't say anything and Ardyn swerves right into on-coming traffic on the highway. A car slams on their breaks and honks at us. We're probably going to crash. And we're driving so fast I realize we might get pulled over. I hope we do. Then the police can help me.

"Where are we going?" I ask.

Ardyn doesn't answer me. I don't even recognize him right now.

When I notice a small picture on the dash, I pick it up. In the photograph, Ardyn is holding Casey in his arms and she's holding baby Graham. Casey does kind of look like me, with her dark hair and olive skin. I flip it over and on the back is Ardyn's handwriting. *Ardyn, Hazey, and Graham age one.*

I feel sick. *Hazey.* Ardyn never loved *me.*

"H-Hazey…" I stammer. "Was Casey?" Somehow holding back the tears.

He looks at what I'm looking at and rips the picture out of my hand and throws it back onto the dash.

My head is spinning and I feel like I might throw up. But I lay my head back on the seat and squeeze my eyes shut.

A half an hour of crazy driving goes by when Ardyn turns left down a secluded dirt road.

"Where are we going, Ardyn?" I ask.

"We're waiting," he says.

"Waiting for what?" I ask nervously.

"I'm trying to figure out where to go. So I can keep you safe. We have to get out of town," he says, pulling off the side of the dirt road to stop the truck.

"I can't leave town Ardyn. I have to go home. I have to go to Will's funeral," I say.

"Please just stop. I have to think about what to do next okay? Just let me think."

Feeling frustrated, I lean back in the seat and rest my head back. I have to come up with a plan. I have to get away.

"Stay here," Ardyn says, opening up his door.

"Wait. Ardyn, I have to go to the bathroom," I tell him.

"Fine," he says.

I open the passenger door and pull down my pants when I hear Ardyn clinking bottles in the back of his truck. He's obviously looking for more to drink. At least he's giving me the decency to pee in peace.

When I'm finished, I stand up and think about running. But before I can, Ardyn comes around the front of the truck.

"Get back in," he demands, opening up the passenger door.

I climb back in and Ardyn slams the door shut. I notice the keys aren't in the ignition as Ardyn gets in through the driver's side.

"When did you start drinking again?" I ask.

Ardyn ignores me.

It's beginning to get dark out. Ardyn starts his truck.

I sit up as Ardyn turns his truck around.

"What are we doing now?" I ask.

"We aren't going anywhere without Graham," he says.

"What are you talking about? We're actually going to get Graham?" I ask.

A frustrated sigh escapes his mouth. "Yes. If we're leaving town for a while, I'm not leaving without my son."

Why on earth are we leaving town?

He won't even look at me as he drives up the dirt road toward the highway.

"Ardyn we can't take Graham. He's with your sister. He's safe," I try to explain.

"I'm going to have my family back," he mumbles as if he didn't even hear me.

I can't let him do this.

"We can't just take him, Ardyn. It's not right."

"No. No! I can't give up on him. I can't give up on you. We're going to get him."

Ardyn was right. He really is a completely different person when he's been drinking. Where's the man who put his son before anything else? I have to try and talk him out of taking his son. Out of taking *me*.

Now I realize that he probably pulled us off to the side of the road because he was waiting for it to get dark, so that Emily and Tyson are in bed when he goes in and takes Graham. Graham will go with him in a heartbeat. He'll do anything for his Uncle Ardyn.

"Ardyn," I say gently, "your wife Casey died. I'm not Hazey. I'm Harper. Casey is gone. And Casey wouldn't want you to take Graham right now. She'd want you to get help. You have to get help. Let's get you to a rehab," I beg him.

"No Hazey! I can't let you go. We're going to be a family," he says as he speeds up the truck.

"Ardyn, please slow down," I say in a calm voice, even though I'm completely panicked.

In the rearview mirror, I notice some headlights coming up behind us.

I have to make a plan and fast. We're getting closer to Graham. I don't know exactly where Emily lives but I know it's in the next town somewhere by his parents' house.

I look into the rearview mirror again, looking at the headlights behind us. They'll see us. I have to stop him.

"Ardyn. It's going to be okay. You're going to get the help you need."

When there's nothing but fields to the side of us, I grab the steering wheel and yank it to the left.

We go flying off the road.

Ardyn yells but I have no idea what he's saying as the truck feels like it's never going to stop. We're rolling and rolling into the field. Then it's black.

Sirens are squealing in the distance as someone pulls me up off the ground.

I open my heavy eyes and Will's holding me while we move into the dark night.

Will's face looks so real.

Will.

I don't want this vision to end but I can't hold my eyes open any longer.

Chapter Fifty

Harper

Machines are beeping as my eyes open. Scout is sitting next to the window in the room with me. I'm in the hospital.

"Harper," Scout says and gets up to hug me.

"What happened?" I ask.

"You were in an accident," she says as Jameson walks into the room.

He says, "We need you to clear some things up for us. But you don't need to do that right now."

The memory of everything that happened causes me more pain than I could have ever imagined would be possible.

My fingers gently touch the stitches in the side of my neck.

"Where's Ardyn?" I ask.

"He's at another hospital. He's okay," Scout says.

"He told me everything. I was just there," Jameson says.

"He has to get to rehab," I say.

Jameson says, "His family will get him the help he needs, Harper."

I nod. "He told you everything? He told you he was the one who took me? That he was planning on taking his son Graham too?" I ask.

Scout gasps. This is obviously news to her.

"Yeah, it took some convincing, but he confessed. I'd still like to hear your side of the story, but only when you're ready. You've been through a lot."

After explaining everything to them, I tell Jameson I don't want to press charges.

"Okay. But maybe give it some more thought. What he did was wrong."

Scout nudges him to stop talking. It's not that I don't think what he did was wrong. I just don't ever want to have to face him again. I never want to see him. But I don't explain that right now. But I need answers. I have to know why he did this. "I don't understand why he all of a sudden felt the need to take me," I tell them.

"I think we can explain that, but first I have to show you something I found," Jameson says.

Scout sits next to me on the bed.

"Are you okay?" she asks.

I nod my head. Even though I'm not even close to okay.

I look at Jameson. Searching his face for answers.

He hands me the box of **Do Not Send** letters I wrote to Will. "I found these in Ardyn's apartment after you went missing. Rafe let me in."

I have no idea how long Ardyn had these. I can't believe this.

"He also crinkled up and threw away Will's last letter to you. The reason he kidnapped you was because he didn't want you to find out," he says.

"Find what out?" I ask.

Jameson nods at the open door.

I cover my mouth with my hands and gasp. I'm in complete disbelief when Will walks in.

He smiles at me and kneels down next to the bed. This can't be real. But he's here.

He's alive.

I can finally breathe. I don't know how else to describe the last few days besides feeling so overwhelmed with grief that I couldn't breathe.

"Harper, I'm so happy you're okay," Will says.

I never thought I'd get to hear his voice again. That's the one thing I had a hard time remembering about him. His voice. Sometimes I found myself trying so hard trying to remember it. I completely forgot the sound of it until now.

"I'm home. I'm alive."

Those are the best words I've ever heard come out of Will's mouth.

My heart feels like it's going to burst through my chest. I've never felt this much relief in my life. Jameson and Scout leave the room.

"But how?"

Will
Four days earlier...

They're going to kill us. I know I've got to act fast before the Taliban soldiers look inside the building. The one in front is getting close.

I tuck my dog tags back in my shirt and whisper, "I'm going to veer him away by running out into the open. He'll follow me."

Ed frantically shakes his head. But before I can let him try and talk me out of it, I dart from the shelter and out into the open. Running as fast as humanly possible, I turn around and see one Taliban soldier chasing after me. As I hear the shots firing, I take Harper's hair clip out of my pocket and hold onto it. I need all the luck I can get right now.

Knowing what I have to do to get him off of me, as soon as I hear another shot coming at me, I drop to the ground face first and I don't move a muscle. I don't look up to see if he's coming, I don't do anything but lay here in the dirt, next to other bodies, praying that the Taliban doesn't come too close. I play dead.

That's when I hear an explosion. The heat of it hits my face but I still don't move. I don't even look up to see if it was the brick building, because I already know it was. My plan didn't work and guilt overwhelms me.

God fucking dammit.

I try not to stir throughout the rest of the night as I hear movement and voices.

It's barely light out when I hear footsteps around me. I still don't move. I hold my breath. They can't see me alive. I can't die. I'm clenching onto Harper's hair clip as I lay here playing dead, not moving until I know the Taliban is gone. I hear a helicopter in the distance. My eyes open and I see boots walking around the dead bodies. I close them shut again and hold my breath. I'm worried if I don't go back soon, I'll get left here.

So a few hours later, when I don't hear or see anyone anymore, I get myself up and sprint to base.

I'm relieved when I see that I haven't been left behind. A few marines in my unit are gathered around and I hear another helicopter coming in to land.

I see Lieutenant Muller and make my way over to him.

I tell him my name is Will Karter and that I was hiding all night. He writes my name down as I ask him about Ed.

He says, "I don't know about your friend but his chances aren't good. We lost a lot of people last night. I'll get back to you on that."

He continues barking orders for everyone to load up. We're moving. I'm sure Shaun knows if Ed and the Afghan man and boy are okay. I don't see him anywhere so I ask around and someone tells me he already left on the first helicopter. I'm glad Shaun made it out okay.

After moving to a new Forward Operating Base the next day, I see Lieutenant Muller charging toward me. He looks pissed.

"Are you Frank Karter?" he asks me.

"Um, yeah. Frank William Karter," I answer.

I realize now that I told him my name was Will Karter yesterday.

"Can you explain to me how the hell you were declared dead two days ago?" he asks, shuffling through his stack of papers.

Holy shit.

What? They declared me dead all because I gave him the name Will instead of Frank? How could that be?

"I'm sorry sir. I messed up. I always go by Will," I tell him.

"You did mess up. You should've told me your full name. But you didn't mess up as bad as Shaun Hartman. He's the one who told me he saw Frank William Karter run with Ed Bradley inside the brick abandoned building that exploded. We weren't able to identify any of the bodies but there were three of them. After what Shaun told me, we assumed one of those bodies was yours."

I shake my head in disbelief.

I explain, "When we were being overrun, Ed showed me the abandoned brick building with an Afghan man and boy. They were letting us hide in it. When we saw the Taliban walking right to us, I ran out of the building to try and veer them away. Then I played dead all night and most of the next day. I can't believe this. There were three bodies? None of them made it out?"

Lieutenant Muller rubs his tired eyes and says, "No. And now I remember you asking me about Ed yesterday. Sorry, I have to admit, it was my fault too. I should've looked at the names closer. It's not on you. The overrun from the night before sure caused a lot of grief." He sighs then he continues, "I need to apologize. We already notified your family to inform them that you were killed."

My heart drops.

"They think I'm dead?" I ask.

Jameson is probably the one who got the news, which means he probably told Harper.

Harper thinks I'm dead.

"Yeah. I will notify them as soon as possible. But do you know what this means, soldier?"

"What?" I ask.

"You're going home."

Will
Now

Harper has so much confusion all over her face. But after I explain to her what happened, she smiles.

"I can't believe you're alive," she says, her voice breaking up. I hug her so tightly, I'm worried it will break her.

"I missed you," I say.

When we pull away I look straight at her. Tears run down her cheeks. She's so beautiful. Even in a hospital bed.

I stand up to pull out the beaded bracelet I fixed for her from my pocket and put it back on her wrist. Her eyes light up.

"You found my bracelet? How?" she asks.

"When I got home yesterday, as soon as I saw Jameson at the airport, I immediately knew something was wrong. Especially when you weren't there. He told me you were missing and I told him I had to help find you. I've never been so worried in my life."

"Yeah, I know the feeling," she says. "Tell me everything."

I tell her I drove with Jameson all over the Bennett's properties looking for her.

"When we got to the house on a hill, I found your bracelet scattered all over the basement floor."

I stop talking when I can tell Harper's hurting. I can see by the look on her face that this isn't easy for her to hear.

"Are you sure you want to talk about this now?" I ask.

"Yes. I have to know. Please," she says.

"After we found the bracelet and we realized you weren't there, someone said they spotted Ardyn's truck driving north so we started driving in that direction. Police were looking all over the highway but we couldn't find it anywhere. Gosh, Harper. I was so sick about it all. I was so angry. I wasn't sure if I'd ever see you again. It was the scariest moment of my life. We were out on some back road looking for you when we spotted Ardyn's truck flying by on the highway. We couldn't believe it. Jameson immediately started following close behind with his flashing lights off and informed the other police on the radio to stand down but to be ready. We didn't want to risk putting you in any more danger by turning the situation into a complete police chase. We followed behind the taillights and I didn't even dare blink. I wasn't letting that truck out of my sight for a split second. I've never felt so scared when I saw Ardyn's truck go rolling off the road."

"Yeah I saw the headlights behind us. I can't believe that was you," I say.

Will continues, "When I got you out of the truck you were unconscious and you had a bad gash on your neck. I stopped the bleeding and then as soon as the ambulance got there, I picked you up and ran toward it. You were looking at me. You were conscious for a second. Do you remember that?" I ask.

"Yeah. I thought I was dreaming. Or dead," she laughs and cries at once.

"I'm so glad you're okay. I have never been so scared, Harper. How's your neck?"

"It feels fine," she says.

She leans into me and touches the cast on my wrist.

"What happened to your hand?" she asks.

"I may have punched a few things while we were looking for you."

Harper lays her head on my shoulder.

"If this is actually a dream, I never want to wake up," she says.

"It's not a dream. It's real," I say, resting my chin on her head.

I pull away from her and stand up off the bed.

"I'm sorry," I say, looking down at her confused expression.

"You're sorry? For what?" she asks.

"For everything."

I sit down on the bed and bring my thumb up to Harper's beauty mark and she closes her eyes. Gosh I have so much to tell her but I know I can't do that right now. Not after everything that's happened.

She opens her eyes and smiles. I love that smile.

Jameson and I wait in the lobby while Harper visits with her parents. I can't believe everything she's just been through.

"Harper said Ardyn mentioned Bert's name as the man in black trying to kill them. I remember Ardyn asking me about my past. About the illegal fighting. I can't remember giving him Bert's name, but I guess I must have."

"Yeah that's weird. You or Harper probably mentioned him at one point," I tell him.

"Yeah. My instincts were screaming at me that something was up with Ardyn the moment he answered Harper's door, and the moment I smelled the alcohol. I shouldn't have left him there. I shouldn't have let him take her," Jameson says, rubbing his face with the palms of his hands.

"It's not your fault Jameson."

"I know. But it still doesn't make me feel any better knowing I could have done something to stop it. But he loved Harper so much, I didn't think he'd ever hurt her. At least when he was sober. Didn't you think dad was a completely different person too? When he was sober?" he asks, looking back up at me with his exhausted eyes.

I flashback to when my dad was teaching me how to tie my shoes.

I hear his voice, "You got it William. I'm so proud of you. The first three year old to ever tie his own shoes."

He picked me up, tossing me in the air. I was laughing and so was he. I remember my mom watching us from the porch swing with a smile on her face.

"Yeah. I do," I tell Jameson.

He looks at me like he knows exactly what I mean. He remembers it too.

Harper

My parents were so relieved that I'm okay. After discussing everything with them, I decided I do want to press charges after all. Ardyn needs help. And he shouldn't get away with what he did. I have to be strong. My parents leave the room and I give a full statement to the police.

When I'm done Will comes back and tells me he's going to get me food. He laughed when I told him I just want a 7-Up and a Twinkie.

Chapter Fifty-One

Ardyn

I 'm sweating like a mother fucker in this jail cell. Alcohol withdrawal might just kill me. I've lost everything. *Again.*

When Will died, I was hoping things were going my way for once. But Will's death brought up a lot of memories of losing Casey. That and seeing Harper so heartbroken over him was too much for me. That's when I knew she loved him more than she could ever love me. I couldn't handle it. I've always been a jealous person even though I know how to hide it. But being jealous of a dead man was painful. I needed a drink more than ever. I couldn't help myself. When Harper left for her walk to the park, I found Rafe's stash, destroyed my sobriety and got drunk while I waited for her. Then Jameson showed up and told me that Will was actually alive. I had to think fast. I had to make a plan.

I remembered the car one of my buddies from work kept parked at the sunset house. We kept that car there to make it look like somebody was home so that nobody would break in again. So I went to find Harper.

I was drunk and thought I had to do something big. Something that would make Harper have to be with me. I was going to rescue her. Be a hero. I wanted to make her believe somebody was actually trying to kill her. So I thought of Bert.

When Will suddenly showed back up at the end of summer after Harper's high school graduation, my blood was boiling. I didn't understand why he was back in the picture. Even though I knew I couldn't pursue her myself, I still couldn't handle watching her with him. It drove me crazy seeing the two of them together again. I knew that what I was doing wasn't going to last forever but I needed her at that time in my life. Will had to be out of the picture. I needed him away from Harper. I knew I had to scare him off, get him locked up, something. At least for a while. I needed more time to feel close to Casey again. But at the time I didn't even know his name. That's when I wore a hat and sunglasses and stopped Will when he got up to use the restroom in that diner he was at with Harper. I disguised myself every time I was around them. I was careful so they couldn't figure out I was watching them. I asked him what his name was and he gave it right to me. When he asked why, I just said I thought I knew him from somewhere and that was that. Not knowing what to do next, at least I knew his name. It was stupid of me but I went to the bar in Harper's small town to clear my head. I almost drank that night but I was able to control my urge. When this guy named Bert came up to me at the bar he was trying to get me in on some bet for illegal fighting he had going on somewhere. I wasn't interested but I pretended to be because I knew this guy wanted money. I could hire him. Being in such a small town, I thought he could potentially know Will, so I asked if he did. And as luck would have it, he did know him. Bert told me he knew "Frank's boy, Will," and that "his pop was locked up and he's been mad at Will ever since some bitch ran him out of town." I had to take a calming breath because I knew he was talking about Harper. I asked Bert if he wanted to make some cash and right away he agreed. I lied and told him Frank actually sent me from jail and that he's looking for Will. I told him his dad, Frank, wanted Will locked up with him. I told Bert that Will was in town so we had to do something fast. Bert was ready to hear the plan. I couldn't believe how easy it was. I told him to get Will to hit him in public so people could witness it. Then to press charges so that he has to go to jail for a while. Bert told me he definitely knew how to piss Will off. When he told me he'll just "threaten the bitch," I couldn't handle my calm anymore. I told him to stop calling her that and punched him. When he gave me a confused, pissed off look I told him I was just getting him ready for the hit. He still looked a little pissed off but he half laughed and took his money.

When Bert confronted Will at the gift shop, our plan had failed. At least that's what Bert thought. Will told Bert that he was getting ready to leave for Afghanistan. I was worried for nothing that Will might show up with Harper at college, but instead, he was leaving for war. I came up with a ridiculous plan for nothing. I ended up giving Bert another black eye when he told me about what he said about Harper to Will. After hitting him, I sent him on his way. I was done with him. I got some kind of thrill out of standing up for Harper when Will hadn't.

Remembering that Bert told me Harper was with Will that day in the gift shop, I knew Harper would remember Bert.

I thought my plan was brilliant. I knew she trusted me. I was going to be her hero so that she'd have to choose me. I wasn't in my right mind when I decided I was going to take her as far away as possible. As drunk as I was, it just made sense. I thought maybe she'd never find out Will was alive or when she did eventually find out, we'd already be married. The plan was never to take Graham. I was just desperate to have my family back. The alcohol took control over me.

I couldn't lose them again. Maybe she would have chosen me if I didn't fuck it all up. I'm so frustrated that I punch the concrete wall. If only I could've gotten her pregnant, then she would've stayed with me. We could've been a family. I fucking needed her. Now, Will is back and I'm stuck here. Hopefully not for too long.

Chapter Fifty-Two

Harper

One month later...

Will is starting school this semester while he works at a Naval hospital in Columbus to finish his military service. He wants to become a doctor. I couldn't be more proud of him.

Scout and I kept the apartment. I thought about moving out after everything that happened, but I decided to stay. Ardyn's trial was last week and he got up on the stand and apologized to me. It was hard seeing him again but it was closure I didn't realize I needed. The judge told him as long as he goes to rehab and therapy to get the help he needs, he'll only have to serve five years with the chance of parole in two. He also signed the adoption papers. I know how difficult it was for him but I could tell he knew he was doing the right thing. Court was hard on his family but afterward, they thanked me and told me this might be Ardyn's chance of changing for good, so that he can be an uncle to Graham and take over his dad's company when he gets out.

Will, Jameson, Scout and I are spending the day at Boulder Beach before summer ends and school starts again.

"I think you guys should have a housewarming party," Scout tells Jameson and Will as we sit on our towels trying to dry off in our wet swimsuits.

"Why would we do that?" Jameson asks. "I've been living in that house for over a year."

"It's different with Will there now," Scout says.

Jameson laughs. "What makes him so special?"

"Okay fine, not a housewarming party," Scout says.

I mention, "We could do a welcome home party."

Will's dum dum sucker is tucked in his cheek as he grins at me. He takes it out and says, "I feel like we've already celebrated me being home enough, but whatever you guys want to do. Every day's a party when I'm not being shot at anymore."

The thought of Will being shot at is absolutely gut wrenching. I hate it. I still have nightmares of him not coming home.

He touches my hand. For a moment I think he might kiss me. There have been a few of these moments since he's been back. But I've already accepted a long time ago that Will just wants us to be friends, even though he makes it difficult when he looks at me like this. My eyes fall on his tattoo of trees and without even thinking, I touch it. "Did you get the trees for Boulder Beach?"

He nods and gives me that same look again. But it's a lie. He doesn't love me. I quickly stand up and throw on the oversized t-shirt I wore as a cover-up.

"I think I'm going to walk to my parents' house. I told them I'd stop by before we drive back to Columbus."

"I'll come with you," Will says with his sucker.

I nod. Even though I wish he wouldn't. I don't want to be alone with Will. That's when the moments between us are hard for me. He throws on a sleeveless t-shirt that looks like he cut himself. The cut-out sleeves are ripped down, exposing the muscles in his sides. His blonde hair has gotten longer on top since he's been home and I find myself wanting to run my hands through it. I wish he didn't look so good.

We're walking down the street toward my parents' house when Will says, "Sorry for what I said back there. About being shot at. Sometimes I forget that me being away at war wasn't just hard for me."

"Do you have any idea how much I worried about you every single day while you were there?"

"I know."

We walk in silence for a minute then Will asks, "How are you doing? After the trial and everything?"

I sigh at the memory of having to go to court to relive that nightmare. But I feel a weight lifted off my shoulders. "I'm glad it's over with."

"How did you feel about seeing Ardyn again?" he asks.

"It was hard. I thought I was falling in love with him."

It doesn't make sense but Will's face shows that this isn't easy for him to hear.

He swallows and says, "Do you think you still love him?"

"I don't think I ever really loved him. At the time I thought maybe I did. But I think I always knew in the back of my mind he was hiding something. Our relationship was a lie. As soon as he saw me for the first time at Copper Hill University I think he saw me as his deceased wife. He really only saw me as Casey. He loved her so much that he thought he loved me. But I got the closure I needed from him after court. I feel a lot better."

Will says, "I'm glad. I haven't told you this but Ardyn looked familiar to me the first time I saw him in a picture. When I told Jameson, he told me there's just no way I could've seen him before. And I guess he's right. It's just weird. How familiar he seemed, especially watching him in court."

"Really? That's strange."

He nods.

We walk silently again when I feel Will's hand brush up against mine. I immediately pull away.

"Harper," he whispers quietly.

The sound of Will saying my name will always be loud, waking me up and filling me with hope. I hate what it does to me, so I ignore him and walk faster. Whatever he's about to tell me, I don't want to hear it.

"Harper, what are you doing?" Will says, speeding up to catch me. "Slow down, I have something I need to say."

"I already know how you feel, Will. It's okay. I don't want to hear about that right now, okay?"

He grabs my hand and stops me from walking. But I can't turn around to face him. My breathing is heavy when he says, "I need you to look at me so that I can tell you this."

I close my eyes tightly and try to brush off any last hope that I'm still hanging on to.

"Harper, please," Will begs. "Turn around."

I finally look at him and sigh. "What, Will? Can't you just let it go?"

"No," he says, "I can't let another day, another hour, another *second* go by without telling you the truth. I've been lying to you. To myself. I was pushing my feelings aside, afraid that I could never be good enough for you or that I would end up hurting you. And that's exactly what I did. I hurt you *because* I held back. The first time I kissed you at Boulder Beach, I knew. But I lied. To both of us."

Hope is pulling me under deeper and deeper. It's drowning me just like the lake before saying goodbye to Will a year ago. But I have that same feeling as I did in the water. I need to be here. I can feel it. But if I stay in here too much longer, I'll suffocate. Then Will helps set me free to the surface.

Will

"I love you Harper. I'm in love with you," I finally say out loud. It feels so good to finally say it, that I have to say it again. "I love you."

I can tell my words hit her hard. It might be too late. She's quiet as she squints her eyes and takes a deep breath. I grab her hand and place it on my shoulder. "That night on the Fourth of July, when you touched my scars, I never wanted to forget the way that felt. That's the exact moment I realized I was in love with you. I got this tattoo for you."

She lets out a breath. I'm not sure she's going to say it back. I wouldn't blame her. But then she smiles before jumping into my arms. I catch her legs as she gleams down at me with her arms draped around my neck. She looks so happy and I want to keep this image of her burned into my memory forever.

"Finally, dummy. I still love you, too. I never stopped." She drops her feet back down to the ground as we're still holding on to each other.

This is the best moment of my entire life. I want to hear her say it over and over again. And I want to say it back even louder than she just did. Like I should've done the first time she told me.

I let go of her and cup my mouth with my hands. "I love you Harper!" I yell out so loud it echoes. She laughs. I bring my thumb up to her beauty mark as she closes her eyes.

"I love you," I say this time in a whisper. She opens her eyes as a tear rolls down her cheek. She smiles again.

"I love that smile."

Then I kiss her and I realize I never want to stop kissing her.

When eventually we pull away from each other, she stares up at me and says, "Please tell me you did not eat that sucker because you were planning on kissing me, dummy."

I laugh. "I was only planning on telling you that I love you. Promise."

"I'm never going to get tired of hearing that," she says.

So I tell her again, before kissing her *again*.

Chapter Fifty-Three

Harper

Jameson and I have been talking about Will and Scout's Christmas gifts for the past month. We're making them open them at the same time on Christmas morning. We are all gathered around the Christmas tree at my parents' house. Jameson looks at me and smiles as they each rip at the wrapping paper.

"You gave us each a key?" Scout asks, looking confused.

Will explains, "Your key is the key to Jameson's house. My key is the key to your apartment. We're switching places apparently."

"It just makes sense," Jameson says, "Will is always over at the apartment with Harper and Scout is always staying with me at the house. So you're officially switching places. If you want to, that is."

Jameson gives Scout a hopeful smile as she squeals and practically tackles him to the ground with excitement.

I look at Will and he smiles at me with his eyes before his mouth. We're sitting on the floor facing each other. I scoot closer to him. "What do you think?" I ask.

"I think moving in with you isn't even a question," he says.

He's staring at my lips then back up at my eyes. It's the look I've seen so many times before, but this time I know for certain that it's his way of telling me he loves me without even having to say it. Before I can respond his mouth lands on mine.

"We're going to need a bigger bed," I tell him.

"We'll go look for one tomorrow. Want to drive to Pennsylvania with me today?"

"What's in Pennsylvania?" I ask.

"I have someone I need to go see. Her name's Laura. Noel was planning on proposing to her today. I need to tell her. For Noel."

My heart hurts for Laura. But Will's right. She needs to know how much he loved her. "A road trip on Christmas. Sounds fun."

Will
The next day...

When we get back home from Pennsylvania, I watch Harper lay down on a mattress at the furniture store since she thinks we need a bigger bed. Personally, I like sleeping on the twin sized one with her.

"Wow. This one's so soft. If we could lay on clouds, this is exactly how I would picture it would feel like," Harper says.

She's so damn cute. I plop down next to her.

"It is soft. Almost too soft. But anything is better than sleeping on dirt. Especially with you."

After grinning up at me, she jumps out of the bed and goes to the next one. She lays down.

"What about this one?" she asks with her eyes closed.

I love that her eyes are closed. Like she's imagining us together in this bed every night.

Laying down on my stomach next to her, I stare down at her face. My thumb goes to her beauty mark. She opens her eyes and smiles.

"What do you think?" she asks.

I can't help but kiss her right now.

I somehow manage to pull away and say, "I think I don't really care where I sleep as long as I get to sleep next to you."

"If you had to, would you sleep in the dirt with me forever?" she teases.

"I could do anything forever if it's with you," I say, feeling cheesy. But I mean it.

She smiles. "Well, I do kind of like sleeping in my twin sized bed with you. It forces us to stay close to each other," she says.

How I ever convinced myself that I wasn't in love with this girl is beyond me.

"I was thinking the same thing," I tell her.

"Why are we here?" she asks and we laugh. We laugh so hard together and it never gets old.

Then Harper's smile fades when she stops laughing. She's now looking at me with a worried expression.

"What's wrong?" I ask.

"Six months ago I thought I was never going to laugh with you again."

I trace my finger along her soft lips. "I told you I'd come back to you."

She still looks worried.

"Harper, I'm okay. I'm right here."

"Are you sure this is what you want?"

It kills me that she would ever think that I don't want her. That I'll change my mind. I've always wanted her. I was just too big of an idiot to admit it.

"I'm going to have billions more uncontrollable belly laughs with you," I promise, bringing her smile back to life. "And I'm never going to let you miss a bright sunset, or go without shoes, or run the universe alone." Making Harper smile has become my new favorite part of every day. "I'll never change my mind about us. I love you." I love the way she's looking at me right now. *I'll convince her every damn day if she needs me to.*

"I'm going to love you forever, Harper. Even when we run out of seconds."

The End.

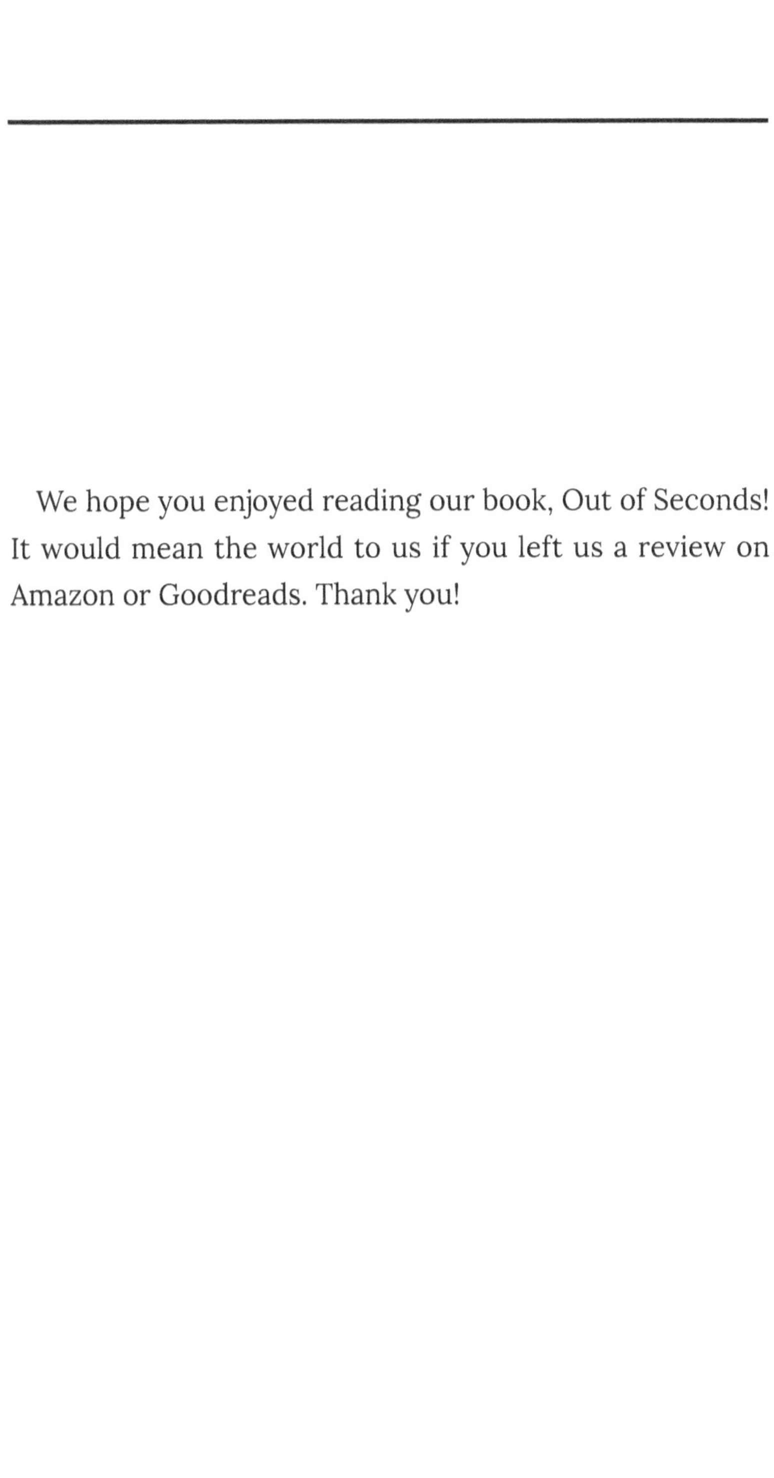

We hope you enjoyed reading our book, Out of Seconds! It would mean the world to us if you left us a review on Amazon or Goodreads. Thank you!

Acknowledgments

First and foremost, we'd like to thank each other. When we say that one of us could not have written this book without the other, we mean that. We argued, we cried, we laughed, and we finished it. We didn't give up, together.

We want to thank our husbands Cody and Chandler. They put up with our late nights, our emotional outbursts, listened to every idea, and encouraged us each step of the way.

We want to thank our Grandpa Twiss for his war stories and for inspiring us to write this book. And we want to also thank our Grandma Twiss for telling us how cool we are and giving us important details we couldn't think of putting into our story. Like her horse Taffy and how she used to call our grandpa dummy.

We want to thank our dad Bryce for always being so proud of us, no matter what. He always wanted to read the book before it was finished and that encouraged us to finish it.

We want to thank our mom for always getting just as excited about our book as we did. And for always supporting us.

We want to thank our babies. Ridge, Kanoe', Cash, and McKray. We hope it inspires them to do whatever they want to do when they grow up. We love them more than anything.

We want to thank all those who have served our country. We can't even begin to understand and describe what war is possibly like and we'd like to thank every serviceman and servicewoman for allowing us to try.

We want to thank our editor Hilari Cohen for being so kind-hearted as she helped us bring our story to life. She wasn't only our editor, but a mentor. We also couldn't have done this without her.

And for every friend and family member who has supported us. We love you all!

We appreciate these sources that helped us with our research on Afghanistan and Navy Corpsmen.

https://www.cfr.org/timeline/us-war-afghanistan

https://www.wearethemighty.com/popular/corpsmen-marines/

https://www.history.navy.mil/content/dam/museums/nmusn/PDFs/Education/Corpsman%20Up!.pdf

About the Authors

Shannah and Mariah are twin sisters, best friends, and co-authors. They both live in Utah with their families and take advantage of the short five minute drive to and from each of their houses. Shannah Bassett is married to Cody Bassett and they have two boys. Mariah Street is married to Chandler Street with one boy and one girl. They both love being moms, reading anything that makes their heart rates skyrocket, and of course, writing together. When Shannah's not writing, reading, or chasing her boys around, she's traveling with her pilot husband, training for a half-marathon, or enjoying the outdoors with her family. When Mariah's not writing or reading, she's listening to Taylor Swift, working in her garden, spending time with her family, or baking her favorite chocolate chip cookies.

Follow us on TikTok and Instagram @twicethe_spice
Join our Facebook group Out of Seconds discussion